The Amerii

Second Rising

We the People

Article 1

The Amerii

Second Rising

J. W. Christie

PROSPECTIVE PRESS

Winston-Salem

PROSPECTIVE PRESS LLC

1959 Peace Haven Rd #246, Winston-Salem, NC 27106
www.prospectivepress.com

Published in the United States of America by Prospective Press LLC

 TRADEMARK

THE AMERII – SECOND RISING

Cover and interior design by ARTE RAVE
© Prospective Press, 2022

ISBN 978-1-943419-30-2

ProP-H009

Printed in the United States of America
First Prospective Press printing, June, 2021

The text of this book is typeset in Alegreya
Accent text is typeset in Aquifer and AquilineTwo

Cover adapted from an image © Matthew Henry/Unsplash. Used under license.

The Amerii — Second Rising

Chapter 1

First Day in the Gray Blazer

I awoke in a magical wonderland. The early morning sun, streamed through my window and reflected off of the crystal-fringed lamp shades in my bedroom. I'd been too busy unpacking my clothing and getting situated to notice their beauty the night before when Uncle Rob had shown me to the room I'd be staying in for the summer. One of the lamps sat on the bedside table and the other, a floor lamp, was nestled behind the beautiful rose tapestried arm chair in the corner. The dancing rainbows leaped around on the walls and pirouetted like tiny ballerinas in shimmering tutus on the floor, and the ceiling as well. I laid there in bed, watching the performance for quite some time before deciding to get up.

It was my first day working for the family paper and I was eager to start writing. I hoped to make a good impression with Uncle Rob and get a glowing review from him for Penn State. Working on the paper was my father's idea. He'd strongly encouraged me, saying, "An internship at the paper would look great on your application." I'd applied to Penn State last fall but wasn't accepted, and I was willing to try anything to increase my chances of getting in. I quickly showered, threw on some clothes, then headed downstairs in search of something to eat for breakfast. Voices met me as I approached the kitchen. Grant, the youngest of my four cousins, and Aunt Theresa were chatting away over their bowls of Cap'n Crunch about today's to-do list. My dad called Grant a permachild and joked he'd never leave the nest.

"We're running low on a few supplies for the paper," Aunt Theresa said, placing her spoon in her empty bowl as she rose from the kitchen table. "I'm sure Aurora might like to see the town and get to know some of the people around here," she added as I entered the room. Her gentle blue eyes glistened and her pale pink lips formed a reassuring smile. She had her long blonde hair drawn back into a loose ponytail, but rebellious curls fought their restraints, and dangled wildly around her delicate features. "It would be nice of you to take her into town with you when you go?" She pushed in her chair, leaving Grant alone at the table and fluttered over to the sink. Aunt Theresa had been a dancer in her early twenties, long before she'd had the boys, but her movements still reflected her training. I admired the way she seemed to float across the floor instead of heavily tromping around like a clumsy elephant, the way most people do.

I grabbed a bowl from the cupboard and sat down next to Grant.

"It would be nice to know where everything is," I said, pouring cereal into my bowl. "Think you could put up with me tagging along?"

"Aw, Cuz, anything for you," he mumbled sarcastically, his mouthful of food.

"Plus, I have a few things I'd like to pick up as well," I added. I searched around for the milk.

"Here you go," Aunt Theresa said. She grabbed the gallon of milk out of the fridge and handed it to me. "It's settled then. Aurora's first assignment will be to get acquainted with the town."

"Assignment accepted." I poured the milk in my bowl. It splashed over the cereal onto the table top. I stretched the hem of my t-shirt out and quickly wiped up the mess before anyone noticed.

But Grant had noticed. "Let's hope you're better at getting to know where everything is in town than you are at pouring the milk," he said, teasing me. "Otherwise you've got zero hope of ever becoming a writer. Well, I guess that's not true, anyone can be a writer. Being a successful one, that's where you need to have good investigative skills. Like noticing when someone spills the milk." He laughed.

I glanced over at him. Wow, had he changed from the last time I'd seen him. He still had his mother's blonde hair, but without her gorgeous curls. Instead, his hair was short and bone straight like his father's. His hazel eyes and pointy nose, also from his father. In fact, we could have been siblings instead of cousins. That's how much our faces looked alike. We both took after our fathers, in that respect, more than our mothers. Grant was no longer the shaggy-haired, booger-picking, frog-catching twit I remembered from ten years ago. He'd grown up. His cargo shorts and Star Wars t-shirt had been replaced with black dress slacks, a neatly pressed white-collared shirt, and a gray blazer. He almost appeared normal, almost. His corny sense of humor prevented him from ever being completely normal.

Uncle Rob strolled through the doorway wearing the same gray blazer as Grant and gave Aunt Theresa a quick peck on the cheek as they passed by one another. His scrawny frame and weak shoulders were drastically different than my father's broad sturdy shoulders. His short dark brown hair was sprinkled throughout with signs of his age. Whereas his big hazel eyes were filled with a youthful wonder seldom seen in the eyes of a forty-eight year old man. I recalled Uncle Rob's love for solving puzzles. Perhaps that's what's kept him young inside. He was always coming up with riddles for me when I was a child. I'd spent hours with my cousins trying to solve them. It made my mom so mad.

She would say, "You're wasting your time, Rob. They are never going to need those skills. Not in this day and age." I still, to this day, have no idea what she meant by that.

"See you at the paper," Aunt Theresa said and off she fluttered.

"Where is the paper?" I asked turning to Uncle Rob. "Is there a building out back or something?" I pointed towards the rear of the house with my spoon. My dad and mom had decided to move away from Stony Creek when I was still very young and it had been ages since I'd been to my aunt and uncle's.

He let out a quick laugh, one that reminded me of my father's. Though their appearances were polar opposites, their laughs were identical.

Grant glanced up from his bowl of cereal. "Come on, Cuz, it's in the formal living room. There's no building out back."

"The formal living room?" I raised my left eyebrow. That's a weird place for a business. How rinky dink is this paper? "This place has a formal living room?" I stared at Uncle Rob, waiting for an answer. I wasn't interested in the sarcastic comment Grant would have to share but Uncle Rob just poured himself a large cup of coffee, then turned to face Grant and me, and leaned against the edge of the sink. He blew at the steam rising from his cup before closing his eyes and taking a sip.

"Oh sure, this house has many wonderful secrets—hallways, bedrooms, there's even a dining room," Grant said mockingly, as if every house in the world had a formal living room. My home in Cary, NC didn't have one and neither did the house we lived in before that.

"What? No bathrooms?"

"Okay, kids, let's stop fighting," Uncle Rob said teasingly. "I've barely just taken my first sip of coffee. I need at least a half a cup to deal with your squabbles." He gave us a fatherly glance over the rim of his coffee cup as he took another sip. "See?" He turned his coffee cup around so we could read the words. Don't talk to me until here, it read, and there was a line drawn halfway down the cup.

"Mom got him that cup for his last birthday," Grant said rolling his eyes. "He thinks it's funny." He shook his head. "It's not."

"Oh, that reminds me. I have a present for you, Aurora." Uncle Rob set his coffee on the counter, and then reached up to grab a package off the top of the fridge. He pulled down a clear plastic bag with a gray blazer, just like the one Grant was wearing, in it. Only this one had Aurora embroidered in big, red letters across the breast pocket.

"Thank you, Uncle Rob." I stood up and gave him a quick hug, then tore the plastic from the blazer and tried it on. It hugged my shoulders nicely, making me feel like part of the team. Even though it wasn't something I would normally wear, it still warmed my heart to be included.

"Now you two finish your breakfast. I trust your mom... Aunt Theresa gave you your assignments for the day?" He looked my way as if to clarify who he was talking about when he said Aunt Theresa.

"Yep," we both answered in unison.

"Grant's taking me into town," I added, then slurped the last bit of milk from my bowl.

Grant did the same and the two of us headed out through the parlor to the front door, leaving Uncle Rob alone in the kitchen to finish his coffee. The ride into town didn't seem to take as long as it had when I'd gotten lost yesterday trying to find the house. I'd even had to pull the car over to ask an older gentleman, who was taking his pup for a stroll, for directions. I chuckled to myself remembering the dark gray trousers and orange, Mr. Rogers cardigan he'd worn.

"Excuse me, sir. Could you please tell me where I can find the Stony Creek Gazette?" I'd asked him. It had taken hours to get from Cary to Stony Creek. I was desperate to find my uncle's and get out of the car.

"I could, Miss?" He started to say then paused, tilting his head to the side and stared at me with a puzzled expression. "I haven't seen you around here before, Miss?"

"Aurora. My name is Aurora VanAgteren," I replied, realizing it was his way of asking me for my name.

"You're one of them. One of those VanAgteren's." He'd dramatically placed his hand on his chest. "Why would such a sweet looking young lady like yourself be looking for that house of lies?" he'd asked. I didn't have it in me to explain to him why I was going to my uncle's, that my father had decided it would look good on my application to Penn State and that I'd do anything to get into Penn State. Plus, it really wasn't any of his business. "I have half a mind not to tell you. To save you from becoming a filthy liar like the rest of those VanAgteren's. Always printing their half truths and unfounded rumors. Whatever sells the papers and makes them money. Not caring who they hurt in the process," he continued when I didn't elaborate.

Liars? Half truths? His words confused me. It didn't sound like something my uncle would do. I'd always known him to be fair and kind to others.

"It's my uncle's," I'd said hesitantly, afraid to say any more than that. I was offended by the accusations. We weren't liars. The whole conversation had been so weird with the man that I'd almost driven off without his directions.

"Hmph," he'd said, angrily throwing his hands in the air, forgetting the leash in his left hand and almost hanging the pup attached to the other end. "A few miles up the road that way," he'd pointed down the road behind my car, "you'll find a dirt road to your left, Miss Aurora, but if I were you I would turn around. Go back to wherever it is you're from. Uncle or not, it's no place for a young lady," he'd said in warning, then turned his back to me and waddled away. The puppy was reluctant to follow, but after a few light tugs on the leash from the old man, he eventually gave in and did. I'd meant to ask Uncle Rob about it when I arrived at the house but hadn't gotten the chance to.

"To your left you will see a rock and if you look to your right, another rock," Grant said, bringing my attention back to the present. "In a few moments we will be passing a tree, make sure to have your cameras ready, you wouldn't want to miss a prime picture opportunity like this, folks," he announced as we drove along, doing a terrible impression of a tour guide. His commentary continued on for most of the ride into town. He had his funny moments, I'd give him that, but most of it I ignored. I was trying to get a sense of where I was in relation to the town. The car squeaked and groaned in defiance as Grant rambled on, unsuccessfully avoiding hitting the multitude of potholes along the road. The dirt drive leading from the house to the main road had become overgrown with bushes and they scratched at both sides of the car. It had been nearly dusk when I'd arrived yesterday and the scratching noises on the side of my car along with the strange conversation I'd just had with the older gentleman had given me an eerie feeling, but now, in the light of day, it all seemed strangely beautiful. Not eerie in the least bit. The overgrown bushes gave way to an open field full of gentle daisies and whimsical black-eyed susans just as we reached the main road. I opened my window and sniffed the air.

"Here we are," Grant said, gesturing out the window at the town. The sidewalks in Stony Creek were much wider than in Cary. Park benches and garbage cans freckled the sidewalks, street lights designed to resemble old, gas lanterns hung on tall posts at the street corners and crosswalks. It seemed most of the people here preferred walking to driving. There were plenty of open parking spots along the roadways and very little traffic. We passed the hardware store Aunt Theresa had talked about at dinner last night. She'd done her best to fill me in on the local gossip between bites of pot roast. Two men were standing out front chatting while their kids happily ate ice cream. Next to that, the grocery store was Bud's Market. Big posters of fruits, vegetables, and sale items hung in the large glass windows that covered most of the storefront. Across the street from Bud's was a laundromat, and next to that was the pharmacy. They proudly advertised their new store hours. Now open until 8 PM. On the next block we passed several specialty shops—Jenny's Quilt shop, Dan's Butcher shop, CJ's Bakery, and Candles & Carnations, which appeared to be some sort of gift shop. Down a side street, I could see the police and fire departments. Grant parked the car, and we scurried off down the sidewalk toward the office supply store.

"Oh look, Grant, this café is adorable." I peered in the window as we passed by on our way to the supply store next door. "Do you think we have time to stop and get a coffee before we head back?" I loved sitting and sipping coffee out of giant coffee cups while I relaxed and watched people. You can learn a lot about a person when you quietly observe them. I've learned that people all have the same wants and needs. Everyone wants to be accepted and needs to be loved.

"Sure, sure, once we've picked up some paper, some toner, and whatever else mom has on this list. It should only take a minute," he said, not bothering to glance up from it. "My buddy from high school runs the joint. It'd be nice to stop in to say hi. Catch up, ya know."

Nothing was ever quick in a small town and a minute turned into an hour. No one seemed to be in a hurry at all here. In a way, it was kinda nice to take it slow and easy. Things weren't at all like what I was used to in Cary. In Cary, it was *rush-rush-rush*, and no one bothered to ever learn your name. Here in Stony Creek we spent forty-five minutes at the supply store. Down every aisle was another neighbor with another story to tell you. After the tenth time of being introduced and spilling my life story to strangers, I finally had to excuse myself. While it was nice to take it easy, when nature calls you don't put her on hold.

"Excuse me, sir, is there a bathroom I could use?" I asked a young man with a name tag on.

"Sorry, miss, we don't have a public restroom. The café next door does," he replied. Oh thank goodness. I'd wanted to get some coffee anyway and I finally had the perfect excuse to hurry Grant out of the store. I rushed him through the checkout lane and out the front door.

The coffee shop reminded me of one I frequented back home. A long, bar-height table ran the length of the front window, with a half a dozen stools lined up along it, where you could sit and sip your coffee while watching people enjoy the beautiful weather in the small park across the street. There were fluffy couches and oversized armchairs, perfect for reading or relaxing in, and four low tables on the left side of the shop. Meanwhile, on the right side, ten or so high-top table and chair sets invited people to have a muffin or scone with a friend. The order counter and coffee station were centrally located, making for easy ordering or a quick coffee refill from either side of the shop.

"Wait for me to order. I've got to use the restroom," I said with a little more urgency in my voice than I'd realized.

"Sure, I see my friend from school over there." He pointed to two guys sitting at one of the high-top tables on the right. I couldn't believe my luck, or should I say, *bad* luck. There, sitting not more than fifteen feet from me, was Kaylin Becker, the guy I'd been crushing on all last winter. The one I'd totally embarrassed myself in front of in English class. The one I hoped I'd never see again—but there he was, drinking coffee and looking hotter than ever.

I recalled the first day I'd seen him in English class. Our English professor had the desks arranged in a half circle around the room and Kaylin sat opposite from me. Every now and then our eyes would meet. I would quickly turn away, pretending I didn't notice him, but I did. How could I not? He had the deepest blue eyes I'd ever seen, the kind of eyes I could gaze into all day. Sandy blond strands blended nicely into his short, light brown hair, giving him an angelic glow in the sunlight. His hair fell naturally into place, resting just above his strong cheekbones, often hiding his hypnotic eyes when he leaned forward. He would gently place it behind his ear, sending me into a trance. He stood tall, nearly six feet by the looks of it, and was well built. His chest muscles had nowhere to hide under the tight-fitting t-shirts he wore.

I wished Steph were here. Stephanie Abbott was my best friend. She was like no one I had ever met before, full of life and enthusiasm. Steph was the jelly to my peanut butter. Together, we were one hell of a sandwich. Apart, I was a sticky mess you desperately tried to scrape off the roof of your mouth with your tongue. Steph and I had become instant friends the second we'd met. I don't want to say it was fate, because I don't believe in that kind of mumbo-jumbo, but something brought Steph into my life my senior year, and I was grateful for it. I'm not a graceful social butterfly like her, effortlessly fluttering around between friend groups. I was more like a clumsy moth, attracted to the popular kids beautiful glow, getting scorched by their insults and judging stares whenever I got near them, never becoming one of them. Then Steph showed up, and suddenly I was able to float on her wings, navigating through social circles without being burnt.

If Steph were here right now, she'd know what to do. She made situations like this easier. Without Steph here to keep me from saying the wrong thing or laughing too hard at a joke, situations like this were torture for me.

"You're friends with Kaylin Becker?" I said trying to keep my cool, accidentally shrieking the question louder than I meant to. The people standing next to us stopped their conversation and directed their attention to me. I slumped down trying to become invisible. "Of course you are. That's how my luck works."

"No," Grant replied. "Kevin Becker is my friend." Over emphasizing Kevin's name. "Kaylin's his little brother." He thought about it for a moment. "Wait just a minute! You know Kaylin? But you just got here yesterday."

"Not from here. From college," I said, trying to play it off as if it were no big deal, but it was. It was a huge deal. I couldn't let Kaylin see me. "Please excuse me." I marched as quickly and calmly as I could to the bathroom. My heart pounded so hard in my chest that I was sure everyone in the shop could hear it. I made it to the bathroom just as my face started to burn. I could feel it turning bright red. What am I going to do? How am I going to face him? Why was he even here? In this coffee shop. In this town. What were the chances we would both be in the same place? I turned the faucet on and splashed cold water over my face while I got my thoughts under control. The sound of running water reminded me why I was at the café in the first place. I had to use the bathroom! Like, I really needed to go. I stumbled into the stall and locked the door. Maybe I could just stay here forever, I thought as I sat down on the seat. Knowing that wasn't really an option, I took a deep breath, zipped my pants back up, unlocked the stall door, and stepped back over to the sink. My face was returning to its normal color, but my hair looked like I hadn't brushed it in a week. I searched in my purse for a brush—no luck. Of course not. If it weren't for bad luck, I'd have no luck at all, or at least that's what my dad used to tell me all the time. I was forever scrapping up my knees or loosing my books. Things almost never went my way, why should today be any different? The best I could find was a hair tie, some tinted chapstick, and a tube of old, clumpy mascara. I ran my fingers through my hair trying to untangle as many of the knots as I could, smoothed it back into a low pony, splashed my face again with cold water, and did the best I could with the chapstick and mascara. That's when I noticed the blazer in the mirror. Auh! I'm still wearing this stupid blazer with my name in big red letters on it. How embarrassing. I no longer felt like part of a team. At that moment, I felt alone, isolated from the rest of the world, in my own personal hell. A gray blazer with red lettering on it would be my downfall. I took it off, wadded it up into a ball, and tried stuffing it into my purse. It wouldn't fit. I had no choice but to put it back on.

With as much courage as I could muster, I opened the bathroom door, slowly stepped through it—making sure not trip or draw any unwanted attention to myself—and made my way to the table to sit down.

"There you are, Cuz, I was beginning to worry you'd fallen in. We were about to organize a search and rescue party to find you." Grant nudged his shoulder into mine.

All three boys stared at me. I was sure they were looking at the blazer. I clutched my purse tight to my chest. I really could have done without Grant's jokes. I was nervous enough.

"I'm fine, thank you." I wanted to run back to the bathroom and lock myself in the stall.

"Guys, this is my cousin Aurora, she's from Cary. Cuz, this is Kevin Becker and well, you already know Kaylin Becker. Kevin runs this place. It's been in their family for years."

Even if Grant hadn't introduced us I would've known right away that Kevin was Kaylin's older brother. They both had the same blue eyes and strong cheekbones. Kevin's hair was longer, though, and a bit darker, with a slight wave to it. I imagined it was from wearing it in a ponytail when he worked in the kitchen. It was obvious from the looseness of the white t-shirt he wore under his unbuttoned chef's jacket that he wasn't as muscular as Kaylin, but still had a very nice body to gaze upon. I wasn't sure, because he was sitting down, but I had a feeling he might be a few inches taller than Kaylin.

"You two know each other?" Kevin asked with a puzzled expression on his face. "How?" He dragged a cluster of fries through what was left of a blob of ketchup on his plate then tilted his head back and popped them into his gaping mouth.

"We, ah, we attend, we are attending the same college," Kaylin said, stumbling over his words as he spoke. He shifted uncomfortably in his chair. "I think we had a class together or something."

We most definitely did have a class together. I wondered if his awkwardness was because of the embarrassing incident that happened. He probably hated me, I wouldn't blame him if he did, I hated me for it.

"If your parents own this place, then why do you attend college in Cary, down by me? By where I live?" I asked. There had to be a logical explanation for how we could have ended up at the same college.

"This is our mother's place. Our father lives down in North Carolina. I'm going to school there and living with my dad in the winter. He lives alone in—"

"Hey!" Kevin interrupted. "Do you guys want a sandwich or some coffee? We're known for our spectacular sandwiches." He plucked a paper napkin from the napkin dispenser in the center of the table, wiped his hands, then tossed the dirty napkin on his empty plate. "Kaylin, why don't you go make these guys one of your special clubs. Put some extra love into it." He glanced at me. "By love I mean bacon. Lots of bacon. Piled high with bacon." He licked his lips.

"I love me some bacon. How about you, Cuz? You want one." I shook my head no. "You didn't turn into a vegetarian while you were away did you?" Grant teased.

"No." I frowned. I hadn't turned into a vegetarian. I quickly thought of an excuse to leave. "We should really get back to the house, I bet Aunt Theresa is wondering what's keeping us so long. I don't think we have time for a sandwich," I said, faking my disappointment. I started to get up from the table. I was desperate to find a way out of this awkward situation.

"No worries, Kaylin can make 'em quick. Two turkey bacon clubs to go then." Kevin nodded Kaylin towards the kitchen.

Kaylin reluctantly stood up, taking one last big swig from his paper coffee cup before throwing it in the trash as he headed towards the kitchen. I slowly sat back down, helpless.

"And two coffees," Grant hollered as Kaylin stomped away.

While Kaylin was gone, Grant and Kevin reminisced, reliving their glory days as high school rebels and catching up on what had been happening or rather what had not been happening in each other's lives now that they were responsible adults. I couldn't see either of them as being all that responsible and most certainly not adult. Kevin appeared to be interested only in himself and the things that directly affected him. He bragged about his triumphs, barely acknowledging the things Grant was talking about, constantly turning the conversation back around to himself. Grant on the other hand was a prankster, always joking and goofing around, never taking anything in life too seriously. They most certainly did not act like adults.

Kaylin walked up next to me holding a brown paper bag in one hand and balancing the coffee carrier in the other. "Here you go, two clubs with two black coffees to go. There's cream and sugar over on the counter by the register, if you want some." He glanced at the counter.

This was the closest I'd ever been to him. His cologne was musky. It filled my nostrils and soaked into my brain. I wanted to bathe in it, to soak myself in its alluring aroma. His arm brushed up against mine as he leaned forward to hand Grant the bag. It sent a rush through my body. Every inch of me surged with electricity. I was positive my face was about to turn red again.

Had he touched me on purpose? I quickly grabbed for the coffees, almost knocking them out of his hand, and said, "Thank you." Then I turned from the group and rushed for the door. I couldn't let him see me get flushed.

"Guess that's my cue to leave," Grant said, grabbing the bag from Kaylin as he passed by. "Wait up, Cuz! Where's the fire?" He stopped at the counter and tossed a couple sugar packets into the bag, then followed me out the door.

I kept quiet on the drive back to the house. Luckily, Grant was more interested in singing along to the songs on the radio than he was in talking to me. I prayed he hadn't noticed my reaction when Kaylin brushed up against me.

The house was tucked behind a slew of large oak trees that randomly dotted the front yard, almost as if they'd been thrown from the sky and took root right where they landed. The house looked like the child of an Old Plantation style home and a Queen Anne, resulting in a unique but gorgeous style of architecture. It was obvious there had been some recent updates done to it, mostly cosmetic stuff like new siding. The bones of the house had been left untouched and were old. Really old. A sturdy testament of time.

I pictured Scarlett O'Hara, from Gone with the Wind, kissing Rhett Butler on the massive front porch that began on one side of an elaborate white columned entryway, then wrapped around the entire first floor of the house to the other side. On the far right side, two round towers grew tall into the sky above the second floor, their points pierced the plump white clouds overhead. The wooden sills around the windows on each of the towers were adorned with beautifully carved patterns. The size of the house alone was impressive, even without all the extra details carved into it. On the extra-wide front steps leading up to the front door stood Uncle Rob with an un-mistakable smile plastered on his face, holding a lemonade in one hand and giving a big welcoming wave with the other.

"How was your trip into town?" he asked, genuinely interested in our answer.

"The usual," Grant replied as he opened his door. He grabbed the lunch bag from the back seat and exited the car. "You get the coffees," he hollered over his shoulder as he rushed up the stairs past his father and disappeared into the house.

"Good talk," Uncle Rob called after Grant then turned to me. "I don't stand in his way when he's hungry." He took a sip of his lemonade. "Did you get acquainted with the town?" he asked me as I climbed the stairs.

"I saw it a little bit yesterday, but yeah Grant showed me around," I said and smiled as I passed him, eager to eat my lunch. I didn't want to tell him about running into Kaylin. Then I remembered the question I'd been meaning to ask him. "Actually." I turned and faced him. "I've been meaning to ask you something."

"Ask away Aurora. No secrets here."

"Funny you should say that." I stepped closer to him. "That's kinda what I wanted to talk to you about."

"Did your dad say something?"

"What? My dad? No. What would my dad say?"

"Nothing, never mind. Go on with what you were going to say." He motioned for me to continue.

"Okay," I started off slowly. "Yesterday on my way here. I got kinda turned around, so I stopped in town and asked a man for directions, but he was reluctant to give them to me and, to be honest, a little rude. He called this a house of lies, saying you print half truths." I paused to judge my uncle's reaction. I expected anger but the corners of his lips turned upwards into a smile. "What did he mean, Uncle Rob?"

"That must've been old man Witherson. Pay no attention to that silly man. He thinks we're keeping secrets from him. That we know more than we print. He says the town deserves to know everything. He thinks we're more interested in making money than printing the facts."

"What kind of secrets?"

"You know you come from a long line of influential people, right?" Uncle Rob stepped down the stairs to the gravel pathway.

"No." I shook my head. "What people?"

Uncle Rob rolled his eyes in disbelief. "Your father," he said sadly. "I'll never understand why he chose to move away from here." I suspected Uncle Rob wanted to say more. I set the coffee on the porch railing and leaned against the nearest white column. Allowing him the opportunity to go into more detail.

"I suspect your lunch is getting cold," he said still shaking his head and wandered off down the driveway towards the mailbox.

I grabbed the coffee and headed inside to find Grant. We finished our lunch, then Grant took me to the newsroom. It was a larger room than I had pictured in my head. It was packed to the point of exploding with boxes and file cabinets. Three desks lined the far wall, all of them with older-looking computers on them. The first one was neatly organized, with labeled paper bins and pencil holders. The second had no system at all for keeping things in order, while the third was piled so high with old files that I wasn't totally positive there was actually a desk under all of it.

"This is where you will be working," Grant said, pointing to the third desk.

"You've got to be kidding me! How will I get anything done with a mountain of papers on the desk?" I asked, annoyed. I lifted a few of the papers up off the desk.

"Your first task will be to go through all the old lead files, see if there are any stories in there and, if not, recycle the folders." He seemed very pleased with giving me the grunt work to do. "I've got a story to write, so I'll leave you to it." He laughed as he headed over to the second desk. I should have known his desk was the unorganized one.

I spent the rest of the afternoon sorting the folders into three stacks while he clicked away on his keyboard. One stack for good story ideas, one for possible stories that needed more research done, and one stack for who-the-hell-cares-about-this-shit. I had hardly made a dent in the mess when Aunt Theresa hollered from somewhere down the hall, "Dinner time."

"Wow!" I mumbled out loud. I looked over to see Grant was no longer sitting at his desk. When had he left?

I felt discouraged. I'd been at this for hours and could barely see any progress. It would take me days to sort through the mess. I was anxious to start writing a story, even if it is just a small town paper. I still wanted to uncover a juicy story and report on it. It didn't seem like that was going to happen anytime soon, so I wandered to the dining room.

"Aurora ran into Mr. Witherson yesterday," Uncle Rob said to Aunt Theresa as she handed him her plate to load full of lasagna.

"You still like lasagna, right, Aurora?" She smiled at me. "I made it because I remembered it was your favorite."

"It is, thank you. I can't wait to try it." I said politely as I sat down.

"Mr. Witherson, huh?" Aunt Theresa glanced back at Uncle Rob. "I bet that must have been interesting." They shared a look.

"She sure did." He handed her back the plate and reached for Grant's. "He asked her if she was a liar."

"Hmm," Aunt Theresa took a bite.

"That old man's dee-ta-dee," Grant said, taking his plate back from his dad. "I see him in his front yard talking to the flowers in his garden all the time."

I held my plate up for Uncle Rob to fill. "There've been studies that say talking to your plants helps them grow," I told Grant. I had read it in one of my science books. I found Plant Science to be captivating, but not as much as English. If I couldn't make it as a writer, my backup plan was to be a botanist.

"Yeah, but he acts like they're talking back, and that's not normal," Grant said with his mouth full.

I agreed, taking my first bite of lasagna. "You made this?" I said to Aunt Theresa. "It's wonderful." The lasagna tasted just like my mom's.

"I called your mom and got her recipe. It's okay?"

"It's more than okay, it's perfect." I couldn't believe how much trouble Aunt Theresa had gone through to make me feel at home. "Thank you."

"You're welcome, dear. And don't let what Mr. Witherson says scare you. His family has lived in Stony Creek for generations, like ours. He thinks we know more about the A—"

"Not now," Uncle Rob cut in and shot a disapproving look at Aunt Theresa.

"Very well," she said, adjusting her position in her chair. "He thinks we know more than we do." She returned Uncle Rob's look back to him.

Uncle Rob quickly changed the subject, asking Grant something about the article he was writing for the paper.

I looked at the two of them, ignoring Grant going on and on about his story. Maybe Mr. Witherson was onto something. It did seem like they were keeping secrets.

Grant monopolized the conversation for the rest of dinner. I had a feeling that Uncle Rob intended for that to happen.

After dinner, I took a break from the daunting task of file sorting and headed up to my room to call Steph instead. As I walked down the long hallway to my room past the numerous portraits of my ancestors, a picture of the house caught my eye. *VanAgteren estate 1701* was inscribed on a small gold plate at the bottom of the frame. It amazed me. This house, or at least part of it, was almost three hundred and twenty years old. The front porch had been added on, along with a few other minor changes, but all in all the basic style of the house remained the same. I hadn't realized our family had lived here that long. As I dialed Steph's number, I wondered if our family had come over on the Mayflower. Steph and I spent the rest of the evening chatting. I told her all about running into Kaylin at the café, the excitement I felt when we touched, and how I rushed out. Being the good friend she was, she reassured me he probably didn't even notice my reaction. "Guys can be so oblivious when it comes to stuff like that," she said. We talked about the house and the mountain of files I was sorting through. She filled me in on the dorm parties she'd been to, as well as her plans for the summer. She was taking a few summer classes, but would have a break sometime in August and hoped to be able to come visit. I couldn't wait to see her.

Chapter 2

The Summer Heat

Our morning breakfasts had become a routine. The four of us met in the kitchen to discuss the day's assignments over a bowl of cereal, or two in Grant's case, then head off in our own directions to start work on them. It had taken almost two weeks but I finally managed to unbury the desk and get it set up the way I liked it. I sorted all of the folders into piles, got rid of the garbage, and had picked my first story to write.

The spring flowers were done blooming, and the yard was no longer filled with their vibrant colors. The yellows and oranges had been replaced with a sea of green leaves that rippled in the summer breeze and made a rustling sound as it blew across them. The summer heat was starting to set in, with high temperatures soaring in the mid ninties. Uncle Rob warned me that the townspeople tended to get a little batty when the temperature neared the triple digits. Next weekend, the town would be holding their annual Fourth of July Picnic in the Park Celebration, with fireworks at dusk. This year they were celebrating their one hundred and eighty-eighth anniversary. Our family was one of the first settlers in Stony creek. When the VanAgtern estate was built, the whole area around it was a hearty forest full of trees prime for logging. The men who built the estate saw the income potential and brought their families to the area. One hundred and thirty-one years later they named the town Stony Creek and held their first picnic.

I had successfully managed to keep my distance from Kaylin, avoiding any further embarrassment for most of the spring, and things were on track to start Penn State in the fall. I'd applied for every grant and scholarship I could find online and I was starting to get responses. I had almost finished the research I needed for my first article. It was nothing groundbreaking, like a corrupt government conspiracy or an alien invasion, but I was proud of the work I'd put into it. I planned to head into town today, to the park, to get the final pieces I needed to finish the article. Someone had been throwing trash all over the town park at night. I'd hidden a motion activated camera high up in the branches of a tree the day before, to catch the culprits in the act, and I needed to retrieve it. I'd become an expert at avoiding the potholes on the drive into town and I was getting to know all the locals by their first names. Things were going well. Perhaps my luck was changing.

As I pulled into one of the parking spaces at the edge of the park, I noticed Kaylin standing under the very tree I'd hidden my camera in, with something in his hands.

"It better not be my camera," I muttered to myself, quickly getting out of the car. If he so much as touched my camera he's going to be in for it.

"Miss Aurora," called out a voice from behind me. "Miss Aurora, wait. I have something I must tell you." I knew without turning around it was Mr. Witherson. Most people would find it difficult to mistake his squawky old voice for anyone else's.

"I'm in a hurry, Mr. Witherson." I spun around to face him. "Can't this wait? I really need to get my camera." I glanced over my shoulder to make sure Kaylin hadn't run off.

"No, it's very important, Aurora," he said taking a moment to catch his breath. His puppy sniffed at my shoes. "You need to know the truth about your family," he said, sputtering.

Not this again. I didn't have time for one of his foolish conspiracy theories about my family. I needed to get my camera. He plunged his hand into the pocket of his trousers and pulled out a handkerchief, dabbing the sweat from his brow. "Boy, it's a hot one today."

"Yep, in the nineties, but I really need to go," I insisted looking back to see Kaylin leaning against the tree, laughing, his eyes glued to the object in his hands. He did have my camera. What could possibly be so funny? "We can talk tomorrow," I assured Mr. Witherson as I darted off in Kaylin's direction.

"It's you, Miss Aurora. You're the key," he hollered after me.

I'm the key? What was he talking about? The key to what? "You better not have my camera," I told Kaylin as I ran. "You're interfering with an investigation. That's official equipment." I pointed to my camera.

Kaylin raised his hands in the air, pretending to surrender. "I wouldn't want to interfere with official business," he said, laughing, as I came to an abrupt halt in front of him. "Good news though." He lowered his hands.

I yanked my camera away from him, immediately forgetting about Mr. Witherson and his nonsense.

"You caught the culprits red handed! Or should I say red pawed?"

"What gave you the right to watch my recording?" I said angrily. I quickly rewound the footage to see what he thought was so funny.

"The masked bandits have been caught and will do time for their crimes against humanity," he said in a commanding tone, as if he were the city commissioner making an official announcement. He held his side and bent over in pain, laughing hysterically at his own joke. His hair, falling over his eyes, didn't look as adorable when he was making fun of me.

"It was raccoons, Aurora. Get it? Masked bandits...because raccoons look like they're wearing masks." I got it, but I didn't think it was funny. Not one bit.

I stormed off to my car, my ears burning with anger. I could feel the tears welling up in my eyes. I'm not going to let him see me cry. This was supposed to be my big story, not a fluff piece about raccoon bandits trashing the park. I was going to catch some deviant kids doing deviant kid things. I was wrong. My luck hadn't changed. I was still the awkward unlucky girl that never said the right thing at the right time. The girl who embarrassed herself in front of the whole class.

"Oh come on, Aurora, don't be like that. It's funny," he hollered after me. He stopped laughing, but the damage was already done. My feelings had already been hurt. "I didn't mean anything by it, honest."

I sped back to the house trying to get my emotions under control, but my thoughts raced around in my mind. All my research was for nothing. There was no story in raccoons. How could Kaylin be such a jerk? I'd worked so hard on this story. What did I ever see in him?

I pulled up in front of the house and slammed the car into park. I leaned forward and rested my forehead on the steering wheel. I was defeated. Or was I? Maybe there was something I could salvage from the video. A story I could find. I hadn't had a chance to go over all the footage at the park. Maybe my camera caught something else, something more interesting than raccoons. I snatched the camera off the passenger seat and took a second to watch three raccoons take turns knocking over garbage cans in the park on the video recording. Nothing. My heart sank. Not even a shadowy figure in the background. I was about to head inside when an old Jeep pulled up behind me and Kaylin got out. I watched him walk up in my rearview mirror. He plodded up to my window, his head hanging low.

"I'm sorry, Aurora," he said sincerely, his icy-blue eyes apologetic. "I shouldn't have laughed. I didn't mean to hurt your feelings." He brushed his hair away from his eyes and leaned closer to the window.

I didn't know what to say. I'd been avoiding him ever since that day at the café, but now here he was. He'd followed me home. I thought about shoving my door open, running past him to the house, and locking the door behind me, but something held me in place, a force of nature that left me helpless. I couldn't fight the attraction I felt for him. I could hardly even glance in his direction without turning red, but I couldn't run away, not this time. Not like I had the day our English teacher held my essay up in class with the words Aurora + Kaylin scribbled on the back page for all of my classmates to see, including Kaylin. I was mortified. I ran out of class that day, hoping

I would never see him again. Then I came to Stony Creek only to find him here. And now he was here, in my uncle's driveway, apologizing to me. I couldn't seem to avoid him, no matter how hard I tried. The universe kept throwing him into my path. So I sat there, frozen in my seat, melting a little more inside with every word he spoke. He had the most soothing voice. I didn't ever want him to stop talking to me.

"Are you mad at me, Rory?" he asked sympathetically. He rested his forearm on the roof of my car and peeked in the open window at me. His face a couple of feet away from mine.

He called me Rory. I wanted to die. My name sounded so beautiful when he said it like that. No one had ever called me Rory before.

"No, yes, I don't know." What was I saying? I sounded like a damn fool. I couldn't think straight. I took a deep breath and asked myself what Steph would do. I carefully formed the sentence in my head before speaking. "I wish you wouldn't have taken my camera, but I forgive you." There, that made more sense.

"Would you like to go with me to the Picnic in the Park this weekend?" He lowered his eyes towards the ground trying not to make direct eye contact as he said it.

OMG, could this be real? Was he really asking me on a date? My heart fluttered in my chest. "Yes," was all I managed to get out.

"Great," he said with a big smile as he lifted his gaze back up to meet mine again. Our eyes locked and for a moment I thought he was going to lean in and kiss me, but then he pulled away and said, "I'll come by and pick you up around two on Saturday."

"Okay," I answered. Couldn't I have come up with a more beautiful response. Something poetic or at least something with more than two syllables? How did I ever expect to be a writer?

"You do have to admit, Rory, the raccoon thing, a little funny," he said teasingly. I smiled and nodded. He patted the roof of my car then headed back to his Jeep and got in.

It *was* a bit funny, I supposed. I smiled and waved, my rear still frozen in place as he drove off down the driveway. As soon as he was out of sight I was finally able to move. I grabbed my things from the passenger seat then burst out of the car with a newfound sense of excitement. I ran to my room and called Steph. I spent the rest of the day in a fog, thinking only about Kaylin. My emotions soared and life coursed through my body.

The next few days took forever to go by. I couldn't wait to see Kaylin again. Finally, Saturday arrived. I woke up early, I was too excited to sleep. I tried to get a little work done to pass the time but I couldn't focus. My mind kept fantasizing about how our date would go. Would we instantly hit it off? Would he hold my hand? Would he kiss me? I decided on a stroll around the house to help me clear my head. It was a beautiful day out. I hoped the lazy summer day would help to distract me but everything outside was buzzing with the same energy I was feeling inside. Even the fat little bumble bee that floated from empty stem to empty stem in search of the last remaining spring flowers was doing so with more pizazz.

After a few laps around the house, I headed inside and began to get ready for my date with Kaylin. I wanted to look my best for him. I showered and shaved my legs, not just to the knee like I usually did, but all the way up my thigh. I dried off and retrieved my pretty red slip dress, with little white polka dots, out of the closet and slid it over my head. It was the perfect dress for a Fourth of July picnic. I curled my hair in big, loose curls, then pulled most of it up into a messy bun, leaving several strands down to frame in my face. I admired myself in the mirror. Something was missing, I had the red and white on my dress but I was missing the blue. I dug through my jewelry box searching for the necklace my grandmother had given to me when I turned eighteen. It was an etched gold medallion with a large blue sapphire in the center of it and twelve small diamonds forming a circle around the sapphire. She told me it had been passed down from first born female to first born female for generations. Someday, I would pass it down to my daughter or granddaughter, whomever the next female born would be. It was a beautiful addition to my wardrobe, completing the theme perfectly. I headed out of my room. Thud! I kicked the leg of my bed. "OUCH!" I shrieked in pain. I grabbed my toe and hopped around, eventually collapsing on my bed.

Shoes! I'd forgotten shoes. I glanced down at my throbbing toe. Once the pain subsided, I rummaged around the pile of shoes in the corner of my closet and pulled out a pair. I decided to go with my flat, strappy sandals. I didn't want to press my luck and try to wear a pair of heels. There, now my outfit was one hundred percent complete.

I waited patiently in the front parlor for Kaylin to arrive, awkwardly sitting on the arm of a floral patterned chair next to the front window, where I was able to peek out and see Kaylin, without him seeing me.

Aunt Theresa and Uncle Rob had already left. They apparently had a ritual for finding the perfect picnic spot. One with just enough shade to be comfortable but that still had optimal viewing for the fireworks later. Aunt Theresa had explained their process to me but my mind was elsewhere, and I hadn't been paying attention. It wasn't long before I heard Kaylin's Jeep coming down the drive. I peeked out the window. He exited his Jeep and began waving his arms around in front of his face, battling the cloud of dust he stirred up.

I waited for him to climb the front steps before eagerly throwing open the door.

"Hello, Rory," he said, his arm lifted in the air to begin knocking. He awkwardly lowered his arm.

I scolded myself for being so impatient. He's going to think I'm desperate. I reminded myself to act cool.

"You look nice." His eyes lingered on my chest. "I really like your necklace," he said pointing at my chest. "It looks old. Not old, like worn out. Like vintage." Our eyes locked. "May I?"

"Oh, yes. Thank you." I lifted the necklace from my chest to let him see it closer. "It was my grandmother's." He leaned in, taking the necklace in one hand and inspected it. He was wearing the same cologne as the day at the café. I breathed as much of his scent as my lungs would allow. "It's been in our family for generations." I turned my head slightly so as not to talk directly into his face.

"Are you ready for the most thrilling day of your life?" He smiled a sheepish grin at me and winked, before resting my necklace down on my chest.

Um, duh, of course I was ready to be thrilled!

"Best date of my life, huh?" I played it cool on the outside, but inside, my heart was racing.

"Absolutely. A day filled with fireworks." He escorted me to the passenger side of his Jeep and opened the door. My dad would've been impressed with his chivalry. "Our town puts on a pretty amazing fireworks display," he added, winking again. He waited for me to get situated in my seat before closing the door.

"Something smells really delicious," I said once he sat down in the driver's seat.

"I made my famous chicken noodle soup and some sandwiches for the picnic." He reached into the backseat and lifted the cover off the basket sitting there. I noticed he'd also packed a bottle of wine.

Is he older than me? No, I was pretty sure he wasn't twenty-one yet. Maybe he had Kevin pick it up for him, or maybe he took it from his mom's stash?

"Isn't it a little warm outside for chicken soup?" I asked, deciding not to bring up the bottle of wine. I glanced out the window up towards the cloudless sky. The sun's rays blazed down on me. I could already feel my shoulders starting to burn and I'd only been outside for a few minutes. "You do know it's July, right?" I added teasingly as I fastened my seatbelt.

"My chicken soup is the best. It's perfect all year round. Wait until you try it, you'll see." He fiddled with the radio, finding a song he liked before putting the Jeep in reverse and backing up.

Grant flew out the front door. "Guys! Wait! I need a ride into town." He waved his hands in the air like a madman trying to get our attention. "Guys!"

Kaylin stomped on the brakes. "I guess we have company." He glanced over at me. "Do you mind if we give Grant a ride?"

"So much for our perfect date," I mumbled sarcastically. Our romantic twosome was about to become an awkward threesome.

"If you don't want to, I can tell him to find another ride."

"No, it's fine."

"You sure?"

"Yeah, yeah. It's fine."

"Thanks, guys," Grant said hopping into the backseat. "Hey, you guys on a date or something?" He shoved the picnic basket across the seat, oblivious to the fact that he'd just inserted himself into our perfect day.

We drove into town not saying much, but I caught Kaylin glancing over at me every now and then. At a stop sign our eyes met, I could see he was just as unhappy as I was about having Grant tagging along.

"Are you meeting someone in town?" I asked Grant, hoping he wouldn't be hanging out with us all night.

"Yep, Kevin and I are in charge of tonight's musical entertainment. We set the DJ booth up last night. It's going to be great." Grant pretended he was scratching a record.

I did a little dance for joy in my mind. Kaylin and I would be alone after all.

We parted ways with Grant in the parking lot then set out to find a perfect picnic spot of our own. Our perfect spot was at the far edge of the park. A spot where we could have some privacy but still be close enough to take part in the festivities. The afternoon flew by, filled with tons of eating and group activities. Activities like the one-legged race, the egg toss, and a silly game where you had to pop a balloon by squishing it between you and your partner's bodies. Kaylin and I won first place at that one. The town had built a dance floor in the center of the park out of plywood and vinyl flooring. The trees were wrapped in twinkling lights, and everywhere you looked were red, white, and blue ribbons. As the sun set, the trees started to shimmer, turning the park into a romantic fairytale land. It was turning out to be the perfect first date. Better than I could have ever imagined.

"Would you like to dance?" Kaylin stood up, extending his hand out to help me up from the picnic blanket where we'd been lying, watching the sunset and holding each other.

"I would love to, sir." I accepted his hand and he led me onto the dance floor.

"I'm not very good at this," he admitted before putting his hand around my waist. "Is this okay?

I nodded and we began to gently sway back and forth.

"Are you having a good time?" he politely asked. "You seem a little tense."

My arms were rigid leaving a large gap between us. I smiled and nodded then forced myself to step closer. I nervously glanced around at the other couples on the dance floor. He pulled me closer to him, closing the small gap between our bodies. I closed my eyes and laid my head on his shoulder. My nervousness vanished. He felt so right. I wanted this moment to never end. The world around us melted away, leaving just the two of us holding each other tightly on the dance floor. The music played, and off in the distance fireworks filled the sky. It was like a scene in a movie. He spun me around in our little corner of the dance floor. Time stood still. We were the only two people on the planet. I gasped as my lips grazed his cheek. He pulled back and our eyes locked. I wanted so badly for him to kiss me. We hadn't realized the music had stopped playing or that the only people left on the dance floor, other than us, were the groups of friends saying their goodbyes.

"Kiss her already. Everyone is leaving. Can we get a ride back to the house?" Grant's words echoed in my head as reality crashed in around us.

Kaylin quickly stepped back. I spun around to see Grant and Kevin a few feet away making kissing faces at us.

"Grow up!" I said angrily. How many times was Grant going to ruin my perfect date? I stomped off towards our blanket to gather up the picnic basket.

"Real nice," Kaylin said, quickly following behind me.

"We are having an after party at the house, if you two love birds would like to join us." Kevin yelled from the dance floor. He held up two bottles of Jack.

Kaylin stared at me. His lips gently puckered in one corner of his mouth and his eyebrow raised. "Want to?" He shrugged. "Might be fun." He tried to read the expression on my face. "It's fine if you don't. Hanging out with those two probably isn't what you had in mind." He gathered up the two empty wine glasses we'd left lying on the blanket and carefully tucked them away in the basket. He was right. I didn't really want to, but I doubted we were going to get any more alone time.

"I guess," I replied. Hanging out with them was a better option than having our date come to an end. He paused for a moment and gazed into my eyes. "We can go," I said, assuring him it was fine.

Kevin shook the bottles he was holding up, waiting for an answer from Kaylin.

"Yeah, sure. Just give us a minute," Kaylin hollered to him, then tossed the last of the picnic supplies into the basket.

"I don't know, Cuz! Maybe we shouldn't invite you. You're not twenty-one yet," Grant said in a teasing tone as the four of us headed towards the Jeep.

"Shut up, Grant," I replied, punching him in the shoulder.

"Just kidding! No need to get violent." He rubbed his shoulder. "Geesh."

We piled into Kaylin's Jeep and drove off. Grant and Kevin started to party in the backseat on the drive and were feeling pretty good by the time we made it to the house. Kaylin and I had some catching up to do. I ran inside and quickly changed out of my dress into a comfy t-shirt and a pair of jean shorts, then returned to the party.

"Let me see that bottle." Kaylin grabbed one of the bottles from his big brother, took a big swig then handed it to me. "Want some?"

I took the bottle and sat down on a lawn chair. Grant had dragged four lawn chairs out of the garage while I was changing and set them up in a circle around the sticks and branches Kevin and Kaylin were gathering into a pile.

"I grabbed a lighter on my way out." I slid the lighter out of my pocket and tossed it to Kaylin. "I had a feeling you might need it."

"That was very thoughtful," Kaylin said as he caught the lighter, his smile sheepish.

"Light the fire already, Lil' bro," Kevin said impatiently. He grabbed the bottle of Jack, took a swig, then passed it to Grant. "If you can stand to take your eyes off her for a minute." Grant took a swig and passed it to Kaylin.

Kaylin did the same, then passed it back to me before leaning down to light a pile of leaves. "This house is huge," he said, changing the subject. He sat down in the chair next to me. "Here's your lighter back." He handed me the lighter. "This is great. Being outdoors. Enjoying what mother nature has to offer. Look at those stars." Kaylin pointed to the sky. "You can't see stars like that back in Cary, can you?" He admired the sky for a moment. "How about a tour of the house?" He glanced over at me. I wasn't sure if he was really interested in taking a tour or if it was his sly way of asking me to take him upstairs to my room.

"Sure, let me be your tour guide. Ask Aurora, I'm great at it," Grant said. His words slurred from drinking too much.

"Yep! Best ever tour guide," I said, relieved Grant offered to take Kaylin on the tour. I looked down at the empty bottle of Jack in my hand. The bottle clinked against the metal leg of the chair as I set it on the ground. Perhaps I was a little tipsier than I'd realized. I probably didn't have the best judgment right now. "Hey, listen, listen guys! I have something to say." I waved my arms to get their attention. "I want to go in the towers and be a princess with my pretty dress on. See my pretty dress?" I peered down at my t-shirt and shorts, forgetting I had changed when we'd gotten home. "Okay, not in my dress, haha, look I'm not wearing one, but you, Grant." I pointed an accusing finger at him. "You're still an evil dragon."

"What'd I do?"

"Trying to ruin my fun with Kaylin." I waved my finger around in the air.

"Ignore her," said Kevin. He reached over and pushed my arm down to my side. Kaylin glared at him. "Oh, forget you too."

"So, yes a tour?" Grant floundered as he tried to get up from his chair. He watched the rest of us stumble to our feet then led us to the tower. "Ta-da, the tower." He tried to bow but fell to the ground instead. "Here you goes, Cuz. Be a prin...prinscesseses," he said, using the wall to help himself up. His words were making less sense the longer the evening wore on.

"It's only a stairway to the second floor? Where's the rest of it?" I was disappointed. I'd expected there to be more to it. A spiral staircase leading to a lookout or something. Not just an open stairwell to the second floor.

"What do you mean, rest of it?" asked Grant, confused. He rested against the banister. Kevin had his back to the wall trying to stay upright.

"The rest of it, the rest of it," Kaylin sang. "Where is the rest of it?"

I grabbed Kaylin's hand and dragged him back outside. Grant and Kevin followed, singing the ridiculous song with him.

"Looks up at the top, there's two towers, and look at the windows, there are two of them, one on each tower. There's not two windows in the stairway. We need to look in the windows."

"Are you nuts?" asked Kevin, no longer singing along with the other two. "Did you know how high that is? Are you trying to commit homicide?"

"You said *homicide*," Grant said, busting out laughing. "Homicide. I think you meant suicide, unless she's going to throw your drunk asses off the roof. If that's the case, I'm in."

"You want to throw me off the roof? That's cold man, real cold."

"Just kidding, Bro, I couldn't let that happen, I love you guys." Grant started hugging everyone.

"Okay, okay, stop. Look, she's right. Something isn't adding up, up there," said Kaylin.

"Thank you, Kaylin. See? Kaylin believes me." I shot an I-told-you-so glare at the other two, who for some reason were still hugging.

"However, I'm pretty sure none of us is in any shape to go climbing around on roof tops tonight. First thing in the beginning of the morning we will do it. For now I think it's best if we get some sleep." Grant finished his nonsense sentence with a disgusting belch then added. "You guys can't drive home like this. You can sleep in the parlor on the pulled out couch bed thing. I'll get you some pillows and blankets and stuffs." Grant stumbled into the house. "I've got this!" he called out from just inside the door.

Chapter 3

The Next Morning

T he sun shone in through my window as it had every morning since I'd arrived, but now the beautiful rainbow ballet didn't seem to be as spectacular. In fact, it made me feel nauseated. My head throbbed.

"How much did I drink?" I recalled the events of last night. Kaylin! Oh my gosh, Kaylin and Kevin spent the night. They were downstairs.

I threw on the same jean shorts I'd worn the night before, a clean t-shirt from the dresser, and quickly fixed my hair. It was still curly. I didn't appear half as bad as I was feeling. I bounced down the stairs to the kitchen, ignoring the pounding in my head. All three of the boys were sitting around the table, eating breakfast.

"Mom.... Aunt Theresa, made us pancakes before she and dad headed out this morning." Grant pointed to a big pile of pancakes over by the stove.

"Where did they go?" I asked. I grabbed a plate and loaded it full of pancakes.

"To Cary to visit your parents," Grant said, reminding me. I had totally forgotten they were heading out today.

"Oh, right. They will be gone for the week."

"How are you feeling today?" Kaylin asked as I sat down next to him. "We were all pretty wasted last night. "

"Ugh!" I groaned, putting one hand on my head and one on my stomach. "I feel like I've been hit by a truck."

Everyone nodded their heads in agreement as they continued to devour their pancakes, desperately licking the dripping syrup off their forks as if it were some kind of magic hangover cure.

"Hey, listen," Kaylin said, then leaned over and whispered in my ear. "I'm sorry if I said or did anything I shouldn't have last night." Then he sat back and asked, "Were you serious last night about climbing on the roof?" I nodded yes. "I'm still game, if you are."

"I think we should," Kevin said between bites.

"Yeah! Me too," Grant agreed. "It does seem a little weird. We should investigate. We are, after all, reporters, are we not? Or at least Aurora and I are. It's our job, no, our *duty* to uncover the truth," Grant said, giving us more credit than we deserved. He wasn't the ace reporter he claimed he was, and I hadn't even written one article.

"Okay then, sounds like we're all in agreement. We're climbing up on the house," Kaylin said. It was nice having them all think one of my ideas was worthwhile. It wasn't often I came up with a good one.

We finished gorging ourselves on the sweet pancakes, then headed to the garage to find some rope and ladders. Climbing onto the roof of the porch was easy, but getting from there up to the second floor roof took a little more skill and group cooperation than we'd anticipated. It was late afternoon by the time we'd finished creating an elaborate rope and pulley system to hoist us up. The guys stood on the first floor roof using the rope we'd flung over the branch of a nearby tree to hoist me up in a makeshift harness to the second floor roof. Once I finally got up there, I was able to make my way over to the first tower and peer through the window.

"What do you see, Cuz?" hollered Grant. He stood on his tiptoes trying, unsuccessfully, to see over the edge of the roof. "What's in there?"

"It's the stairway," I yelled back over my shoulder. "I have to get to the second tower, just a minute." I carefully navigated around the first tower, taking small, well-placed steps on a ledge that ran around the base of the tower over to the rooftop that separated the two towers. I made my way across the roof to the second tower and knelt down in front of it. I gripped the window sill on both sides and pressed my nose against the glass. My eyes widened. "There's a room in here!". I rubbed the dirty glass with my hand and took a second look. It was difficult to see what was in the room. I felt along the base of the window. "I think I can get in." My hunch was right; there was more to this old house than anyone knew.

I shimmied the window open and slipped inside. The window slammed shut behind me as I dropped at least eight or nine feet to the floor. Everything in the room had a thick layer of dust on it. No one had been here for years. Shelves filled with books lined three of the walls. Several paintings hung randomly on the fourth wall. A larger painting near the center of that wall drew my attention. Two figures in white, hooded robes, the edges of which were intricately embroidered with blue and red symbols, stood prominently as the main focus of the painting. Circled around them were more hooded figures, some of them in red robes with blue symbols embroidered on them and some with blue robes and red symbols. In the lower left corner was the name John Smybert.

"Must be the man's name who painted this," I muttered to myself. My eyes left the painting, continuing to scan over the mysterious room. Stacks of documents and maps were spread out over the large table in the center of the room. I ran my fingers along the rough plastered walls in search of a light switch, but there wasn't one. Scanning the room for another source of light, my eyes settled on an old oil lamp in the center of the table. I remembered I still had the lighter in my pocket from last night. I prayed there was fuel in the lamp and that it wouldn't explode when I lit it. Who knows how long it had been sitting there? Judging by the inch of dust on everything, it had to have been close to a hundred years. I cautiously lifted away the glass globe and a snug, brass cap to expose the wick, then I held my breath and flicked the lighter. It worked. The room filled with a soft, warm glow. The smell of burning dust wafted to my nostrils as I replaced the globe. Holding the lamp up, I wandered over to the bookcase closest to the window. There were so many books; books from all over the world, in languages I'd never heard of. I removed an old, leather-bound volume from the shelf. I felt the raised, gold, lettering on the cover. It was written in French. I opened it, only able to make out a few words, before closing it and placing it back where I'd found it. I'd forgotten most of the French I'd learned in high school. I picked up the book next to it. English, antiquated English, but still English. I was able to recognize enough of the words in the sentences to piece together the meanings, so I took the book with me over to the table.

"Aurora, are you all right? What's going on? Aurora?" I glanced up to see Kaylin standing outside the window. He held it open and leaned his upper body in.

"Careful, it's a long drop," I warned as he made his way through the window, landing on the floor with a loud thud. The window slammed down again.

"We were calling for you. Are you all right?" He brushed himself off and strolled towards me.

"Look!" I said holding up the lamp to illuminate the room. "Can you believe it?"

"Holy crap, this is amazing!" He stopped dead in his tracks and waited as the lantern lit up the room, then strolled over to the table in the middle of the room and started rummaging through the papers on it. "This stuff is old, like really old."

"I know! We should be careful. Some of it might be fragile," I warned. I set the lantern on the table next to the book from the bookcase and traipsed back over to examine a few more of them. I started reading aloud the titles on the spines.

"You guys should've seen Grant try to shimmy up the rope by himself." Kevin said as he swung his legs over the edge of the window sill. "I had to practically pull him up with the rope." Kevin slid off the sill and onto the floor.

"It wasn't like that." Grant said as he too landed on the floor with a big thud. "You remember in gym class where you had to climb the rope and ring the bell at the top? It was like that."

"Yeah, only if I hadn't been pulling you up from the other end we'd still be waiting for you to ring *the bell*." Kevin made air quotes with his fingers.

J. W. Christie   35

"Whatever, dude. You don't know what you're talking about." Grant dusted himself off. "So what did you guys find?"

"I'm not sure, but it's awesome," Kaylin replied excitedly. "Come look at this." He motioned Kevin over. "It's got our last name on it. Look! Becker!" He held up the book and pointed to their name.

"Your last name? Why would a book in my house have your name written in its pages?" Grant asked as if one of us might know the answer.

"Weird," Kevin said and stepped up beside Kaylin. He glanced at the page over his brother's shoulder. "Maybe there's a book with your name in it too, dude."

"Maybe?" replied Grant. "Maybe in one of these." He started scanning the shelves alongside me. He grabbed a book off the shelf every once in a while to take a peek at what was inside, then replaced it when he didn't find what he was looking for.

The four of us spent hours carefully searching through the papers, inspecting the paintings on the walls and rummaging through the books.

"Listen to this, guys." I walked over to the table and stood next to Kaylin. "It's some sort of creed." I read the paper out loud.

"Who can right the wrongs of injustice?
The Amerii can.
Who can keep our nation's beliefs alive?
The Amerii can.
Who can forge a path of freedom and individual rights?
The Amerii can."

I looked up at them. "There's more here but I can't figure out what it says, it's just a bunch of random words and numbers that don't make sense."

Kevin, sitting across from Kayin with his feet up on the table, asked, "Who are the Amerii?"

"According to this book, we all are," Kaylin said, holding up the book he'd been reading nearly the whole time we'd been in the room. "This book has a list of last names, not just Becker but yours too. VanAgteren is here also." He glanced at Grant and me. "It goes back hundreds of years to the first settlers of America. It has which countries each of our families originated from. What their purpose for coming here to America was and what position in the Amerii they held. There's twenty six names here. Thirteen men and thirteen women from all over the globe, they called themselves the Amerii." He listed off the men and women's names. "Their mission was to make sure everyone in America had equal rights, that no man would have to live under the tyranny of an unjust government any longer in this New Wo—"

"Ah, guys, I hate to interrupt. This is fascinating stuff, really, but I think we might be about to run out of fuel for the lantern." Kevin let his legs fall from the table to the floor. "And has anyone else noticed there's no door?" He stood up and glanced around.

The rest of us surveyed our surroundings. We'd been so busy going through the books, none of us realized that we had no way out. Scaling the wall back up to the window was out of the question. There was no way any of us could reach it. We were trapped. My palms began to sweat and my stomach churned.

"There has to be a way out," Grant said with panic in his voice. His eyes darted around the room. "A secret door or something."

We spread out and frantically searched for a way out.

"Feel the walls, check the bookcases, look for anything that doesn't belong," Kaylin said feeling along a bookcase. "He's right. There has to be some way out."

"That's not very helpful, Kaylin," I said, fear coursing through my veins. One by one, I skewed each of the paintings on the wall so that they were all tilted to the right in hopes that moving them might trigger something to happen. "Nothing here seems like it belongs." I threw my hands in the air when nothing happened. "This whole room doesn't belong."

"I think I found something." Kaylin motioned for us to come over. I rushed to his side. "There's something weird about this wall. There's a seam here." He ran his fingers along the wall. "Everybody search this area for a latch or a button, anything that could open it."

"How about a loose board?" I asked, tapping on the baseboards.

"This one's flimsy, like there's nothing behind it." I rapped my knuckles more intently on the board. "Hear that?" I said excitedly. "Someone help me push this board in."

Grant hurried over. "You're right. Stand back, I'm gonna kick it in." Midway through Grant's kick the lantern sputtered. He missed the hollow board and kicked the one next to it.

"Son of bitch! I think I broke my toe!" Grant hopped towards a chair on one foot, holding his other foot in his hand, and cursing like a sailor. He collapsed onto the chair and quickly slid off his shoe.

Everyone frantically talked at once. The sun had already set, leaving only a sliver of moonlight streaming in the window when the lantern flickered again and the flame vanished. I yanked my cell phone out of my back pocket. Only nineteen percent battery left. The power wouldn't last us long, but I had enough to turn on my flashlight and examine Grant's foot, which was already starting to swell.

"What do we do now?" Kevin said angrily. "It was your idea to come in here. Now we're trapped." His accusations infuriated me, but I ignored them and helped Grant elevate his foot.

"Don't get mad at her, she didn't force you to come in," Kaylin said, defending me as he felt for a way out. Even though Kevin was right. It was my fault. We wouldn't be stuck in a room with no door if I hadn't said I wanted to be a princess. Why had I suggested we find out what was in the second tower? I got my wish. A princess locked in a tower.

"Grant broke his toe. We have no way out and no one is ever going to find us in here." Kevin stomped angrily around the room. "Don't defend Aurora just because you have the hots for her." Kaylin glanced at me and smiled. "I'm your brother, man. Bro's before Ho's."

"Excuse me?" I said angrily. I let Grant's foot slip from where I'd rested it on my thigh.

"Aurora." he howled, but I was too offended to apologize to him.

"How about instead of bitching, you come help me find a way out," Kaylin suggested to Kevin, defusing the situation. Kevin shook his head in contempt but did as his brother asked and knelt down beside him. I picked Grant's foot up and placed it gently on the table, the whole time giving Kevin an irritated stare.

The two of them diligently searched the wall from top to bottom. They moved the pictures and books around, trying to find a lever or something, anything to open the door.

"I know there's a door here, I can feel it. We just need to figure out how to open it," Kaylin said positively. "Can you shine the light over here, Rory?"

I stepped next to Kaylin and bent down beside him, focusing the light where his hands were.

"Turn the light off," Grant said urgently.

"What?" We all turned to face him. "If I turn the light off, we won't be able to see." I crinkled my nose and tilted my head slightly to the side, raising my left eyebrow. His suggestion didn't make sense to me.

"No, I could see light coming from the wall when you moved, turn your light off."

I hesitantly switched the light off. He was right. There was light shining from inside the house through a crack in the corner of the wall. Kaylin ran over to the light.

"There's something here," Kaylin exclaimed, feeling along the edge of the bookcase closest to where the light was coming in. "I feel it!"

There was a loud popping sound, then the wall jerked. The entire wall from top to bottom, along with everything on it, swung inwards, opening up to reveal the second floor hallway. The same hallway I walked down every day to get to and from my bedroom.

How had I not noticed something was strange in this part of the hallway?

"I think we should keep this a secret for now. I don't even think we should tell our families about it," Kaylin said as he stepped out into the hallway, with Kevin quickly on his heels. I helped Grant to his feet. Grant leaned on me as he hobbled out of the room. A sense of relief greeted me in the hallway.

I was free.

The four of us agreed to keep the secret room between us, then pulled the wall shut and headed downstairs to discuss what we had found.

Chapter 4

The Amerii Room

We spent every second of our spare time sneaking into and out of the secret room, making sure each time that Uncle Rob and Aunt Theresa didn't catch us. Most of our time in the room was spent researching the Amerii, what their beliefs were, how they came to be, and where they were now. We had more questions than answers. Were there still active Amerii out there in the world, influencing the country? If so, what were they doing? How were our family's involved with them? Late in July the answers finally came.

"Rory, look at this chest." I glanced up from the book I was reading to see Kaylin dragging a chest out from between two of the book cases. The chest wasn't very big, about the size of a laundry basket, but it was well built, with thick wood boards and iron brackets, making it very heavy and hard to maneuver.

"What do you suppose is in there?" I asked, strolling over to him. I ran my fingers over the curved lid as if I could magically sense what was in there just by touching it. "Maybe it's jewels or gold coins." My eyes widened.

"Let's open it and find out." He swiveled the chest so that the latch was facing towards us.

Of course, it's locked, why wouldn't it be? You're not a lucky girl, Aurora.

"What kind of lock is this?" I studied the bizarre looking indentation. There wasn't a keyhole like you would normally find on a chest. It seemed like when it came to the Amerii, nothing was ever going to be easy. Everything was top-secret. "It doesn't look like any lock I've seen before."

"It looks like something fits in here." Kaylin traced the shape of the indentation with his fingers. "It kinda reminds me of the necklace you wore for our date. You remember it? The one from your grandma."

"You're right, it does have the same shape to it." I smiled proudly. The possibility that my necklace could be the key to opening the chest thrilled me. Mr. Witherson's words popped back into my head. *You're the key, Aurora.*

"Go get it! Let's see if it fits!" The tone of Kaylin's voice matched the excitement in my body.

I successfully sneaked out into the hallway with no one noticing and quickly ran to my room to retrieve the necklace from the jewelry box.

What could be in the chest? I wondered. It's already a secret room. What would they need to have a locked chest in a secret room for? What could be so important?

I was just about to open the wall up and slip inside when the sound of footsteps on the stairs stopped me. I pretended to be studying at one of the portraits on the hallway wall.

"There you are, Aurora. I've been searching all over the house for you. It seems like you and Grant have been impossible to find these last few weeks," Uncle Rob said as he stopped in front of me. He leaned against the wall. His hand dangled inches away from the door release. I felt a tiny bit of panic creep up the hairs on the back of my neck. Was he toying with me? Did he know about the secret room? I stared at his hand. "That must be some story you guys are working on."

We'd told Aunt Theresa and Uncle Rob we were working on a big story as an excuse for us being absent from the paper and why we were so secretive lately. It wasn't a lie, not really. We were, after all, uncovering a big story, just not one for the paper. I hated not being able to tell anyone, but we had all agreed not to say anything yet, not to anyone, so I kept my promise. I didn't even tell Steph. "I need you to run into town and pick up toner for me." He stepped away from the wall. The hairs on the back of my neck laid down. It was just a coincidence, that's all.

"Again? Didn't we just pick some up a few weeks ago?" I didn't want to run into town, we were just about to uncover something big. I could feel it. "Can't Grant do it?" I pleaded with Uncle Rob.

"Grant's editing tomorrow's paper. We can't miss our deadline. The town counts on—"

"Okay, okay, I'll go." I cut him short. We were wasting time arguing about it and Kaylin was behind the wall waiting for me. I sent him a text as I trudged down the hall with Uncle Rob.

> Uncle Rob caught me in the hall.
> I have to go to town.
> Be back as soon as I can.
> Sorry.

I drove into town as fast as I could, disobeying every speed limit and stop sign I passed. I almost drove into a mail truck at one of the intersections. The mailman honked his horn angrily. I shrugged my shoulders and made an I'm-sorry face as I swerved around him, not stopping. Kaylin was waiting. I needed to get back to find out what was in that chest. I avoided eye contact in the supply store, making it in and out in record time, then zoomed back to the house. I threw the toner on the desk in front of Grant. It landed on the desk with a thud, causing Grant to let go of the mouse. He shot an irritated glare at me, grabbed the mouse again, and continued to drag articles around on the screen to find the best layout for tomorrow's paper.

"Gotta run, Kaylin's waiting. We found something big..."

Aunt Theresa glanced up from her desk.

"What did you find, dear?" She asked curiously. She set the paper she was holding down on the desk and waited for me to answer.

"Something for the story," I said trying to quickly cover up my slip. I couldn't tell her what we'd really found. I had to keep up our cover story. "We are still putting all the pieces together, Aunt Theresa."

"You two have been working really hard on this story. I'm proud of you. It's nice to see you guys working so hard together. It shows a lot of responsibility." My heart sank. She's proud of us and we're lying to her. Grant and I exchanged a guilty glance. He didn't like keeping the secret any more than I did.

"I'm almost done with the layout. Give me a sec, Cuz, then we can go together."

I took a deep breath. "Okay, but make it quick." I peered over at Aunt Theresa to see if she was still listening. She was. "Ah, we need to talk to our source before he changes his mind." There, that sounded professional. Like something a reporter would say when he was following a lead. She returned to her work. Grant quickly put the finishing touches on the layout, then saved it on his computer.

"Okay, Mom, it's saved and ready for your approval." He stood up and pushed his chair in.

We made a quick exit before she had a chance to disapprove of it and keep us there longer, or worse, ask us more questions about the story we were working on.

"Do you think your mom bought it?" I asked Grant as we headed upstairs.

"I'm pretty sure she suspects something, but there's no way she could know what it really is we're keeping from her."

"Did you hear something?" I asked Grant as he was about to force in the hidden door latch.

"No." He paused for a moment. "Did you?" He stretched his neck to see down the hallway.

I stood perfectly still, listening to the silence around us and waited to hear footsteps. "I guess I'm just paranoid," I said when I didn't hear anything.

We sneaked into the room to find Kaylin sitting at the table, scanning over some old maps of North Carolina.

"Sorry it took me so long. Grant wanted me to wait." I joined Kaylin at the table. Grant wandered around the room.

"That's okay, Rory, I kept busy looking at these old maps. I found some interesting stuff." He held one of them up to show us.

"You can show me after we open the chest," I said, eager to find out what was in it. The excitement had grown inside me now that I was back in the room.

"Do you guys think we should call Kevin?" Grant asked. He started to lift his phone from his pocket.

"He's working till six. We can fill him in later," Kaylin said. He too was eager to see what was inside. "Now let's see if we can get this thing open."

I was thankful Kaylin didn't want to wait for Kevin. The suspense was killing me. How Kaylin was able to patiently wait in the room and not try to smash the chest open was beyond me. Kaylin and Grant lifted the chest onto the table.

"Did you get your necklace?" asked Kaylin. He was practically jumping up and down he was so excited.

"Yep, I've got it right here." I took the necklace out of my pocket and held it out for Kaylin to take.

He shook his head. "I think you should do the honors, it's your necklace. Whatever's in here must belong to you." He stepped back from the chest, allowing me to get closer.

I hadn't really thought about it like that. Did whatever was in the chest belong to me? What secrets had the women in my family kept all these years? Did my grandma know about this room?

I stepped up to the chest and placed the necklace medallion in the indentation. It fit perfectly.

"Nothings happening!" I peered at Kaylin and Grant, feeling disappointed.

"Try turning it or pushing it in or something cuz," Grant said, extending his hand out to help me. "Or, do you need me to kick it?" I held my hand up to stop him from climbing on the chair.

"No, I've got it. Besides your toe hasn't totally recovered from the last time you tried kicking something," I teased. He stepped back to the floor.

I gently urged the medallion deeper into the slot. Pop. "It worked!" The chest lid creaked as it opened just a crack. A plume of dust puffed into my face. It smelled like what I'd imagine an Egyptian pyramid would smell like—old, musty, and earthy. I squeezed my eyes tightly closed and hesitantly stuck my fingers in the crack then flipped the lid the rest of the way open. I prayed there wasn't a rat, or worse, spiders crawling around in the chest. I absolutely hate spiders, with a passion. When no one shrieked, I opened my eyes and stared into the chest. There were no rats or spiders. In fact, there wasn't much of anything at all. Just some old linens.

"Clothing?" Grant said, let down by the contents. We weren't feeling the wonder and awe we'd expected to be feeling. "We needed a secret, medallion necklace to open a box of clothing?"

I stuck my arm in and started lifting pieces of clothing out one by one. There has to be something spectacular at the bottom. Something of value. There has to be. My fingers found something hard.

"There's something in here. It's wrapped up in the clothing, something heavy, it feels like a...rock?" I lifted out a large, smooth black stone with letters engraved on it.

"Oh, much better! Clothing and a rock!" Grant's tone was sarcastic. He grabbed the stone from my hands. "It's just gibberish." He tossed the stone back to me. I wasn't prepared for him to throw it at me and I nearly missed catching it. "I'm beginning to think the Amerii were nuts." He scoffed then marched off towards the door.

"Wait," Kaylin shouted at Grant. "It's not a rock, well it is, but no, not just a rock, here let me show you." He said excitedly. He was way more excited than any normal human being should be about a rock. He rushed over to the book on the table and picked it up. "Look, look here!" He thumbed through the pages of the book. When he found what he was looking for he set the book back on the table and pointed to the page. "It's a Dare Stone."

"What's a Dare Stone?" Grant asked. He let go of the door. Kaylin had piqued his interest. He wandered back over to the table and studied the page. "Oh, I see. It's a—"

"It's a cypher. A code!" Kaylin grabbed another book and frantically flipped through the pages. "Look, we need it to decipher some of the text on these pages. I've been trying to figure out where the stones are ever since I found this journal entry the other day. Take a look." He pulled a small black leather book, with the initials A.V. stamped on the cover in gold, out of his back pocket and held it out for me to read. I traded him the stone for the journal. The binding cracked as I opened the cover. Kaylin had marked the page with a torn piece of scrap paper. I read the passage out loud to Grant.

> "August 5, 1695. I fear I may not be able to protect my family's secrets for much longer. There is a traitor in our midst. I have informed Mr. Dupont of my suspicions and requested his help in separating the stones. He agreed to take swift action. I pray it's not too late. I will be taking one of my great grandmother's stones home. Should you need to retrieve the stone, remember this poem: Two will rule, one for all, when three stones are recovered, none will fall."

"Who is A.V.?" I asked, handing the book back.

"Anna Hunt-VanAgteren, Virginia Dare's granddaughter."

"Virginia Dare? Like the lost colony of Roanoke Virginia Dare?" I asked.

"Yep, that's the one." He smiled at me. "I'm surprised you know that. Not many people know the story." He glanced at Grant. Grant shrugged his shoulders.

"Never heard of it," he said.

"Well forget what you know, Rory, 'cause there's way more to the story than you think. Virginia Dare married Alexander Atterberry, a general appointed by John White to defend Roanoke in his absence and they had a daughter Eleanor, named after Virginia's mother."

"But—?"

"I know what you're going to say and they didn't disappear." Kaylin held his finger up to hush me and continued on. "Eleanor Atterberry married John Hunt. John and Eleanor then gave birth to a daughter named Anna. The names Atterberry and Hunt are on the list of the original thirteen men in the Amerii. So now, I understand how the name Atterberry became involved with the Amerii. Alexander was one of the Roanoke colonists. The name Hunt however, has me still a little confused. Other than the marriage of John Hunt to Eleanor

Atterberry, I haven't found any mention of his name anywhere and when I googled Roanoke colonists, he wasn't one of them either. He must have come into the picture another way."

"Who's Mr. Dupont then?" I asked. I hadn't recognized any of the names he'd listed.

"I have no idea. I haven't found the name in anything I've read other than the journal entry," Kaylin said. He set the stone on the table and began to decipher one of the pages in a book.

"Anna's talking about a traitor and having to hide the Dare Stones. She said she was taking a stone home to hide. What do you think she means by that? Where is home?" I asked, trying to get a better understanding of what happened all those years ago. Everything I had ever read about Roanoke said that the colonists had all disappeared without a trace. There shouldn't be an Anna or an Eleanor.

"That's what I was going to show you when you guys returned. I found a map, I think I know where home is."

"How many are there?" Grant interrupted. "How many stones?"

"Well, I've found three completely different codes spread out over several books. I believe there should be a different stone for each one of the codes." He pointed to a second book. As we'd been talking, he'd been grabbing books from the shelves and putting them onto a growing pile on the table. "See here! Three separate codes, each in a different handwriting. How many stones are in the chest?"

"Just the one." I peeked back into the chest, double checking that I hadn't missed one. The chest was empty. "Nothing but dust in there."

"Hold up, I'm confused," Grant said trying desperately to follow Kaylin's rantings. "Three stones, three codes, we have one stone and one stone is hidden at her grandma's."

"So, let me finish what I was telling you. We have a Dare Stone here." He lifted the stone off the table. "And I'm pretty sure I know where the second stone is." Kaylin said frantically. He was acting like a madman, pushing papers around the desk, flipping through books, pulling even more books off the shelves.

"Kaylin, slow down. We don't know what you're talking about." I was also having a hard time keeping up with him.

"Here!" He pointed to a spot on the map. "We need to go to Roanoke."

"We have to go to North Carolina?" I asked, raising my eyebrows. "Why?"

"We need all three Dare Stones to be able to read their communications, we have one, I'm positive there's another one in Roanoke and I'm pretty sure once we get the second stone it will lead us to the third." Kaylin finally sat down and took a deep breath. "Eleanor Dare, the daughter of John White, the Governor of Roanoke and mother of Virginia Dare, who, we all know, was the first English child born in this country and as it turns out, your great, great, great, great Aunt Virginia, was one of the Roanoke colonists and an Amerii. Eleanor Dare made these Stones as a way to send secret messages back and forth between the Amerii. No one knows for sure what happened to the colonists of Roanoke, but these books, this room, and you being alive proves they didn't just vanish in 1590. The only way we're going to find out more about what happened to them, who the Amerii are, and if anyone is still doing their work is to get the rest of the stones."

"Holy crap, that's some heavy shit, man." Grant sat down beside Kaylin to let it all sink in.

I stood there for a moment, trying to wrap my head around everything he'd said. Our families at one point in time were a part of a secret society that helped build and shape this nation into what it is today. I wondered how deeply our families were embedded into our country, our government. What history had our families made?

Chapter 5

Roanoke Museum

We spent the next few days planning our trip. We gathered as many maps as we could from the secret Amerii room as well as any of the books we'd deemed would be helpful in our search. We'd concocted an elaborate story—that we were going to visit Steph in Pennsylvania—to tell Aunt Theresa and Uncle Rob in order to keep them from getting suspicious. The list of lies we'd been telling them was growing by the day. They couldn't know we were heading three hours south-east to Roanoke Island, North Carolina, where the Roanoke colony used to be, in search of the second Dare Stone. They'd have too many questions and we didn't have the answers to give them. Plus, they might try to stop us from going. I doubted they'd understand.

"Did you remember to pack your necklace, Rory?" Kaylin asked, while he helped me pack a bag. "We might need it again."

"I hadn't thought about it. It's in my jewelry box on the dresser. Could you grab it for me and throw it in my bag please?" It was a good thing Kaylin was there to help. My head had been spinning for days, my adrenaline in overdrive.

"Hey," Kaylin said and handed me my necklace. I tossed it in my bag. "We haven't had any time to talk about us." He followed me around as I searched for the clothes I wanted to take on the trip. "There's been so much going on we haven't even been able to go on a second date." I tossed a shirt in my bag, zipped it closed, then glanced up at him. His face was sincere. "I don't want you to think I've forgotten about us."

Not only was he proving himself to be a terrific leader of our group, keeping everyone focused and on task, but he was also so sweet. I'd fallen completely head over heels for him.

"I would like a second date very much." I smiled. I'd been craving some alone time with him. It seemed Grant and Kevin were always around. "Maybe once we get back from Roanoke we could go out, just you and me, without the others."

"I was hoping you'd say that." He returned my smile and kissed me on the cheek before picking up my bag. My pulse quickened. "I didn't want you to think I wasn't interested. We've just been so busy with all this Amerii stuff." He explained, but I couldn't hear what he was saying over the pounding of my heart. "Guess we'd better start loading the car." He headed toward the door.

"Kaylin, wait!" I grabbed his arm. He spun around, his gaze meeting mine. I couldn't take it any longer, I had to kiss him. If he wasn't going to make the first move, then it was up to me to do it. I touched the side of his face. I'd been dreaming about kissing him ever since the night in the park. I wanted to hold his body close to mine. I wanted to feel his lips on mine. I lured him closer to me and whispered in his ear, "Kiss me." He dropped my bag and gently grabbed the back of my head, drawing my lips closer to his. I trembled, our lips finally meeting. His kiss was soft at first, then harder as the urges in our bodies took over. I'd been waiting so long for this moment, I wanted to give in to the feeling and his kiss told me that he did too. He slid his other hand around my waist and held my body tight against his, kissing me more passionately. It's going to happen. Right here, right now. I was finally going to lose my virginity and it would be with the most wonderful man.

"It's time to go. You guys ready?" Grant hollered down the hall to us.

My heart sank. Kaylin slowly pulled his lips from mine. Neither of us wanted the kiss to end.

"Be there in a sec," Kaylin replied, slightly out of breath, then whispered to me. "We've got to get some alone time." He gazed deep into my eyes, still holding my waist.

Stupid Grant, always getting in the way. I nodded and sucked on my bottom lip with his kiss still fresh on it. We reluctantly separated, then headed down stairs.

Kevin was sitting on the porch steps, keeping himself entertained on his phone by watching random videos of guys doing stupid stunts. Grant was tossing his bags into the back of the Jeep.

"Grant and Kevin, you're in the back." Kaylin tossed our bags in the back of the Jeep then shut the hatch. "I'm driving." He strolled up to the driver's door. "Rory, you're up front with me," he said before opening the door and climbing into the driver's seat. The rest of us piled into his Jeep, which took off down the driveway.

"We should play the license plate game," Grant said once we'd reached the highway. "But let's skip Alaska, I doubt we're going to see any plates from Alaska."

I spent the first half of the car ride replaying the kiss in my head, while the boys chattered on about some sports games they'd watched the other day and randomly shouted out a state's name as they spotted the plate. I tried my best to tune them out. Somewhere just after we crossed the North Carolina border, Kevin's words broke into my daydream, stealing my attention.

"Do you know where to look once we get there, little bro?" Kevin leaned forward between the front seats and asked Kaylin. "Delaware!" he suddenly shouted.

I rubbed my ear and gave him a dirty look.

"Aurora's been doing some research online about the Roanoke lore, with what she's found and the information I was able to dig up in the Amerii room we've got a pretty good idea where to start." Kaylin said as he turned the radio off. "Rory tell them what we've found."

"Okay," I said, lifting my phone out of the cupholder and finding the page I'd bookmarked. I turned in my seat, facing towards the rear of the Jeep. "According to historical reports, in 1584, Sir Walter Raleigh dispatched an expedition to the New World, where they soon established relations with the local natives, the Secotans and the Croatans. They then returned to England with two native Croatans who described to the Queen the politics and the geography of the area. Based on their accounts, a second expedition was sent out in 1585. Five ships departed for the new world to establish a settlement. Due to a storm at sea the ships were separated."

"Were there pirates?" Grant asked. He closed one eye and made his finger into a hook shape, gesturing excitedly.

"No, it's not that kind of story," I said, shaking my head. Grant's such a goofball.

"Bummer. Pirates would be cool." He seemed genuinely disappointed. I wondered what it would be like to see the world the way Grant did.

"So anyway," I continued, "the plan was to meet up in Puerto Rico if something such as that happened. Two of the ships landed in Puerto Rico, where they built a fort and established relations with the Spanish. Tired of waiting for the other ships to arrive, the two ships left the fort, departing Puerto Rico again for the New World to see if they could locate the others. They arrived in Roanoke to find two of the ships, the third had already dropped off its passengers and supplies and headed for Canada."

"To get maple syrup?" Grant interrupted again.

"No! Not for maple syrup. Geesh, Grant."

"Then tell me, Cuz, why did the ship go to Canada?" He asked with a know-it-all expression on his face. "Huh?"

"I don't know. I didn't research why they went to Canada."

"Then it must have been for maple syrup," he said, then shouted, "Florida!"

"Fine, it was for maple syrup," Kaylin said, obviously getting tired of Grant's nonsense. He then said, "Georgia."

"Now where was I?" I scrolled through the page to find where I'd left off. "Oh, yes. So, the plan was for a fort to be built at the northernmost point of the island near the settlement, but there's no records of its actual location, there's only speculation as to where they built it or even if they actually did. But, we know more than they did." I smiled at Kaylin. "We will get to that in a second, though. So anyway, in 1586 a passing ship, coming from the Caribbean, captained by Sir Francis Drake, passed by, offering to take anyone who wanted to go home a ride back to England. Due to lack of food and native attacks, many decided to head back. Then in 1587, Raleigh sent out a second group of around one hundred men and women, this time under the command of John White, Eleanor Dare's father, to the abandoned colony. Shortly after arriving in Roanoke, White returned to England to inform the Queen of the conditions in Roanoke and acquire more supplies, leaving behind his daughter and newly born baby grand-daughter, along with the other colonists. Due to the Spanish War, his return was delayed until August 18th, 1590. His granddaughter's, our Aunt Virginia's, third birthday." I looked at Grant. "But when he re-turned, the colonists were gone. No sign of them anywhere. The only clue was the word Croatan carved into a fence post. From there it's all speculation as to what really happened to them. Some say they died from illness and lack of food. Some speculate they went to live with the Croatans and had written the word on the fence post to tell John White where to find them.

"John White was beside himself, desperate to get his family back. An expedition was formed in 1602 to investigate the disappearance of the colonists and to search for them in the Croatan village, but by then there were no signs of them there. Still another speculation was that the Croatans slaughtered them and buried their remains some-where. In that case, the word was written as a warning for White not to trust the Croatan.

"Here's the good part. We were able to use the Dare Stone we have to decipher some of the text in the books, giving us a better idea of what really happened. When the two ships left Puerto Rico they brought with them Jose Huerta, a Spanish man they had befriend-ed. Huerta is one of the names we found in the Amerii book. We also know the fifth ship that headed for Canada had returned with sup-plies and an Irish gentleman by the name of Ian MacCarrick, another name from the Amerii book. The two men didn't accept the ride from the passing Caribbean ship."

"See? Maple syrup. I knew it," Grant said as if it confirmed he was right.

I ignored him and kept going. "When John White and the colonist arrived at Roanoke the settlement wasn't abandoned like they had assumed. Ian and Jose had hidden themselves deep in the woods when they saw the ships arrive. It wasn't until the village was under attack from the Croatan that they reemerged to save Victoria and her mother Eleanor. We know some of the other colonists also survived the attack. We're just not sure how many or who they were. We also figured out that Raleigh's men did in fact build a fort, we found a diagram of it in the secret room back at the house. And if that wasn't proof enough, we deciphered a message from Eleanor Dare to Mr. Alexander Atterberry, the general, saying that the only place she felt safe was at the fort. She felt betrayed by her Queen and alone in the New World. Our plan is to start where the settlement was, see if we can dig up anything there. If not, we go to the fort. If there's a Dare Stone, it's going to be in one of those two places." I took a breath, then added. "It's been hundreds of years though, so it's going to be difficult, maybe even impossible."

"Have faith! Look how far we've gotten already," Kaylin said and patted my knee.

"Dumb luck," Kevin said. He stared out the window. "Can we skip Hawaii too?"

"Definitely," replied Grant.

"Okay then... Idaho!" Kevin shouted.

"Didn't you guys hear what Aurora just said?" Kaylin asked over his shoulder. "Isn't it amazing?"

"We heard. It's so amazing," Kevin said in a mocking tone.

"Hey, let me see that map, Cuz." Grant held his hand out.

"Which one? The old map or today's map?"

"Both."

I handed him the maps. He placed the old map over the current map and held them both up to the window.

"The settlement should have been here." He pointed to a spot just south of where Manteo is today. "Not at the northern tip, where it's thought to be."

"What about the fort they built?" asked Kevin suddenly interested. He leaned over and studied the map. "Where's that?"

"Here, at the northern tip."

"So, what everyone thinks is the settlement is really the fort?" I asked confused.

"Looks like it, Cuz," Grant said, his expression smug. He rolled the two maps up together. "It wasn't the fort they couldn't find, it was the settlement. They just didn't know it."

"Then Manteo it is," Kaylin said.

I rerouted Google maps on my phone.

"Looks like we go straight on through Manns Harbor and across the Virginia Dare Memorial Bridge. That will put us just south of Manteo," I said to Kaylin. I placed my phone back into the cup holder and settled into my seat.

"Can we stop for lunch before we head over to the island? I'm starving," Kevin asked. He wasn't as excited about the trip as the rest of us and didn't even bother to fake it. I speculated the only reason he came on the trip was to spend time with his brother.

"Me too," said Grant.

"Sure, that will give us a chance to formulate a plan," Kaylin said, turning the radio back on.

We continued on for another half an hour before reaching Manns Harbor. We stopped at a cute little diner where we ate lunch and discussed what to do once we'd located the settlement.

"Here ya go, sweetie." The waitress placed the bill on the table next to Kevin. "You kids here looking for information about the lost Roanoke colony?" The four of us exchanged worried glances. "I couldn't help overhearing," she continued on. "We get kids like you around here every so often. They usually hear about Roanoke in a history lecture or watch the episode of American Horror Story on FX and think they can solve the mystery." She laughed. "No one has, but none of them have what you have." She nodded at the map on the table. "Where'd you get a map like that? It looks like it belongs in a museum."

Grant quickly rolled up the map. "The things you can do on a computer these days," he said as he tucked it between him and Kevin on the bench seat. "All you need is some editing software and you can make anything look old." He avoided eye contact with her and took a drink of his soda.

Kaylin reached in his pocket and pulled out his debit card. He laid it on the bill.

"Well, nonetheless, there's a tourist spot just up the road." The waitress picked up the bill and debit card. "A lot of the kids that come here find it interesting. Has a museum with some stuff in it that looks like your map and there's a gift shop too. Get yourselves some Roanoke t-shirts," she said before she walked away.

"Maybe we should check it out." Grant leaned towards the center of the table and whispered, "Maybe there's some more stuff of Virginia's and Eleanor's."

The waitress returned with Kailyn's debit card and a receipt. "Sign here please."

"What did you say the name of the place was?" Kaylin asked as he took his debit card back. He slid it in his wallet, then tucked his wallet in his back pocket. "We loved the episode AHS Roanoke." He signed the receipt.

The rest of us chimed in, "Yeah, yeah, Horror Story. Our favorite."

"Oh, it's just called the Roanoke Museum. You'll see a big sign. Can't miss it. It's in the old MacCarrick homestead." She thanked us for coming, wished us a good day and walked away.

"Now we definitely have to go," I said excitedly. I took my napkin from my lap and wadded it up before placing it on my plate, then waited for Kaylin to stand up so I could scootch out of the booth. "Do you think it's the Ian MacCarrick homestead?" I asked as I stood up. "I mean how many MacCarrick's could there have been around here, right? It has to be."

"Let's find out," said Grant as we headed out the door to the Jeep.

Not more than a half a block up the road was a large wooden sign with Roanoke Museum painted in big, black letters on it. Kaylin turned into the drive and parked in one of the many empty spots.

"This place looks abandoned. Are we sure it's open?" asked Kevin. He peered out the window at the empty lot.

"The sign on the door says open." I pointed out. I exited the Jeep and walked over to the door. I pulled on the handle. A bell jingled as the door swung open. "See, it's open."

"Hello, how are you today?" said a friendly woman as we entered the gift shop. She was standing near the register, wiping the dust off a display of polished rocks. "Can I interest you in a Dare Stone?" she asked.

I couldn't help but laugh. "No thank you."

"We were told there was a museum here," asked Kaylin.

"Check this out," Grant said from the far side of the store. "How do I look?" He tried on a tan leather jacket with fringe on the breast. "I feel like Davy Crocket." He spun around. The fringe spun out around him and made a slapping sound as it hit against his upper chest and back.

"Here," said Kevin. He walked over to Grant and held up a coon-skin hat. "You need this." He placed the hat on Grant's head. "King of the wild frontier."

We all chuckled. Even the saleswoman couldn't help but smile.

"The museum is at the back of the store, through the archway." She lifted her hand with the rag in it and motioned to an opening at the rear of the store. "I ask you not to horse around in there though," she said with a straight face. "The stuff back there is irreplaceable."

Grant quickly took the hat off his head and apologized. He hung the jacket back on its hanger and kept his head low as he followed Kevin to the rear of the store. "What's her problem?" he whispered once he'd gotten out of earshot.

"Look at this, Aurora." Kevin stared into a glass display case. "I bet this is important."

Grant strolled up beside him. "What makes you think it's import-ant." He glanced at the object as he passed by on his way to a shadow box display of a torn soldiers uniform. "It's just a barrette."

"Oh, I don't know, Grant," Kevin said slightly irritated. He glared at Grant. "Maybe because it has the initials A.V. engraved in the silver."

"What?" asked Kaylin. "Let me see." He hurried over to the case. Kevin stepped back. "He's right, Rory."

I peered over Kaylin's shoulder at the silver hair comb in the center of the display. "It's beautiful." I touched the glass. The silver hair comb was adorned with tiny silver rose buds along the top edge and, in the center, a scalloped circle with the initials A.V. It struck me as odd that there were missing teeth. The third, fifth, ninth, and tenth teeth were missing. Otherwise it was in immaculate shape. "I wonder if it's for sale?"

"That's a magnificent piece isn't it?" The woman strolled up behind us. "It was found not too far from here, out by the old fort. It's said to be over three-hundred years old." She tapped me on the shoulder. "Please don't touch the glass."

I returned my hand to my side. "Is it for sale?"

"No, never," she quickly responded. "Didn't you hear me say it was over three-hundred years old?" Her eyes scanned over me. "And even if it were, I doubt you could afford it. That's pure, handcrafted silver in there."

I frowned. She didn't need to be rude.

"I think we'd better go," said Kaylin. He pulled on my arm. "Grant," he hollered. "It's time to go."

"I'm not done looking," he said in protest. He stepped over to the next display.

"I said it's time to go," Kaylin said firmly.

"Fine," Grant said, but stopped at one more display case and peered in before he followed us out to the parking lot.

"Hey, you guys get in the car," said Kevin. "I think I left my phone in there. I must have set it down when Grant was trying on the clothing." He patted his pockets then turned and headed back into the store. A few minutes later, he rushed out of the door and jumped into the backseat. "Let's go," he shouted.

The saleswoman burst out of the doors. "Get back here," she yelled. "I'm going to call the cops!" She ran towards the Jeep, waving her arms in the air.

"Go, now." Kevin hit Kaylin on the shoulder.

Kaylin shoved the Jeep in reverse and stomped on the gas then hit the brake, stopping inches away from the woman. She pounded on the back of the Jeep with her fists, yelling all the while. He slipped it into drive and sped off, watching the woman take her phone out of her pocket in the rearview mirror. The tires squealed as he tore out of the parking lot. "What did you do, Kevin?"

"Here," Kevin said and tossed the silver hair comb into my lap. I picked the comb up and stared at it. "This is yours. It was your great great grandmas or whatever. You should have it."

"She was my grandma too, ya know," Grant said jealously. "Not just Aurora's."

"Fine." Kevin snatched the comb out of my hand and stuck it in Grant's hair. "You want to wear it? It's all yours."

Grant shook it loose from his hair.

"I didn't think so," said Kevin. He picked the comb up off the seat and handed it back to me, then turned and checked to see if the woman had followed us. "I think we're in the clear. You can slow down now," he said.

"I saw her calling the cops," Kaylin said, his voice booming. "You've made us accomplices." He glared back at Kevin. "I think we should take it back."

"If you go back now, you're definitely going to jail. Just slow down, act like you're out for a Sunday drive and everything will be okay." Kevin reassured Kaylin. "I promise."

Just as Kevin finished speaking, a police car, heading in the direction of the museum, sped past.

"I think we better lay low for a bit." Kaylin turned off the road into a parking lot full of cars and backed into a parking spot. "Just to be safe." He sank down into his seat. "Get down. Make it look like there's no one in here."

We silently crouched in our seats for what felt like hours. After the third time someone pulled up beside us, went into the store, shopped, and returned to their car, Grant said, "I think the coast is clear." He stretched and sat up. He glanced in every direction. "There's not a cop in sight. Maybe it was just a coincidence."

"No, I'm sure she called the cops. I saw her," Kaylin insisted.

"Well, they're nowhere to be found, if she did," said Kevin. He groaned as he sat up. "Let's get out of here. This road trip sucks so far."

"Your opinion," I glared at him. "I'm having fun."

"I think we're right by the bridge to take us over to the island," Grant said. He rolled his window down and stuck his head out for a moment. He stretched his neck to see something near the road, then pulled his head back in. "I thought I'd seen a sign when we pulled in the lot. The bridge is that way. If we hadn't gotten off the road, we would've gone across it."

Chapter 6

Roanoke Island

After crossing the bridge, we took a right turn, down a narrow, two-lane road. The road was so narrow that if two larger vehicles were to pass by one another, someone would have had to drive off the edge of the road. Tufts of grass stuck up out of the potholes and along the sides.

"Doesn't seem like anyone's been down this way in awhile," Kaylin said. He continued driving towards the marshes. The Jeep jostled back and forth as he swerved to avoid getting stuck.

"Just up ahead is where the settlement should have been," Grant said to Kaylin. He braced himself as he tried to unroll the maps. "Like maybe a half mile up the road, then a mile or so that way." He pointed out the window. "I don't know for sure. This old map's hard to read."

"Then it looks like we're on foot from here," Kaylin said as he pulled off the shoulder of the road and parked the Jeep. "There's no way I'm driving the Jeep into that stuff." He pointed to the wet marshlands, overgrown with tall swamp grass.

We loaded our backpacks with as much as we could carry, then headed off across the marsh towards a wooded area a few miles away. We had been trekking around for most of the afternoon and hadn't found any signs of anyone ever living here. Our feet were soaking wet and freezing cold.

"Does anyone have bug spray?" Kevin asked, swatting at the air.

I shook my head. "Nope."

We were all miserable and ready to give up when Grant tripped over something.

"Son of a...I'm soaked and I dropped my granola bar! What the hell was that?" he yelled.

"Serves you right for eating all the supplies. How about you save some for the rest of us?" I said as I spun around and started trudging through the tall grass back towards him. As I drew nearer, I saw something wooden sticking up out of the ground. Kaylin and Kevin were also on their way to him. Kevin made it to him first, extending his arm out to help. He yanked Grant to his feet. Grant rubbed at his pants legs, unsuccessfully trying to brush the mud off. The mud had soaked deep into the fibers, and his pants hung awkwardly stiff on him.

"Hey, Kevin, what's that wood thing sticking up?" I asked, still a few yards away from them. "I can't see it from here."

"I don't know," he answered, not bothering to look. Instead, he rummaged through his backpack for something.

"Well thanks for looking," I said sarcastically as I came up to them. Kaylin arrived at the object at roughly the same time, and we inspected it together.

"Give me a hand, Rory. I think we can lift it up." Kaylin tugged on the end of it. "Watch out for slivers though."

"Any idea what it is?" I asked, kneeling down. The cold, wet mud quickly penetrated the front of my jeans.

"I think it's a fence post, but I won't know until we get it out of the ground."

We dug at the ground and jerked the long swamp grass up by its roots to clear off as much of the object as we could before trying to lift it. We were close to the tree line and the ground was firmer here than it was when we'd first entered the marsh, but kneeling on it was still unpleasant.

"Give us a hand, guys." I glared at Kevin and Grant, pleading for some help.

They reluctantly did as I asked, and the four of us managed to break the object free from the ground. It was a fence post, but what did it mean? Was this part of the settlement or just a fence post to some farm that had been here at one point in history?

"I think we've found the settlement," Kaylin said and grinned with excitement.

"Congratulations, you found a fence post," Grant said sarcastically. "You know, you guys get excited over the littlest things. First a stone, now a fence post. You know you can find those things everywhere, right?"

Kaylin glared. "It's not just any fence post. This thing's got to be hundreds of years old."

"My bad! A stone and a really old fence post," Grant said, correcting himself. "I don't see CROATOAN written on it, how do you know it's from the settlement?" He took the fence post out of Kaylin's hands, spinning it around for everyone to inspect. "See? Nothing."

"You're a jerk," I said angrily. Grant's humor could be so mean sometimes.

"I'm done. If you guys want to keep searching, fine, but I'm heading back to the car." He shoved the fence post back at Kaylin, then turned and stomped away.

"I'm with Grant," said Kevin, turning to follow him.

No big surprise there, I thought to myself.

"You can't just walk away. We finally found something," Kaylin called after them.

"We absolutely can. Watch us." Grant took large exaggerated steps towards the Jeep. "See, I'm walking away."

"I can't believe they'd just give up like that. Don't they understand how important finding the Dare Stones is?" Kaylin glanced at me, hopeful. "What do you want to do?"

I didn't want to hurt his feelings, but Grant was sort of right. We couldn't be sure the post was from the settlement, and my pants were soaked from kneeling on the ground trying to dig it up. Some dry clothes to change into would be really nice right now. "I think it's late and we're all tired," I said, putting my hand on his shoulder. "Why don't we find a hotel, somewhere we can get some rest, and then come back tomorrow."

He sadly agreed, letting the fence post slip out of his hands. The muddy hole quickly sucked it in.

We found a bed and breakfast a few miles south of the marsh and rented a room. One room for the four of us. Not really my idea of an ideal situation, but we didn't have a ton of cash, so I made the best of it.

"I call the bed by the window," I said as we entered the tiny room. I threw my bag on the bed closest to the window before anyone could argue. The room was nicely decorated and clean. There were two double beds and a pull out couch.

Someone was going to have to sleep on the floor, I thought.

"I'll take the couch," said Grant plopping down on it. "You two can fight over the other bed."

"We can fit, don't ya think, Bro?' Kevin said as he lay down on it, demonstrating how much room there was.

"Sure, I guess. It'll be like when we were kids and you got scared of the thunder," Kaylin said teasingly.

"It wasn't me that was scared, Little Bro. I was there to protect you," Kevin said, apparently defending his manliness. He grabbed Kaylin and tossed him on the bed, putting him in a choke hold with his left arm and rubbing the knuckles of his right hand on the top of his head. "Noogie!"

That got Grant's attention. He climbed up on my bed, then did a flying jump onto the other two. "Pile drive!"

The three of them wrestled around on the bed like a bunch of ten-year olds.

"I'm going to go search around town and see if I can find a place for dinner," I said. I stepped out the door, not really sure if any of them heard me.

I'd seen several billboards on our drive to the Inn for a market in town that boasted about its deli selection. It seemed promising. I admired the buildings as I walked to the market. The town was filled with old-world charm and character, definitely designed to attract tourists, and the market did not disappoint. I bought some meals from the deli and took them back to the Inn. The boys had settled down while I was gone and were watching YouTube videos on their phones when I entered the room.

"Hey, what ya got there, Cuz? Grant asked as I strolled in the door, only taking his eyes away from the tiny screen long enough to notice I was back.

"Let me help you with that." Kaylin got up from the bed, put his phone in his back pocket and took the grocery bags from me. He set them down on the small table at the far side of the room. He sniffed in the bag. "It smells yummy!"

"I found a market up the road. They had an amazing deli selection of pre-made meals." I unpacked the containers from the bag and set them on the table. The clear plastic lids were cloudy from the steam. "We have fried chicken tenders, mashed potatoes, potato wedges, cabbage rolls, and baked beans. Take your pick." The boys converged on the food like a pack of hungry wolves. "Save me a cabbage roll," I said, trying to wrestle a paper plate off the top of the stack.

After dinner, Kaylin convinced us to go back to the marsh for a second look. We'd agreed on one condition. We needed a clear plan of what we were doing. We couldn't aimlessly wander around the marsh, hoping to stumble upon something, like we had earlier. Once a plan was formulated, we said our goodnights and climbed into our beds.

Sometime in the early morning hours, before the sun began to rise, I was startled by a loud noise. I jerked awake. What was that? I opened my eyes and scanned the room. The thin curtains covering the window, let in a generous amount of light from the streetlamp outside, allowing me to make out the boys shapes. I scanned the room expecting to see one of them heading back from the bathroom, but everyone was still asleep. Kaylin and Kevin were tucked under the covers in their bed as far away from the center as possible. Grant itched his nose, then rolled over and began snoring. Everything seemed fine. I shrugged it off and closed my eyes. It must have been nothing. Then I heard it again.

This time, I was certain which direction the noise had come from. I slowly opened my eyes and turned my head towards the window.

Outside the window stood a man. A clear outline of him silhouetted against the curtain. It couldn't be. I rubbed my eyes, but the man was still standing there. I lay perfectly still, paralyzed with fear, afraid if I moved the man would hear me. I wanted to yell for help, to wake the boys up, but I couldn't, my lips wouldn't form the words. My legs felt heavy, sinking into the mattress like a stone. With every breath I took, my chest heaved up and down. I was sure the man outside the window would be able to see the movement. I started to sweat. The back of my neck became damp, and I could feel my hair sticking to it. The silhouette grew larger as the man approached the window. I heard his fingers prying at the window sill. It wouldn't be long and he would be in the room. Was it the police? Had they found us? Or worse, was it a thief trying to break in and steal something? Did they have a gun? What could we possibly have of any value? The hair comb. There was no way anyone could know we had it. Not unless. Were we being followed?

The man bent forward and disappeared below the window. Now's my chance. My phone was charging on the bedside table next to me. I reached for it. I needed to call for help. I stretched out as far as I could but my arm wasn't long enough. My fingertips barely grazed the edge. I felt for the charging cord. If I can just reach it I can pull it towards me. I found the cord and yanked. The phone slid off the edge of the table and disconnected from the charging cord. Damn it! There was no way I could reach it now. I turned back to the window. The man had picked up something long and thin when he bent over and was now trying to jimmy it between the window and the frame. It wouldn't be long before he'd pry the window open.

Just then Kevin rolled over and fell off the bed. He landed on the floor with a loud thud. The man stopped what he was doing and stood quietly outside the window. Kevin grumbled as he picked himself up from the floor.

"Move over," he mumbled still half asleep as he flopped back down in bed.

The commotion was enough to spook the man. He ran off, disappearing out of view. Kevin instantly started to snore, unaware that the man was ever outside. I breathed in deeply and slid over to the edge of my bed, as far away from the window as I could get. I spent an eternity with my eyes glued to the window, sure the shadowy figure would return once he thought the coast was clear, but he never did. Exhaustion eventually took over, and I drifted back to sleep.

When I awoke the next morning, Grant was brewing a pot of coffee. There was no sign of Kevin or Kaylin in the room.

"Good morning, Cuz. How did you sleep?" His voice was cheerful. He sat down on the edge of my bed and slid his shoes on. "Coffee's almost ready."

I rose out of bed and stepped cautiously over to the window. I pushed back the curtain and peered out. I didn't see any signs that someone had been standing there.

"Not great," I admitted. I pressed my face against the glass to check for scratch marks on the window sill. Nothing. "I saw someone outside the window last night. It took me forever to fall back asleep." I turned from the window.

"Someone was outside the window?" Kaylin asked as he stepped out of the bathroom. He'd just finished showering and was wearing only his jeans. His muscular chest was still damp and it glistened. For a moment I forgot what I was talking about. I cleared my throat.

"I must have been dreaming or something. I thought I saw someone outside last night." I turned my attention back to the window. "But it doesn't look like anyone was there." I pointed at the ground outside the window. The sun was still low in the sky, the grass still damp from last night's dew. There were no footprints in the soil, no broken or bent flowers in the flower bed under the window. Nothing out of the ordinary to imply someone had been there.

"Is everyone ready to go?" Kevin popped through the door with an assortment of muffins in his hand. "I got us some breakfast." A proud smile on his face.

"I need to jump in the shower real quick." I bent over to grab my bag of clothing from beside my bed. Laying on the floor next to my bag was my phone. The hairs on the back of my neck stood up. I shivered as the image of the man outside the window popped back into my head. I shook it off. I picked up my phone and my bag, setting my phone back on the table and slinging my bag over my shoulder. "I'll only be a minute," I said as I walked towards the bathroom. I snatched a muffin from Kevin's hand and took it into the bathroom.

"Make it quick, the day's a wastin'," said Kevin in a better mood than he'd been in yesterday. He stuffed half of a muffin into his mouth.

Maybe he and Grant were finally getting excited about the stone, I told myself and closed the bathroom door. I set my stuff on the counter and jumped into the shower. I was still uneasy about last night, unable to shake the feeling of being watched. If it had been a horrible nightmare then how did my phone end up on the floor? I assured myself that it was just my mind playing tricks on me, and then forced myself to stop thinking about it.

After I'd showered, we headed off to the marsh to find the fence post again. The air had a coolness to it for being August, no doubt a result of the constant, gentle breeze blowing in salty air from the Atlantic. It was nice. Not at all hot and sticky like I was used to in Cary. I'd picked up some bug spray and gardening shovels for everyone at the market last night as well as a pair of rubber shoe covers for myself. I handed out the shovels and offered to spray everyone with the bug spray. The boys graciously took their shovels, then lined up to be sprayed down.

"Thanks," they said as I finished with each of them.

We split up the area surrounding the fence post into four sections, each of us took a section and began digging. The hours passed slowly by. Finally, Kevin hollered, "I've got something. It's full of mud, but I think it's a baby rattle." He held up a tarnished silver sphere, a slim handle with a loop on the end protruded from its side.

"A baby rattle?" asked Grant. "Who in their right mind would raise a baby out here?" He peered out over the grassy marshland

"I don't think it's always looked like this around here," Kevin said.

Kaylin and I stopped what we were doing and trudged laboriously through the thick grass over to Kevin for a look at the rattle.

"Does anyone have any water in their backpack?" I asked, taking the rattle from Kevin and inspecting it. I scraped my fingernail over a small section in the center of the sphere. "I think there's something engraved on it."

Kaylin yanked a half-empty bottle of water out of his pack. "Here you go."

I carefully poured the water over the rattle, using the edge of my shirt to rub the water around over the engraving.

To my granddaughter Victoria.

"Victoria Dare, it has to be!" Kaylin exclaimed. He was so excited he grabbed the rattle out of my hand and began shaking it in the air. Clumps of dirt shook loose and sprinkled over his head.

"Dumbass! You just put dirt in your hair," Kevin said, laughing and pointing.

Kaylin stopped shaking the rattle and began shaking the clumps of dirt from his head. Once all the dirt was out of his hair, he focused his attention back to us and said, "I knew it, I knew we were in the right place. You all doubted me, but I knew it, and now here's proof." He held the rattle up again, making sure not to shake it over his head. "Back to your sections, keep searching, there's got to be more out here."

We did as he said, returning to our sections in search of the Dare Stone. Shortly after lunch, we sectioned off four new plots, each taking one. It continued on like that until late in the evening. By sunset, we'd found three fence posts, a cast iron cooking pot, an arrow head, and a few other smaller objects we couldn't identify, but nothing other than the rattle pointed directly to the Dare family living here.

"I was thinking..." Grant said, digging next to me at the edge of his section.

"What?" I asked not bothering to glance up.

"Anna took the stone to her great grandmother's home, right? Maybe she didn't consider this home. They only lived here for a short time."

I stopped digging and stared at him, thinking for a moment about what he was saying before answering.

"Sure, that makes sense. Victoria and her mother were gone when her father returned from England."

"I wouldn't call a place I lived in less than three years home, would you?" Grant set his shovel beside him on the ground. "Especially if I was a baby when I lived here. Victoria probably didn't even remember this place." He picked his shovel up and rose to his feet. "I think we're searching in the wrong spot for the stone. I think we should be looking at the fort."

I agreed. I wouldn't call it home either. "Let's go tell Kaylin what you're thinking," I said, getting to my feet.

We left our sections, pushing the tall grass out of our way as we trudged over to Kaylin. He'd made it a good way into the trees. Much farther than the rest of us. He was working at an exhausting pace, clearing almost twice as many sections. I admired his determination.

"Kaylin," I said as we approached him. "Grant has a theory."

Grant explained his theory to Kaylin, who agreed. The theory made a great deal of sense.

"Let's call it a day then," he said as he stood up from the ground, clapping his hands together to get some of the dirt off. "Tomorrow, we'll visit the fort."

We told Kevin of the plan then gathered the items we'd found and drove back to the Inn. I cleaned the dirt off our treasures, then locked them into our room's safe. I didn't want the housekeeper to know what we'd been up to. Plus, even though I'd tried to forget the incident from last night, my gut kept bringing it back up. There was always the possibility someone planned to rob us.

"Would you guys mind switching beds with me?" I asked Kevin and Kaylin giving them the best girl smile I could manage. I'd never been good at getting boys to do what I wanted. Not like Steph. She flashed a pretty smile and the boys went crazy.

"Last night still got you creeped out?" Kaylin asked glancing up from the bed.

"Yeah, a little." I sat down on the edge of the bed by his feet. Was I really so transparent?

"Sure, we can switch." Kaylin nudged his brother lying beside him. Kevin had been laughing at memes on his phone and not paying attention to anything Kaylin and I were saying. "Right, we can switch?"

"What? Oh! Fine, sure, no problem. We can switch." Kevin got up off the bed and began throwing his stuff back into his bag.

"Thanks, guys." I stood up and gathered my purse and a few items of clothing off of the bed then tossed them onto the floor beside the other one. I slipped under the covers and closed my eyes. The sheets smelled like Kaylin making it easy to fall asleep quickly. I awoke that morning refreshed, and ready for the day's adventures, before anyone else had even started to stir.

Chapter 7

The Challenge

G rant warned us that the fort was a tourist destination and would be crawling with people. It wasn't going to be easy to hide what we were doing. Searching for the Dare Stone amongst a bunch of tourists was certainly going to be a challenge, but it was one I was ready for. I showered, packed the bags for the day, and brewed the coffee before waking the boys.

"It's time to get up, sleepy heads," I said in a loud voice. "Coffee is ready, everyone up." I bumped the end of the bed a few times with my knees, then went over to the couch and shook Grant's shoulder. The boys arose slowly from their blanket cocoons, filled their mugs, and did their business in the bathroom. Once everyone was ready, we piled into the Jeep and headed north along Highway 64 up the center of the island to the fort.

"We're going to have to keep our eyes open. It's not going to be sitting out in plain sight," Kaylin said, pointing out the obvious. "Look for anything that seems out of place like in the Amerii room back at your place." He gestured to Grant in the back seat. "Illinois," he shouted suddenly. I hadn't realized they were still playing that silly game.

"We should take as many pictures as we can, pretend to be tourists like everyone else, that way if we miss something we'll have the pictures to go through later," I suggested.

Everyone gasped when we pulled into the parking lot. I stared out the passenger window as we circled around the parking lot. It didn't look like a fort at all. I'd visited Fort Michilimackinac in Mackinaw City, Michigan as a child, and I'd expected it to look similar to that, but it didn't. Not in the least bit. It didn't even resemble a settlement. It was basically just an amphitheater on the waterfront. A huge wooden wall separated the water from a bunch of stadium seats. A cast of actors in full costumes were putting on a musical rendition of the Roanoke story. Their music rolled past the stadium seats and seeped into my partially open window like a dense, threatening fog.

"This is not what I pictured it would look like." Grant's comment perfectly summed up my own thoughts. "I pictured it bigger. With a bunch of old buildings and stuff."

"This can't be it," Kaylin said, his disappointment evident. He shifted into park, then leaned forward over the steering wheel. "There has to be more, there just has to be."

We exited the Jeep, bought our tickets at the gate, and found a seat in the audience. I could feel everyone's frustration as we quietly waited for the performance to be over. Luckily for us, there weren't many people in attendance. We wouldn't have to fight any crowds as we looked around like we'd thought we would. We'd be free to take our time and really inspect the place. I just wasn't totally sure there was much to inspect. The performers took their bows, welcoming people to come up on the stage and have a look around. The four of us got to our feet, clapping for the performers as we made our way up to the wall. No one said a word, but I knew what everyone was thinking. Is this where our journey would end? Have we come all this way for nothing? I followed behind Kaylin, glancing at my phone. I figured it wouldn't hurt if I still took pictures. I was capturing the structures, the trees, and the rocks—when I crashed into someone. We hit so hard, it knocked my phone out of my hands.

"Excuse me," said a well dressed man. His clothing seemed out of place. He looked like he should be in an office building, not at a tourist attraction. He bent down and picked up my phone. "I'm a terrible klutz." He gripped my phone in his right hand. I stared at him as he began to walk away.

"You have my phone." I chased after him.

He stopped and turned around. "My apologies." He handed me my phone and went on his way out to the parking lot, not once looking back. I couldn't place it but something about the man seemed familiar, like I'd seen him somewhere before.

"Geez, what a jerk. Are you all right, Rory?" asked Kaylin, coming over to check on me.

"That guy totally ran into you on purpose," said Grant, coming up behind us. "I watched him do it. He headed right for you."

"Why would he do that?" I asked.

"Check your pockets," Kevin said. "Did he take anything? That's a pickpocket trick. They bump into someone and steal their wallet."

I patted myself down checking in each of my pockets. Everything was still there. My cash was still in my pocket. Even my necklace and hair comb were still there. I'd been carrying the necklace around in case we needed it to unlock something again. "He didn't take anything," I said as I finished.

We all agreed it was weird, but since nothing was missing and I wasn't hurt, we decided to keep searching for the stone.

"I think we should see what's in there," Kaylin said as we approached a door marked:

Private
Employees Only

He twisted the door handle. It was unlocked. I nervously scanned the area around us to see if anyone was watching. I'd never done anything like this before. I was the kind of person who always followed the rules.

"No one's watching, let's go," I said feeling exhilarated. Breaking the rules made me feel giddy inside and gave me a rush. It felt good to be bad.

Kaylin forced the door open revealing a narrow stairway leading downwards. We crept down the stone steps to the basement. It was filled with costumes, mirrors, and dressing areas.

"This must be where the actors get ready," Kevin said. He rummaged through some of the costumes hanging on a rack. He found a top hat and tried it on.

The basement reminded me of the Amerii room. "I think we're in the right place," I said, wandering around the room. "Look around. Not at the costumes, but at the walls." I reached up and touched one of the wooden beams near the ceiling.

"It reminds me of the room back at the house! Well at least the crown molding does. It has the same pattern carved into the wood," Grant said, noticing what I was talking about. The same excited look he had when he entered the Amerii room returned to his face.

We'd just started to spread out along the walls in search of a hidden latch when a voice boomed out from the stairway behind us. Kevin quickly took the top hat off, tossing it onto the nearest table.

"Hey, what are you kids doing down here?" The man's voice, loud and commanding. "You can't be down here." He stepped down to the bottom of the stairs, revealing himself to us. I recognized him from the performance. He was the man who portrayed John White.

"Sorry, sir," Kevin apologized. "We were trying to find a bathroom."

"There are no bathrooms down here. Now let's go, everyone out," the man said. His stern look told us he wasn't buying our excuse. He led us back up the stairs. "The bathrooms are over there," he added as he shut the door. He took a set of keys out of his pocket and locked the door before going to rejoin the other actors.

"Crap, now what are we going to do?" I said softly so no one around us could hear. "He's locked the door. Now how are we going to get in?"

"We're going to have to come back tonight," Kaylin said and headed towards the parking lot. "After everyone goes home for the night." We followed him to the parking lot.

Grant sang along to the radio as Kaylin drove us back to the Inn. Kevin joined Grant when the song "The Sound of Silence" came on the radio. Their voices harmonized well. I even caught myself humming along with them. Even though our trip to the fort hadn't yielded any results, we knew right where to look when we came back that night. Everyone was having fun, and that's all that mattered to me.

Kaylin put the key in the lock and pushed open the door to our room. We stopped dead in our tracks. The laughter that surrounded us in the car was nothing more than an echo far off in the distance now. Our room had been ransacked. Someone had come in and turned the place upside down while we were gone. The sheets on our beds had been torn off. Our clothes had been emptied out of our bags and spread out all over the floor. The garbage cans were dumped out, used coffee cups and paper scraps were mixed in with the clothing. Someone was searching for our treasures, but who?

"This day just keeps getting better and better," Grant said as he stepped over a pile of garbage near the door. "My favorite t-shirt." He bent down and tugged a white shirt out from under last night's discarded dinner container. "It's ruined." He threw the shirt back on the floor.

I darted to the safe, ignoring my own clothing on the floor. I prayed they hadn't found what they were looking for.

"It's all still here," I informed the others. My heart pounded in my chest. They hadn't gotten the Amerii items we'd been collecting. The image of the shadowy figure outside the window that first night, rushed back into my mind, sending a shiver down my spine. "I don't think we should stay here tonight."

The boys agreed.

We quickly shoved our belongings, clean and dirty, into our bags and left the room. We didn't bother to stop at the front desk and return the room keys as we rushed through the lobby. I prayed we wouldn't come face to face with the people if they were still lurking around. We headed back across the bridge to the mainland in silence. No singing or laughing just awkward angry silence. Kaylin found a hotel in the same town we'd eaten lunch, on the way to the island.

"We will be okay here," Kaylin said as we pulled into the hotel parking lot. "I kept glancing in the rearview mirror the whole drive. No one followed us." He drove around the corner of the hotel. "But just to be safe, I'm going to park back here." He pulled into a spot behind a large van. "Plus, if that lady at the museum did call the cops like she said she was going to, they won't be able to see the Jeep from the road."

We grabbed our things from the back of the Jeep and stopped at the front desk to get a room for the night.

"This place has a pool." Kevin said. The shock and feeling of being vulnerable had obviously worn off. He flipped through a brochure as we rode the elevator up to our room. "We should go for a swim before we go back to the fort. It might help relax us. Ya know, sooth our tense muscles and stuff."

Swimming did sound like fun. Maybe it would help clear our heads if we had a little fun. I know I think better when I'm relaxed.

"I'm going to rinse my clothes out in the shower before we go. Try to get some of the garbage off them," I said to the boys once we'd gotten in the room. I unzipped my bag and dumped all the contents onto the shower floor. "Does anyone want me to do theirs too?"

After I'd finished hanging everyone's clothes around the room to dry, we put on our suits and headed down to the pool. The pool room was located down a hallway off of the main lobby. A large glass wall separated it from the recreation center. I could see families on vacation enjoying themselves in the pool as we approached the doors. Children splashed about, not a care in the world, while their parents sat on slatted white plastic lounge chairs along the pool's edge. A parent would glance up every few minutes to make sure their children were all right, then bury their nose back in the book they were ready or continue on with the conversation they were having. A good sized square pool took up most of the room. Off in the far corner sat the hot tub.

"I'm going to the hot tub," I said as we found some empty chairs to lay our towels on. I slipped my shoes off next to my lounge chair. "It's going to feel so nice. Riding in the car as much as we have has really got me twisted up."

"Have fun. I'm going for a swim," replied Kevin. He jumped into the pool, joining Grant who'd wasted no time getting into the water.

"Is it okay if I go with them?" asked Kaylin politely. I could tell he wanted to hang out with the boys.

"I'm not stopping you. Go have fun," I replied playfully as I sauntered away from him towards the hot tub.

I dipped my toe in the water. Mmmm, nice and hot. I slowly eased the rest of my body in. It took a minute to adjust to the heat, but once I was accustomed to it, it felt incredible. No way was I ever leaving. The boys were going to have to drag me out of here kicking and screaming.

I positioned myself so the jets pounded on my shoulder blades. I hadn't realized just how tense I really was. My muscles ached from all the digging we'd been doing. I laid my head back and closed my eyes, letting the water soothe my sore body. I could hear the boys splashing around in the pool. They made more noise than the little kids did. It sounded like they were having a ton of fun. I raised my head and opened my left eye to see what they were doing. I was jealous that Kaylin had gone with them, but not jealous enough to go splash around in the cool water of the pool. Nope, I was fine where I was. I laid my head back again.

"You shouldn't stay in there more than a half hour," a voice said. I opened my eyes to see a plumpish man standing a few feet away from the tub. I remembered seeing the man putting swim rings on the arms of a complaining toddler when we first entered the pool room. "Dad! I'm too old for these," the little boy had said in protest.

"Thank you, I'll keep that in mind," I replied. I figured he must have felt obligated as a parent to let me know I was cooking myself like a lobster, otherwise what business was it of his. He nodded at me and returned to his lounge chair. I glanced back over at the pool. The boys were getting out.

"We're going to the rec room," Grant hollered at me as he snatched his towel from the chair and vigorously rubbed it on his head. Kaylin stared at me as he wrapped his towel around his midsection concealing his toned abs.

"Few more minutes, then I'll get out," I replied, ignoring the urge to go over and rip the towel off of his body so I could continue to gaze upon his muscles.

I watched as the boys headed off to the game room. Once they were out of view, I returned to my relaxing position. Suddenly, I got the feeling I was being watched. I opened my eyes expecting to see the plumpish man with another hot tub warning, but he wasn't there. In fact, no one was anywhere near the hot tub. Some of the families had cleared out and the pool room was nearly empty. That's when I noticed a man standing outside the pool room, behind the glass wall, peering in. I studied the familiar figure with its out-of-place clothing. It was the same guy who'd run into me at the fort earlier today. Was he following me? Fear spread through my body. The same heart pounding fear I'd felt when the man was outside my window.

I slouched down in the hot tub, just barely keeping my nose above the water. I wasn't sure if he'd spotted me. He continued to stare into the pool room, just standing there and staring for another several minutes before continuing down the hall and out of sight. I waited to make sure he wasn't coming back before jumping out of the hot tub and rushing over to the lounge chair. I grabbed my towel and slid my shoes onto my wet feet then hurried to the door. I poked my head out into the hallway, scanning both directions. The man was gone, nowhere in sight. I ran to the rec room, dripping a trail of water along the carpet behind me.

I quietly slipped into the rec room. I did a quick sweep of the room with my eyes to make sure the guy hadn't come in there. The room was empty except for the boys, who were at the floor hockey table, playing a game.

"Hey," I said as I approached the boys, finally taking a moment to dry off. "I think I saw the guy from the fort."

"The guy who ran into you?" asked Kaylin, momentarily glancing up from the game. He stood at the side of the table, his fingers gripping the edge.

"Yeah, he was staring at me from the hallway when I was in the hot tub." I glanced over my shoulder at the door. "I swear it was him."

"That's creepy, Cuz," Grant said, too focused on beating Kevin to look at me.

"Will someone walk back up to the room with me?" I asked. "I don't feel safe walking alone."

"We're done here, we'll all go. Besides we need to figure out what we're doing tonight," Grant added. He tried one more time to score a goal against Kevin. Kevin yanked on the rod, lined his man up, waited for just the right moment, then spun the rod and blocked the ball from going in the goal. "You win." Grant threw his hands in the air.

Kaylin put his arm around my shoulder and gave me a quick squeeze. "Maybe it wasn't him," he said trying to make me feel better. He smiled and gently jiggled me before letting go.

As we strolled down the hallway to the elevator, I kept checking to see if anyone was behind us. I felt very uneasy. Too many strange things had happened for it to be a coincidence. First the figure outside the window, then our room getting torn apart, and now the man that nearly knocked me down at the Fort was stalking me. Peeking in on me as I soaked in the hot tub like some kind of perverted creeper. My skin crawled. I felt dirty, my confidence stripped away, leaving me naked and vulnerable.

"Do you think we should call the cops?" I asked once we'd made it safely into our room.

"And tell them what? That we stole a comb from the museum and now we're planning on breaking into the Roanoke Fort?" asked Grant, mocking me as he threw on the same t-shirt he'd worn earlier. All of our other clothing was still drying.

"No, about all the weird stuff happening," I replied angrily. Of course I wasn't going to tell them we planned on committing a B and E.

"Oh yeah, sure." Grant pretended to hold a phone to his ear. "Ring ring, hello, officer? My cousin thinks she saw a figure, and someone broke into our room while we were casing a joint to break into. Now my cousin thinks a pervert's stalking her." He took his hand away from his ear. "Not the best idea, Cuz. I think it's better if we keep quiet. Besides, we're not even positive a few of those things happened. No one but you saw the figure outside the window and you can't know for sure if it was the same guy staring at you in the hot tub."

"So, no one believes me. Is that how it is?" I glanced around at the guys' faces. "Nice. Thanks a lot." I grabbed my clothes and locked myself in the bathroom to change. I couldn't believe how the guys were acting. How could Kaylin be on their side?

"Rory, are you all right in there?" Kaylin knocked on the door. "You've been in there for a while."

"Go away," I mumbled through my tears. "I don't want to talk to you." I grabbed a piece of toilet paper and dabbed my nose.

"It's not that I don't believe you, we just didn't see some of it," he said. "Please let me in."

But his apology was weak and I didn't believe he was truly sorry. It shouldn't matter if they'd seen the man outside the window, he should trust me when I say I did.

"Bring me my phone," I said.

"You can't call the cops."

"I'm not, just bring me my phone."

He was silent for a minute then knocked on the door again.

"I have your phone."

I opened the door a crack and stuck my hand out. He gently placed the phone in my hand. I quickly drew my hand in and shut the door again.

"Rory, please let me in," he pleaded. Pounding on the door more vigorously.

I ignored him, I wasn't going to fall for his nice guy act. Instead, I did the only thing that I knew would make me feel better. I called Steph. I spilled everything to her. I told her about the room we had found, the Amerii, where we were, what we were doing, and about all the weird things that had happened. I needed someone to believe me. I needed my friend. She listened quietly as I spilled all of our secrets.

"I'm on my way," she said once I'd finished. "I believe you."

I exhaled, finally feeling relief. The secret was out. I didn't have to lie any more. As an added bonus, I would no longer be the only girl in the group. My friend was coming. I would have someone I trusted here with me. We said our goodbyes, then I hung up the phone and exited the bathroom to find Kaylin sitting just outside the door. Had he been sitting there the whole time, I wondered. If so, had he been listening to our conversation.

He stood up and hugged me, placing his hand on the back of my head and forcing my head closer to him. I laid it on his chest, giving in to my romantic feelings for him and forgetting I was mad at him. I wanted so badly to be able to trust him. So much so that I was willing to ignore that he'd hurt my feelings.

"I'm sorry, Rory. Are you feeling better now?" He leaned back just enough to get me to look at him. I gazed into his eyes. They appeared sincere. Could I trust him?

"Yes," I replied, laying my head back down on him. "I'm okay" I contemplated telling him about Steph. I would have to sooner or later. He'd figure it out when she showed up. "I called Steph," I admitted, lifting my head from his chest and glancing up at him. I decided it was better to get it out in the open now then to wait and have him find out later. "I told her everything. She's on her way. She should be here by tomorrow."

"I know," he said, resting his chin on the top of my head. "I heard." We continued our embrace for a few more minutes before parting and stepping over to the table where the other two were drawing up plans.

They heard me tell Kaylin that Steph knew everything, but neither of them dared to say a word about it to me. Kaylin and I sat down at the table with them. Kevin had drawn up detailed diagrams of what the fort looks like now. The drawings were scattered around on the table in front of him. Grant held the old fort plans from home in front of him. They made comparisons, noting the differences between old and new.

"Most of the fort is gone now, except the wall we saw today. That wall lines up with this part of the original fort." Grant pointed to a section of the plans. "The door down to the basement is here." He traced his finger along the drawing. "There's a body of water to the north of the wall, so we know there can't be much behind the north wall of the basement. I think our best bet is to try the south wall. That would put us about here." He pointed to a symbol on the old fort plans.

"What's that symbol?" I asked, leaning forward. It felt good to be working as a team again. "It looks like a shell."

"That's exactly what it is. It's an old sailing symbol representing something enclosed, it can also mean treasure if the shell is open," Grant explained.

"How did you know that?" I questioned, fascinated he had such knowledge.

"Dad took us for sailing lessons one summer. I can tie a bunch of knots, too. I'm full of hidden talents." He smiled, pulling his shoulders back and puffing up his chest. He proudly grinned as he glanced around the table.

"Yeah, you're full of something all right," Kevin said, tapping on the plans. "Can we get back to planning, I don't feel like going to jail tonight."

"Fine." Grant slumped back down in his chair like a deflating balloon. "So anyway, our best bet is to search for a secret room like the one back at the house. The Fort closes at six." He looked at the time. "It's almost six now." He turned to me. "Hey, Aurora, do you still have the pictures you took on your phone?"

"Yeah, why?" I asked. We knew where to search. What was the point in going over the pictures?

"I want to see if you got any pictures of their security cameras. I'd like to avoid them if we can."

I pulled the pictures up then handed him my phone.

"Scroll back from there," I said. Grant scanned through the pictures, showing Kevin where to mark the cameras on his drawing.

"It will be dark in a few hours. I think we should wait until then," Grant said. He set the pencil down on the table and inspected Kevin's work. We all agreed, waiting until after dark was the best idea. That gave us a few hours to rest, have a bite to eat, and pick up a few flashlights from the gas station down the road.

It was close to eleven by the time we arrived at the Fort.

"Park outside the gates, over behind that sign." Kevin leaned forward from the backseat and pointed out the front window to a big billboard sign just past the parking lot. "The parking lot is loaded with cameras. We need to go on foot from here," Kevin said as he exited the Jeep. He jogged out closer to the road to make sure the Jeep was hidden from the passing cars. "No one should be able to see it from the road there." He joined us back at the Jeep.

We grabbed our backpacks out of the back. It seemed they were becoming a part of our everyday attire lately.

"Try to keep your flashlight off until we're down in the basement, and keep your voices down" Grant instructed as he skillfully led us through the invisible maze of cameras to the employees only door.

"It's locked. Anyone know how to pick a lock?" Kaylin asked as he tried turning the knob.

"I got this, little bro." Kevin shoved Kaylin to the side. "Watch the master at work." He pulled something pointy out of his back pocket and bent down in front of the key hole. "I had a feeling I might need this."

"Do I want to know why you have a lock pick set in your pocket or why you know how to use it?" Kaylin asked, his arms crossed in front of him.

"I used to sneak girls into the café. Impress them with some late night meal, romance them, you know, that kinda stuff." He jiggled the pick in the keyhole. "Oh man, Grant... you remember Melissa Warren? From tenth grade math. The stories I could—"

"Let's save the story telling for a time when we're not trying to break in somewhere," I cut him short. I really didn't need to hear about his conquests. "Did you ever sneak in and do that kinda stuff?" I asked Kaylin, leaning in close so the other two couldn't hear. He shook his head. I smiled, relieved to know he wasn't like that.

"There, I got it." Kevin proudly swung the door open. "We're in. Now you know why you brought me along."

We headed down the stairway, closing and locking the door behind us before turning on our flashlights. The place was a lot creepier at night. The seventeenth-century costumes and wigs gave it an eerie feel, like there was someone in the room with us.

"I don't like this place," I whispered to Kaylin, getting as close to him as I could.

"Me either." His fingers intertwined with mine. "It's creepy." He shone his flashlight around the room.

We pushed our way through the racks of clothing and the wig stands, passed the changing areas that were sectioned off from the rest of the room by big, folding, four-paneled curtains, the kind you'd see in Japan, and then maneuvered around the makeup tables, loaded full of products, to the south wall. The room smelled of sweaty, unwashed costumes, probably worn multiple times a day by different actors.

"You guys know the drill, start searching for a lever or something. It's probably going to be something similar to what we found back at the house," Grant said, briefly taking over Kaylin's leadership role. It was nice to see him in a role other than comedian.

We fanned out along the south wall, scanning for imperfections in the wood panels and feeling for loose objects with our hands. It didn't take long before Kevin found a small imperfection along one of the large beams that framed the wall. We were getting good at the secret room stuff. I let out a quiet squeal, happy we didn't have to spend a long time searching. I was eager to see what secrets the Amerii had hidden behind the wall.

"Okay, this is a little different than back home," Kevin said. He scratched his head as he pointed his flashlight towards a spot higher up on the beam. "Instead of opening up a door when I pushed in this knot on the beam it opened a panel, exposing this small box."

We hurried over to him, curious to see what he found. About halfway up the beam from the floor was a square panel. Inside were three wheel shaped dials strung along a metal rod like beads on a necklace. Each dial had multiple different symbols carved into it.

"We must have to turn them," Kevin said trying to spin one of them. "Line up the right set of symbols or something." It took some effort but he was eventually able to get all three of the dials to spin freely on the rod.

"I bet that notch at the top of the dials means something," I said pointing in the box at the faded white lines notched into the wood above the dials. "Maybe the symbols need to be near the top and not in the center."

"There's hundreds of possible combinations." Kaylin said, seeming exasperated by the odds of figuring out the right combination. "How are we ever going to find the right one?"

"What symbols are on each of the dials?" asked Grant as he rummaged around the makeup desks for something to write with. He found an eyeliner pencil then sat down at a desk near Kevin. He pulled one of the diagrams Kevin had drawn out of his back pocket and placed it on the desk. "Okay, I'm ready."

Kevin described the symbols to him. "The first one has a cross, a square with a gem like shape in it, a circle with an eye in it, at least I think it's an eye, a triangle divided into three smaller triangles, and then a stick figure with the top half of a second stick figure above it. On the second dial there's an anchor, a line with two lines coming off of it kinda like an F, a square with an X in it, two fish, and a shell. The third has the triangle from the first dial, another shell, another anchor, a sun, and the weird stick figure again."

"Okay give me a few minutes." Grant studied the symbols he had drawn on the paper. "Try the cross, the stick figure, and the shell," he finally said, looking up at Kevin.

Kevin reached into the box and spun the dials. "Nope."

Grant looked back at his drawings for a moment then said, "Okay try the stick figure, the shell, and the triangle."

"Still nothing."

"I don't get it. That should have worked." Grant scratched his head.

"Let me see," Kaylin said pushing Kevin aside. "Shine your light in here for me would you Rory?"

"You don't think I know how to spin a dial?" Kevin said angrily as he stepped back. "I'm not a meathead." He wandered over to the desk next to Grant. "Maybe Grant doesn't know what he's talking about." He lifted the paper off the desk and studied it.

"I do so," Grant argued, reaching for the paper. Kevin raised it over his head and glanced up at it.

I peeked over Kaylin's shoulder. "What do you suppose those tiny holes are?"

"I was looking at those too." Kaylin ran his fingers across the dials. "At first I thought they were random but look. No matter what symbol is showing the holes are in the same pattern. It's like they were drilled into the dials on purpose."

I studied the holes. "There's thirteen of them." I tilted my head, racking my brain for an answer. "Where have I seen thirteen of something before." I sat down in one of the chairs and laid my flashlight on the table.

"Your necklace has twelve diamonds and one sapphire. That's thirteen," said Kaylin

"My necklace wont fit in those holes."

"Was it in the Amerii room? Maybe in one of the books? Or in a painting?" suggested Grant.

"There were thirteen men and thirteen women's names in one of the books, but that's not it." I shook my head. "It was more recent." I tapped my fingers on the edge of my seat.

"One of the objects we found when we were digging? The baby rattle?" said Kevin. "Was something carved in the rattle?"

"I don't think so." I recalled the rattle. "It's right on the tip of my brain." I put my hands on my face. "If only I could just remember." I leaned back in the chair and ran my hands over my head. "Oh my God!" I pulled the hair comb from my ponytail and sprang from the chair. I ran over to the dials and held the comb up. The hair comb was the exact length of the dials but the teeth didn't line up with the holes. "I thought for sure this would be it." I sadly pulled the comb away. "Some of the teeth are missing. They don't fit in all the holes."

"Maybe they're not supposed to," said Kaylin. Here let me see the comb. I handed him the comb. "Remember the poem Anna wrote. Two will rule, one for all, when three stones are recovered none will fall." He held up the comb. Two teeth, then a space one tooth then a space three teeth then a space and another space. Two, one, three and none. It was a code telling him which holes to leave empty."

"Bet you're glad I stole that now," Kevin proudly sauntered over to the dials. "I think I should do the honors." He reached for the comb. "Since without me we wouldn't be able to open the door."

I looked at Kaylin.

"Just let him do it." Kaylin shrugged. "At least he's taking an interest."

I handed Kevin the comb and stepped to the side. Kevin lined the teeth up and slid the comb into the dial. "It's doing something!" Kevin said, quickly jerking his hand back. "I'm not sure it's doing what it's supposed to. Something doesn't sound right."

I grabbed for the comb, yanking it out of the box just before the panel slammed shut.

"Did you put the symbols back in the order I told you to?" asked Grant standing up and backing away from the wall.

"Yes," I shouted over the noise.

"What the hell is going on? Is it a trap?" Kevin asked stepping away from the loud humming noise inside the wall.

"Something's moving in the wall. It sounds like gears spinning," Kaylin said approaching the wall instead of backing away from it like the rest of us were doing.

"Get back," I shouted as he pressed his ear up against the wall. "You don't know what's going to happen."

"It's okay," he yelled back over the grinding and clunking. He waved for me to come closer. "It's opening."

I questioned whether I should believe him. My head told me to run away from the horrible noises in the wall as fast as I could, but in my heart I knew Kaylin would never put me in danger. I stepped closer, ignoring my instincts.

Without warning a three foot wide by ten foot long section of the floor sank just below the level of the rest of the floor, then slid towards the wall revealing a stone staircase just like the one we'd walked down into the basement. This door system was definitely not like the simple latch at home. Someone with significant engineering knowledge had designed it.

"See." Kaylin shone his light down into the dark stairway. "Told you it was working."

The three of us hesitantly stepped closer to the edge and peered down into the dark. Kaylin, without hesitation, eagerly bounded down the deep stairway.

"You guys coming?" He waved his flashlight up the stairs at us.

I looked at Kevin and Grant. Neither of them showed any inclination that they were planning to follow Kaylin down the stairs into the darkness. I certainly didn't want to be the first to follow him.

"Hey, Rory, did you pack a lighter?" Kaylin disappeared under the floor at the bottom of the stairs. Just a faint glow from his flashlight was visible.

"Yes, just a sec, it's in my pack." I dropped to my knee, slipped my pack from my shoulder and found the lighter. "Here it is," I yelled down to him, hoping he would come back up the stairs to get it. I flung my pack back onto my back and held the lighter out.

"Bring it here." He replied. "I found something."

Oh crap! I stood up. Guess I have no choice. I slid my foot forward so that the toe of my shoe hung over the edge. I'm going to have to go down, or risk looking like a scared baby. I carefully placed my foot on the first step. You've got this, Aurora.

As I made my way down the stairs a small landing appeared at the bottom. I slowly stepped deeper down into the earth using the wall for balance until I reached the landing and found Kaylin. He was fidgeting with something protruding from the stone wall.

"Look, it's an old lantern" he said excitedly. "Let's see if we can get this working. It should give us a ton more light than these cheap flashlights."

I stepped up next to him. The walls were made of the same stone as the stairway. Large, smooth rocks that varied in color from gray to a pinkish-brown formed a seemingly endless path into the earth. Occasionally a stone with a blue hint to it would interrupt the monotony of earthy tones. Those were my favorites. It was eerily beautiful. I handed Kaylin the lighter, and he lit the candle wick. The lantern threw a warm light onto the cold stone, exposing a longer hallway than I'd been able to see with the flashlight. There were lanterns mounted about every ten feet, alternating from side to side down the hallway.

"Put this in my pack." Kaylin handed me his flashlight then turned his back to me. I unzipped his pack and threw both of our flashlights in. We strolled down the hall, lighting each lantern as we came upon it. By the third lantern it became clear to us that the hallway opened up into a larger area just ahead. We hurried to the last lantern, eager to see what was in the opening. I couldn't believe my eyes. The light from the last lantern revealed an unimaginable wonder. I gasped and stepped out into a huge underground cavern. A town. Hidden in the center of this enormous cavern was a town. The ceiling of the cavern soared thirty feet overhead. Massive wooden beams reinforced the cold, rock walls. The stone pathway from the hall ran out into the cavern and then along the edge of the walls. We followed the path around the cavern to a post with another lantern on it. Kaylin lit the lantern, and my gaze darted around as I tried to comprehend what I was seeing. Could this be real? I felt giddy inside, like a child at an amusement park. A complete underground town modeled to look like any old town on the surface, appeared right before my eyes. There were even fake trees carved out of wood in the backyards of the houses. Multiple cobblestone streets lined with shops ran from the stone path to the town's center, forming a giant wheel shape. Homes made of wood and stone were scattered about along the path and streets. I looked over to Kaylin, who was frantically searching for more lanterns to light. With every lantern he lit, more of the astonishing town revealed itself. I wandered down the main street peering in the shop's windows as I passed by them, my mouth open wide with shock. I didn't know what to look at first. I continued down the main street to the hub of the town, where the streets met and encircled a round stone well that was filled with water. An old decaying bucket sat on the rim of the well.

"Are you seeing what I'm seeing?" Kaylin's voice echoed down the abandoned streets.

"A freaking town? Are you seeing a town...cause that's what I'm seeing," Grant answered. Grant and Kevin were standing just inside the cavern with their eyes wide and their mouths hanging open. "We found a whole damn town!" he shouted excitedly pointing at the buildings.

"This is the craziest thing I've ever seen," said Kevin, not holding back his excitement. He looked around then changed his tune. "I mean if you'd seen the stuff I've seen this wouldn't be that impressive. It's cool but whatever."

The two boys strolled down the main street towards me, stopping every so often to examine something they found. Kaylin came up one of the side streets and sat on the edge of the well. I sat down next to him.

"Where do we start?" I asked, hoping he had some sort of clue.

"Honestly, I have no idea," he said, shaking his head in disbelief. "There's no mention of an underground town in anything I've read so far. This is as much a surprise to me as it is to you."

"So then, why don't we split up and start searching the buildings. Tomorrow's Saturday, the fort doesn't open up again until Monday. We have all weekend before we need to get out of here," I said.

"We didn't pack enough food for two days," Grant said as he and Kevin approached us. Kevin sat down beside me, while Grant stood in front of us with his arms crossed. "We'll starve by Monday."

"Grant you know where the cameras are, you go up and get some food. I saw a concession stand when we were here this morning, check there, see what you can find. The rest of us will split up and start searching," Kaylin said as he stood up. He dug around in his pocket and pulled out a twenty dollar bill. "Leave this to pay for whatever you find."

"I think we should start with the houses. Eleanor said she was taking the stone home. One of these houses must have been her grandmother's," I said and got to my feet.

"Good thinking, start with the houses," Kaylin said, changing his original orders.

Grant headed back up stairs while the rest of us searched the houses. The first house I entered was small, a single-story building with only a few rooms. I quickly scanned the cupboards for any signs this was Eleanor Dare's home. I found a desk in one of the back rooms with papers on it. It was amazing how well preserved everything was. It had been hundreds of years, but I would swear the house's owner had just been there yesterday. There was very little dust on anything, not like there was when we discovered the Amerii room back at the house. It was like I'd stepped back in time, and at any moment the owner would appear, demanding to know why I was in their house. It left a very uneasy feeling in my stomach. I rummaged through the papers on the desk expecting to get caught. Nothing in them led me to believe this was the right house. I continued on to the next one. The second house was a bit bigger than the first. It even had a second story to it. I entered through the front door, making my way through the parlor to the kitchen. The table was set and ready for dinner with five plates placed neatly around it, one in front of each chair. There was a pot on the cooking stove. It seemed like someone had been making dinner in it, but time had eaten away at whatever was left inside. They must have left in a hurry. I made my way into one of the bedrooms. Two overly large wooden-framed beds rested their heads on the far wall, their feet extending out almost the entire length of the room. In the next room was a cradle and a smaller bed.

There must have been children living here. It's possible this could be the Dare home we're searching for. Victoria was only three when they disappeared. That could have been her cradle.

Excited by the thought that this was the right house, I meticulously searched every inch of it, but was unable to find definitive proof that it was in fact their home. I made a mental note to come back to this house if we couldn't find any others that fit the bill. I continued, searching each house on the street, but just like in the first two, I found no proof of who lived there in any of them. Could the people who lived in these houses have done that on purpose? I wondered. Is the reason I can't find any proof of who was living in them because they didn't want anyone to know who they were?

"Are you having any luck?" Kaylin asked as I exited the last house on the street. He'd finished searching the houses on the street next to mine.

"There's one possibility on this street, but nothing for sure." I answered, looking back at the house that might have been the Dare home.

"Let's find Kevin and Grant." He wiped the sweat from his brow and glanced up at the top of the cavern. "I think we need a break." He paused for a moment. "Do you think there's bats flying around up there?"

I giggled. So bats are his thing. "Bats? No. I don't think so."

He nodded. "Yeah you're probably right." He turned and strolled down the side yard of one of the houses on his way to the next street. I strolled along behind him, close to the picket fence dividing the two houses.

We found Grant searching a house on the next street. He'd been successful in getting food from the concession stand, but was having the same amount of luck that Kaylin and I were having in the houses. Kevin finished up searching the street on the far side of Kaylin's and had already headed towards the well when Kaylin, Grant, and I wandered around the corner. We gathered in the town center and discussed our findings over the popcorn and cotton candy Grant brought down for us.

"This place is truly amazing," I said between bites of popcorn. "I mean think about it. The Amerii built this town hundreds of years ago. It would be a difficult task to do now, even with the technology we have."

"I could do it," bragged Kevin, ripping a large chunk of cotton candy from the bag and wadding it up into a ball before cramming it in his mouth.

"Maybe in your dreams," teased Grant, grabbing the bag of cotton candy from Kevin before he ate it all.

"Or if you lived in a Jules Verne novel," Kaylin said. Our hands touched as we both reached for another handful of popcorn. He pulled back allowing me to take a handful first. "This place is straight up Journey to the Center of the Earth kinda stuff." Everyone laughed at his comment, but he was right.

"We better get back to it," Kaylin said, taking one last handful of popcorn. He handed me the twisty tie he'd been holding onto since he'd opened the bag. I tied the popcorn bag closed and tossed it into my backpack. "There's still a lot of houses left to check out," he said, wiping his greasy fingers on his jeans. We set off again in search of the Dare family home. I was halfway done with the third house on my street when I heard Grant screaming.

"There's someone in here. There's someone in here." he shrieked hysterically.

I quickly ran out into the street to see what he was yelling about. I scanned the area. Where is everyone?

"Come here, everyone come here," he yelled. His voice echoed off the cavern walls.

I ran toward the well, trying to remember which street Grant was on. I peered down each one as I passed by, making a circle around the pool of water. I'd made it almost all the way around when I spotted Grant bending over, holding his stomach at the far end of one of the streets. Had someone attacked him? Kevin had reached Grant first and was standing next to him with his hand on Grant's back. Kaylin was running down the street towards them. I chased after him, frantically scanning for any signs of another person as I ran, fearing someone would jump out and grab me as I passed.

"What's going on? Are you okay? Did someone attack you?" I asked, taking in deep breaths between each question. I hadn't run like that since I was on the high school track team. I definitely needed to get back into shape. I knelt down beside Grant, trying to catch my breath. I inspected him for any signs of injury. No blood.

"No, no. I'm fine." He stood up and glared at me, wiping the corners of his mouth with the back of his hand, his face a pale greenish color. That's when I noticed the vomit on the ground inches away from where I'd knelt down. I hurried to my feet, taking a step back.

"What happened?" I asked, concerned.

"Inside! There's someone inside that house." He pointed to the house across the street from us. "Someone's dead."

"Someone's dead?" Kevin asked. "In that house?" He glanced over to the house Grant had pointed to.

"Dead," repeated Grant, bending over again and grabbing his stomach. He gagged but stopped himself from vomiting a second time. "As a doornail."

"Did you kill them?" asked Kaylin.

Grant stood up and frowned. "Did I kill them? No I didn't kill them. Jesus!" he said angrily. "How could you suggest I'd kill someone." He distanced himself from Kaylin. "He was dead when I found him and from the looks of it he's been that way for a long time."

"I'm not going in there," I said matter of factly. There was no way I was going in there. Not with a dead body in there. Death creeped me out. I couldn't bring myself to go near the casket when my own grandmother passed away a few years ago. I was certainly not going into a house with an unknown corpse just lying around in it.

"You're going to have to," Grant said, joining Kevin near a hitching post in front of what I presumed to be a stable. Had they really brought horses down here or was the town built this way to make the people living here feel like they were above ground? "I'm sure this is the house we've been looking for."

"How do you know that?" I asked skeptically.

"Look up at the peak of the roof." He pointed to a wooden carving nestled in the peak of the roof. "See that carving? Seem familiar?" My eyes widened. The carving was the same shape as my necklace only much, much larger. "Plus, I'm pretty sure the guy in there died searching for the stone. He's caught in a trap."

"A trap?" Kevin asked, leaving the post. He inched towards the front door. Enchanted by the thought of a trap. "Like a booby trap?" His voice got excited. He pivoted on his heels and stared at us with hope in his eyes. "A real life trap with sinking floor boards and shooting poisonous arrows and huge rolling boulders. Like in the movies?"

"I doubt there's rolling boulders," Kaylin said. "It's not like you could fit a boulder in a house." He paused for a moment. "I don't think a booby trap is as exciting in real life as it seems in the movies."

"Exactly," replied Grant. "Cool, but not cool, because this one will actually kill us." Grant shook his head in disbelief. "Why would anyone want to be caught in a trap?"

"Just thought it might bring some excitement to the trip," said Kevin. "Spice things up a bit." He shrugged his shoulders. "Okay, Kaylin, what do we do then? How do we avoid getting caught in a booby trap?" He raised his left eyebrow and glared at Kaylin.

"Why are you asking me? How should I know what to do?" Kaylin responded. He began to pace back and forth on the street.

"You've spent the most time out of all of us reading the Amerii books. You're the one who knew where the Dare Stone would be. Was there anything in there about booby traps?"

"No." He shook his head, pausing for a moment before returning to his pacing. "Nothing. This is uncharted territory."

"That's awesome." Grant said sarcastically. "We're just winging it from here I guess?"

"We go in," replied Kaylin matter of factly. He stopped in his tracks and stared at us.

"Or we go home," Kevin suggested. He stepped over to his backpack and picked it up off the ground then tossed it over his shoulders. "Here." He grabbed Grant's pack and tossed it to him.

"We can't go home now. We are literally standing right outside the door from the Dare Stone," I said, surprising myself. I couldn't believe I'd implied we should go in the house. I honestly didn't want to, not with a dead person in there, not to mention the threat of our own lives hanging over our heads, but we were so close to having another piece of the puzzle. We couldn't stop now. We just couldn't.

Kaylin strolled up beside me. We exchanged glances. He touched my hand giving it a slight tug towards the door of the house.

"We've got to do this," he told Grant and Kevin.

They agreed and followed us to the front door. I sensed none of us wanted to be the one who took the first step through the doorway. No one wanted to find out what was waiting for us on the other side.

"Grant, you go first," I said turning to make sure he and Kevin weren't chickening out.

"Why me?"

"Because you've already been here. You know where to go." I reached back and yanked him closer to the doorway.

He stared at everyone. His eyes pleaded with us to take his place. No one volunteered. Not even Kaylin.

"Okay," he said in unwilling agreement.

He pushed on the front door. It easily swung open. He'd run out of the house so fast earlier that the door hadn't latched closed. I held my breath as he stepped inside. He stood just inside the doorway, slightly trembling. His eyes tightly closed and his arms braced for whatever was to come his way, but nothing did. Kaylin stepped through the doorway next, coaxing Grant forward.

"Ladies first," said Kevin bowing to me. He waited in his bent over position for me to enter the house.

It's funny how, now that his life was in danger, he all of a sudden became a gentleman. I thought to myself sarcastically, how chivalrous of him.

I stepped through the door, scanning the room in search of the corpse. I was more worried about stumbling upon the corpse than I was about getting entangled in a trap. In fact, I wasn't worried about the trap in the least bit. After all, we'd scaled the side of a house, found a secret room filled with books left by a secret society our ancestors founded, we'd found our first Dare Stone and that Dare Stone led us to unearth a lost colony. Not to mention we'd figured out how to break the code to get into a mysterious underground town. So far, when it came to figuring things out, we were experts. We'd done amazing things. It had to be in our DNA. It was our ancestors who'd created all this. A part of them had to be still alive in us. We were born Amerii. I had faith we would know exactly what to do when, or if, we found a trap.

"It's just up ahead," Grant said as we continued to trek farther into the house, past the parlor and through the kitchen to a hallway at the back of the house.

"The body?" I asked. My voice uneasy and my throat dry. I tried to swallow.

"Or the booby trap?" asked Kevin a small hint of excitement still in his voice.

"Both," Grant replied.

I clenched my jaw and prepared myself for what was about to come. Kaylin grabbed my hand. Now that's true chivalry. I squeezed his hand tightly as we drew closer to the end of the hall. Grant stopped at the end of the hall, his posture stiff. He peered through the door before entering the last room on the right.

"It's gone," he said in disbelief. His eyes darted around the room. The body was gone. His shoulders relaxed. "It vanished." He confidently stepped into the room.

"What do you mean it's gone?" demanded Kaylin. He let go of my hand and hurried into the room. "Bodies don't just get up and walk away. Are you sure we're in the right room?" He headed for the door.

"Yes, I'm sure. He was right here." Grant opened his arms. He swung them around in a circle. "Right here next to the bed. Trapped in a net." Grant stood next to an enormous four-poster bed on the opposite side of the room from the door. The kind of bed I'd always dreamed of having. I imagined beautiful, flowing fabric hanging around it. Kaylin stopped before he'd exited the room and spun around then stomped over to the bed.

"I'm out." Kevin said angrily and twisted around, storming off down the hall. "You guys are nuts. I'm done. I'm done with all of you." His voice trailed off.

"Kevin wait. Where are you going?" I yelled after him but it was too late. He was already gone.

"Let him go," Kaylin shouted at me. His anger surprised me. He was usually so level headed. "I'm sorry," he said, seeing the expression on my face. "I didn't mean to yell at you. It's just best to let him go when he gets like this. He'll be back. You'll see." He said to comfort me but his words had already done their damage. My eyes glazed over. He hurried over to me and put his arms around me. "I really am sorry," he whispered. I pulled out of his embrace and wiped my eyes.

Things weren't going like I'd thought they would. Everything was falling apart. The corpse and the trap disappeared along with any clues they might have given us as to where the next Dare Stone could be. Kevin ran off. Our group was falling apart. We had never really been a super close group, but we'd been growing stronger every day, and up until now we've been in this together. I wanted it to stay that way. I'd grown fond of our mismatched group. Kevin and Grant seemed to have their doubts about the trip to Roanoke, but for the most part had been willing to go along with the plan, even coming up with some of their own theories about the Amerii organization and what it stood for. We had become a team. We couldn't fall apart now.

"Someone must have come in here and stole the body," Grant said, still insisting he was in the right spot.

"Maybe it was your mind playing tricks on you," I suggested, in the same mocking tone he'd used when I'd insisted someone was stalking me. The shoe was on the other foot now.

"I know I haven't been sleeping the greatest in the hotel beds. Maybe you're just overly tired," Kaylin said, sympathizing with him.

"No, I'm one hundred percent positive it was here. The corpse was sitting up against the wall by that bed with one arm resting on the bed. His head was turned away from the bed like this," he replied. Moving his own body into a similar position.

"Okay, let's say there was a body here, and let's say he was looking at something, but what would he have been looking at?" Kaylin said leaving my side and wandering over to the side of the bed.

I sniffed, wiping my nose with my sleeve. I took a breath and put on a smile. We had work to do. I wandered over to the opposite side of the bed. I wasn't ready to fully forgive him just yet.

"The only thing in that direction is a portrait." Kaylin pointed to the painting of a man and a woman with their small child on the wall behind me. I stepped over to the painting. It surprised me it was there. There were no portraits in any of the other houses. I inspected the painting for clues. The family pictured in the painting was well dressed. I traced the outline of the child's face with my finger. Could this be a painting of my Aunt Virginia? I scanned the background but didn't see anything in the painting that could be a clue. I lifted the painting off the wall and turned it over. The back was blank, not even a name or a date.

"There's nothing here," I said as I rubbed the wall where the picture was hanging. "Maybe the body wasn't looking at something maybe he was pointing to something with his hand," I suggested gazing to the other side of the room by the boys. I avoided making eye contact with Kaylin. "Maybe there's a clue on the table."

A large stone sculpture of a chalice sat on the wooden bedside table. The chalice's main cup resembled a large bowl trimmed at the top and bottom with beautifully detailed carvings of fruit. The stem mimicked the shape of a man. The man was hunched over as if the bowl he carried on his shoulder had considerable weight to it. The base where the man stood was even wider than the bowl on top. I hurried around the foot of the bed to the table, passing Grant and Kayin on the way. I picked the heavy chalice up and inspected it. Something about the base seemed out of place to me.

"Guys we're trapped!" Kevin burst into the room. "There's no way out!" he said, flushed and out of breath. His hands and face smeared with blood. He had a large gash under his eye, the skin around it already swelling and turning purple.

"What happened to you?" I dropped the chalice on the bed and ran over to him. The chalice bounced off the bed and crashed to the floor, scattering pieces of broken stone everywhere.

"The chalice," Grant called out.

I ignored him and frantically rummaged through my backpack for a bottle of water.

"Someone give me their shirt," I said. Kaylin and Grant stared at each other. "Come on, someone give me a shirt. He's got blood everywhere," I said again. "I need to clean him up. I can't tell if he's still bleeding." Grant removed his shirt and threw it at me. I poured the water on the shirt and gently dabbed Kevin's face with it.

"How did this happen?" I asked Kevin once I was sure he wasn't still bleeding.

"I was going to leave, so I went back to the hallway, but when I got there, there was a man in the tunnel dragging a body to the stairway—"

"See, I told you there was a body in here," Grant interrupted. He all but patted himself on the back.

"Not the time, Grant" I shot him a disapproving glare, then turned my attention back to Kevin. "Go on."

"When I got to the hall there was a guy... with a body." He nodded at Grant. "I yelled at him to stop, he let go of the body and started running towards the stairs. I ran after him and caught him before he could make it all the way up the stairs. We fought, then he knocked me down the stairs. He got away." He backed away from me and sat down on the bed. "He shut the door." He looked up at us. "He locked us in." He glanced down at the floor. "I tried but I can't get it open. We're trapped in here."

"It's not your fault." I knelt down in front of him and leaned on his leg. "I'm sure you did your best." I turned to Kaylin. "Tell him it's not his fault."

"Who cares whose fault it is," Grant said angrily. "Didn't you hear a word he said. We're trapped."

Of course I'd heard him. It just hadn't sunk in yet. "How were we going to get out?" I reached over and picked up a piece of the broken chalice. I stared at the jagged shard in my hand. "Are they going to be waiting for us if we do get out?" I set the piece on the bedside table and mindlessly grabbed another one off the floor. I faced Kevin. "Are there more of them?" My mind jumped from one question to the next. "Are we all going to end up looking like Kevin?" I turned to Kaylin. Kevin placed his hand on my shoulder. I sat the second piece of chalice next to the first. I pulled away from Kevin and began sweeping the broken pieces into a pile. "We're going to have to stay here. It's safer here." Kaylin stepped closer to me. "Nobody can get us here."

Kevin held his hand up. "Let her go, dude. I think she's having a meltdown."

"Are you cleaning?" Grant asked angrily. He stormed over to the table and swatted the pieces of chalice onto the floor.

"What did you do that for?" I replied angrily. I blinked. Why was I picking up the pieces? "At least I'm doing something." I rose to my feet. "Which is more than I can say for some of you." I glared at Grant. "What have you done, other than eat all the food and complain nonstop?"

"I haven't done nothing," he argued. Spit flew from his mouth. "It's your fault we're in this mess." He glanced from me to Kaylin. "I was fine staying at home. I like editing the paper. You guys dragged us to Roanoke in search of some stupid stones." He raised his foot and stomped on a piece of chalice, smashing it into tiny particles.

"They're not stupid," Kaylin said, setting his backpack on the floor. "No one forced you to come. I'm sick and tired of you blaming us every time something goes wrong." Kaylin's voice boomed. He took a step closer to Grant. Kevin stood up.

"Oh yeah! What are you going to do about it?" Grant said, getting in Kaylin's face, his body inches away from Kaylin's. "Are you gonna do something or are you just gonna stand there denying the fact it was you who got us into this mess?" He poked Kaylin in the shoulder with his index finger, provoking him.

"Maybe, I'm gonna kick your ass." Kaylin shoved Grant. Grant stumbled backwards. "Maybe then you'll stop blaming everyone else for your problems." He shoved Grant again. Grant floundered then caught his balance and lunged towards Kaylin.

"Stop!" I shouted. They ignored me and continued to antagonize each other. Both of them fuming, waiting for the other one to throw the first punch.

Kevin rushed over next to Kaylin. "Do you have a problem?" He asked Grant. I was shocked. I was sure Kevin would take Grant's side.

"Now you're on his side?" Grant said, just as surprised as I was. He stepped in front of Kevin. "You told me yesterday this trip was a waste of time, that we would never find the stones, and you didn't really care even if we did." He turned to Kaylin. "He said the Amerii were probably some sort of cult and he wasn't going to drink their Kool Aid."

"They're not a cult," Kaylin yelled, redirecting his anger as he spun to face his brother. "Drink their Kool Aid? What the hell, dude?"

"You're my brother and I'm not going to let you get your ass kicked by Grant's scrawny ass, but this whole Amerii thing, well, it's BS. I'm sorry, but it is."

Kaylin took a step back. "How could you?" he said in shock. The anger disappeared from his face and was replaced by a look of disbelief and pain. "You should just go back to Stony Creek then." Kaylin's voice was monotone no emotion whatsoever in his words. He backed up to the wall then slowly slid down it to a sitting position on the floor. He lifted his knees up, resting his elbows on them. His hand on his forehead. He sat there, staring at the floor, defeated. I hurried over to sit next to him, while Grant stormed angrily out of the room. Kevin stared at Kaylin for a moment, waiting for Kaylin to glance up, but Kaylin didn't. He just kept looking ahead. Kevin shifted his gaze to me. He shrugged, his eyes pleading for Kaylin's forgiveness, then he turned and followed Grant out of the room.

"Don't listen to them," I said once we were alone. "They don't know what they're talking about." I put my arm around Kaylin's shoulder. "The Amerii were an important part of American history. They will come to realize that."

"Maybe they're right," he replied. His face covered in disappointment. "We don't know much about the Amerii yet. Maybe they are some whack job cult, like Kevin said."

"I don't believe that, and I don't think you do either." I rested my head on his shoulder. I stared under the bed. "What's that?" I lifted my head and pulled my arm out from around his shoulder. I leaned forward on my hands and knees.

"What's what?" He questioned removing his hands from his face.

"That." I pointed under the bed at a large piece of the chalice. "It looks like..." I crawled over to the edge of the bed, reaching my hand underneath, feeling around for the piece. "The stone!" I exclaimed happily once I'd retrieved the piece and was sure that's what I'd found. "It must have been hidden in the chalice." I got up from the floor and flipped it over in my hand. "Look." I held it up for Kaylin to see. "We did it!"

Kaylin slowly got up off the floor. He shuffled over to me and inspected the stone in my hand.

"We did do it!" he said, astonished. The defeat disappeared from his face. "We can find out more about the Amerii, we can prove to Kevin and Grant it's not a cult." A renewed sense of purpose resonated in his voice. We quickly gathered up our things and rushed out of the house. Kevin and Grant were nowhere in sight.

"Maybe they went to see if they could open the door?" Kaylin said. With all the fighting going on and then finding the stone, I had completely forgotten we were trapped underground.

Chapter 8

A Mummy and a Way Out

We set off towards the hallway to find them. As we neared the edge of the town, almost to the hallway, I paused.

"Why are you stopping?" asked Kaylin, turning around.

"Kevin said the body is in there," I replied, backing away.

"Hold my hand and close your eyes." Kaylin offered his hand to me. "I will lead you past it." He waited patiently for me to take his hand.

I thought about it for a moment. At some point in time I was going to have to get over my fear. "Just hold my hand tightly, please. Don't let go," I told him. I accepted his hand but kept my eyes open. You can do this, I told myself.

"It's more like a mummy than a body," he explained as we passed it. "The skin is dried and shrunk around the bones."

"I don't need to know what it looks like," I replied, trying to avert my eyes. I searched the stone walls for something to focus on. I found one of the pretty blue stones and stared at it intently. "Please keep your mummy commentary to yourself." It was impossible to think I could completely get over my fear on the first try. "Just keep going," I pleaded and nudged him forward.

"Wait a minute." He let go of my hand and hurried over to the corpse. He hovered over the body, studying something on it.

"What are you doing?" I asked, panicking. "You said you wouldn't let go." I stepped backwards quickly. My back arched as I slammed into the stone wall and my head smacked into one of the lanterns. "Ouch." I rubbed the back of my head.

"There's something around the man's neck," he said amazed. He knelt down beside the corpse. "It's a chain!" he exclaimed glancing back at me. "With a ring on it." He grinned before turning back to the corpse.

"A ring? Like a wedding ring?" I asked. I stopped rubbing my head and stepped forward. I quickly scanned the corpse. Kaylin was right. It did look like a mummy. A mummified corpse wearing what appeared to be a military uniform. The mummy was laying against the wall of the hallway still entangled in a net. I shifted my gaze to Kaylin and locked my eyes on what he was doing, blocking out the face of the mummified corpse.

"It's possible this is a wedding ring. I have a feeling it's much more than that though. It's similar to your necklace." Kaylin appeared calm as he coaxed the chain up the corpse's neck. Wow, he really has no fears. I smiled. "This must be what the man was after," he suggested. He gently tilted the corpse's skull forward and slid the chain off. "I think we should take it with us just in case." He inspected the ring. "Look! Twelve diamonds just like yours only this has a ruby in the center instead of a sapphire." He lifted the ring closer to my face.

"Wow, it is just like mine."

Kaylin slipped the chain over his head and tucked the ring inside his shirt, then took my hand and we strolled down the hallway to the stairs.

"See, that wasn't so bad was it?" He let go of my hand. "Let's not say anything about the ring just yet," he whispered in my ear. He checked to make sure it was still tucked in his shirt, out of sight. "I'm not sold they want to be a part of the Amerii like we do. Let's wait until we're sure this is something they're interested in."

I glanced up the stairs to where Kevin and Grant were standing. They were situated as close to the top as they could get without hitting their heads on the door, discussing ways to slide it open. Their hands were above them on the ceiling feeling the edges of the door. I gasped.

Kevin hadn't exaggerated when he'd said we were trapped. The door was sealed tightly shut. The floor that had once slid wide open to let us in was now firmly back in its place. We're going to die here.

I ran up the stairs, forcing myself between Grant and Kevin, and pushed on the ceiling as hard as I could. "Help me push," I shouted. "Kevin, Grant, push. We have to get out of here." I turned and put my shoulders against the ceiling, my head bent uncomfortably to the side. I stepped backwards up another step then pushed with my legs. "Kaylin, help," I cried out. "Why isn't anyone helping?" I flipped around and started banging my fists on the ceiling. "Help, we're stuck in here. Somebody help." I yelled through the door. I felt a hand on my shoulder.

"Cuz, stop." Grant placed his other hand on my other shoulder. "We've already tried all that. You're going to hurt yourself." I stared into his eyes. He pulled me closer to him and wrapped his arms around me. "It's going to be okay, Cuz, I promise. We'll find a way out."

"We could blow it up." Kevin suggested pounding his fist against the hard surface. I knew he was trying to make me feel better.

"With what? You got some TNT in your pocket?" Grant said sarcastically. He sat down on the step where he'd been standing. I sat down next to him and we racked our brains for a solution. "There has to be another way out," Grant mumbled. "There just has to. The Amerii wouldn't trap themselves underground without a back up way out."

"Maybe there is," I said, sitting up straight. "Maybe we'd been looking at it the whole time but just didn't realize it."

"What are you thinking?" Kaylin tilted his head and raised his eyebrows. "Did you see something when we were searching the town?"

"The well in the center of the town." I stood up and stepped down the stairs. "The water has to be coming in from somewhere, right?" I waited at the bottom of the stairs for them to follow me.

"You think it's coming from the ocean?" Kevin asked taking a step forward.

"If it's coming in, maybe we can get out." I turned and began walking down the hallway. "Come on."

Grant stood up. "Only one way to find out," he said and began to follow me. "You guys coming?" He turned to look at Kevin and Kaylin.

Kaylin ran to catch up with me. "Hell, yeah."

"Wait for me," Kevin yelled, rushing past Kaylin and me. "Last one there—gets stuck in here."

We raced to the well in the center of town.

"Any volunteers?" Kaylin asked, peering into the water.

"It sounded good when you said it, but now I'm not thinking this is going to work," Kevin leaned over the edge. He reached far into the well and scooped up some water in his hands. He slurped it from his palms. "I was afraid of that. It's fresh water." He shook the remaining water from his hands then patted them dry on his pant legs.

"It still has to be coming from somewhere." My hands brushed some of the loose dirt on the edge off into the well as I leaned over and stared hopefully into the well. The dirt sprinkled onto the water's surface then floated down into the darkness.

"Yea, probably coming from an underground spring," said Kevin.

"We have to do something." I spun around and stared intently at them. "No One knows we're here. No one is coming to save us." I reminded them of just how desperate our situation was. "We will die down here."

"I'll do it," Kaylin said. He slipped off his shoes and socks. He neatly set his shoes at the base of the well then stuffed one of his socks into each shoe. "I did a little swimming back in high school. I can do this." He took his shirt off, tossed it on his shoes, and climbed up onto the edge. Kaylin stared down into the well for a moment, gathering his courage, then inhaled deeply and stepped off the edge, into the water. I rushed to the edge of the well and watched as he sank deeper and deeper, my gaze glued to him until he sank out of sight, disappearing into the blackness.

"How long should we wait?" I immediately turned to Grant and Kevin the second he disappeared. "We didn't come up with a plan. He just jumped in." I stared back into the well. I began to feel dizzy. Is he coming back up when he finds something? Is he swimming out to the ocean? How will we know if he's made it or not?

Grant pulled his phone out of his pocket. "Let's give him one minute."

"And then what?" asked Kevin, leaning into the well. "We all go in after him?"

A tiny bubble rose to the surface of the water, then another. "I have a bad feeling about this," I said watching a third bubble rise to the top of the water. Someone needs to go in after him. "I think he's in trouble." I glanced over at Grant and Kevin, my eyes begging them for an answer or a bit of reassurance that he was okay, but I got nothing from them. "How long has it been?" I asked Grant, staring into the blackness for a small sign he might be coming back.

"Forty-five seconds, forty-seven seconds, fifty seconds." He counted off. Time was moving forward too quickly. He'd been down there way too long. "Sixty seconds."

I had to do something now. There is no time left. I dropped my backpack on the ground, filled my lungs with air, and dove in. The frigid water shocked my body and awakened my senses. I kicked my feet as hard as I could, swimming deeper down into the blackness. I couldn't see more than a few feet in front of me, but I kept pushing on, following the widening shaft of the well down into the earth. The man made shaft eventually opened up into a large pool of water. Which way should I go? I twisted my body around. There's no time just go! My lungs screamed for oxygen. I saw something. Kaylin? I kicked my feet, swimming as quickly as I could. It's light. I saw light! I burst through the surface of the water gulping in air. I wiped the water from my eyes and glanced around. "Kaylin," I screamed out. My words echoed off the stone walls of the cavern. I hadn't made it to the ocean. I looked around at the illuminated stone. It glowed. I gazed down into the water. The glow from the stone made the water crystal clear. I could see all the way to the bottom. Oh my God, Kaylin! He wasn't moving. His body floated motionless in the water about ten yards under the surface. I took a breath and dove. Kaylin's lifeless body bobbed in front of me. I shook his shoulders trying to wake him. His arms, weightless, lifted up from his sides. I wrapped my arms around his chest and kicked towards the surface. He was stuck, anchored in place. I pushed away from him. He swayed back and forth in the water as I swam around him trying to figure out what he was stuck on. Every movement I made sent water rippling around his body. I tugged at the seaweed dancing near his ankles. Then I saw it. His pant leg was entangled on a twisted piece of metal. I yanked hard on his pant leg. It didn't budge. I tried again, still nothing. I had to get him free. He was drowning. What should I do? I quickly un-buttoned his pants, slipped him out of them and pulled his body free from the twisted piece of metal that was trapping him in an icy grave. I swam towards the well, pulling Kaylin along with me. It seemed so far away. I needed air. Keep swimming, I told myself. The entrance to the well was just up ahead. I kicked as hard as I could. We entered the bottom of the well shaft, but I struggled to find enough energy to get us to the surface. I glanced up. Light! We were almost there. You can do this Aurora. One last big kick. I closed my eyes and kicked, swiftly pushing us up the narrowing shaft. We're going to make it. I felt someone's hands on my head and body.

"Grab him," I said, out of breath as I broke the surface of the wa-ter. I pulled Kaylin's head out of the water.

Kevin grabbed ahold of him and with strength like I've never seen before, pulled Kaylin's body from the well with one hand. Kevin im-mediately began trying to resuscitate him. Grant slid his arms under mine and heaved me upwards onto the edge of the well. I rolled over the side and landed on the ground.

"Help Kevin," I said out of breath. I curled up into a ball and breathed deeply. Grant stared at me. "I'm fine," I assured him. "I just need to catch my breath, that's all." The expression on his face told me he was still leery but he did as I asked and quickly ran to Kevin's side. Grant took over the chest compressions while Kevin did mouth to mouth. I laid on the ground in a ball, coughing, my chest heaving up and down. Every muscle in my body burned. I was too weak to help Kaylin. "You have to save him," I cried out.

Kevin quickly pulled away from Kaylin. He turned his head and spit. Water gurgled up out of Kaylin's mouth. He coughed, spewing water down the side of his face. He opened his eyes.

"He's okay," Grant exclaimed, stopping the chest compressions. Kevin rolled him on his side. The remainder of the water flowed from Kaylin's airways. Kaylin took a deep breath and looked over at me. Thank God he's alive. I closed my eyes, rested my head on the hard, stony ground and took a long breath.

"Are you okay?" I heard Grant asking Kaylin. "You scared us."

"If it wasn't for Aurora..." Kevin's voice trailed off. "I don't even want to think about it. I'm just glad you're alive."

"Hey, Aurora?" asked Grant.

"Huh,"

"Now that Kaylin is okay. I gotta ask, Where are his pants?" I opened my eyes and giggled. It probably did seem odd. "You have time to stop off for a quickie or what?" He laughed. Kevin glared at him. "Sorry, I know I shouldn't joke at a time like this, with Kaylin almost dying and all but, really. Where are his pants? I know he had 'em on when he jumped in."

"Dude, this isn't the time for jokes," Kevin said angrily.

"I said sorry. Plus he's all right, she's all right, everybody is all right," Grant pointed to each of us as he said it.

"His pant leg was stuck on a piece of metal. It was the only way I could get him free," I explained, rising up into a sitting position. I grabbed my chest. My lungs still ached.

"Thank you." Kaylin put his hand to his throat. He coughed, sputtering out droplets of water. Kevin, still kneeling beside him, rubbed his back. Grant got up and walked over to the edge of the well.

"Did you find a way out?" he asked as he peered in.

"No, it opened up into a small glowing cave. I didn't have time to look any farther."

"Bioluminescent algae," Kaylin said, his voice getting stronger.

"You saw it too?" I crawled over to his side.

"Yeah, I had a chance to look around before I got..." He placed his hand on mine. "Thank you," he said again. I lifted his hand to my mouth and kissed the back of it.

"You don't have to thank me." Our eyes met. I couldn't imagine what it would be like if I never got to stare into his beautiful blue eyes again or smell his musky cologne or feel his strong arms holding me tightly. I shook my head, the thought of it all was just too much. I felt the tears welling up in my eyes.

"It's okay, Rory. I'm all right." He placed his arm around me, pulling me closer.

"You're right. We're okay," I said, burying my head into the crook of his arm. "But when I saw you floating in the water." He kissed the side of my head.

"Well, we aren't exactly all right." Grant pointed out. "We're still trapped."

Kevin stood up. I looked up at him from Kaylin's chest. Kaylin released his arm from around me and pulled away, trying to get to his feet. Kevin rushed to his side and helped him. I stared up at them, reluctant to stand. My legs were so tired but I knew I had no choice. We needed to find a way out or we'd die. I stood up. I had to put what happened in the well behind me and focus on getting out of the Amerii town. I may have saved Kaylin from drowning but it would be all for nothing if we died of starvation.

"We could try to call for help," I suggested. "Steph should be in town by now." I dug my phone out of my backpack. I looked at the time. It was almost two o'clock in the afternoon on Saturday. We'd been underground in the Amerii town all of Friday night and most of Saturday. "I don't have a signal here. If we get as close to the opening as we can." I shrugged. "We might be able to get a signal." The boys stared at me like I had just said something truly amazing.

"Why didn't we think of that earlier?" Grant said stepping away from the well.

Kaylin put his arm around my shoulder, Kevin grabbed my other hand and Grant put his arm around Kaylin's waist. We helped each other limp back to the stairway.

I dialed Steph as soon as we got back to the opening. She answered in a frantic voice.

"Where the hell are you?" she asked. "I've been trying to call me all day. Your phone kept going straight to voicemail." I explained where we were and everything we'd been through then gave her detailed instructions on how to get to the Fort.

"She's going to call me back when she gets here," I explained to the boys. I placed my phone on the top step, ensuring I didn't lose service again. Almost an hour passed before she called back.

"We have a small problem," Steph said as soon as I picked up. "There's a bunch of five o here. I can't get anywhere near the place."

"The cops are here? Where are you? Did they catch you?" I rapidly fired off the questions.

"No, I'm hiding in the bushes. They haven't seen me."

"Ask her why the cops are here?" Grant hollered. "Do they know we're here?"

"They probably found the Jeep. The lady from the museum did call them. She gave them my license plate number. I know it." Kaylin growled at Kevin. "I knew this would come back to bite us in the ass."

"Do you know why the cops are here," I asked her.

"I overheard one of them saying there was a break in. They think it's a robbery. A few of the buildings have been vandalized."

"We didn't do that," I told her then turned to the boys. "Someone tore the place up. They're not here for us."

"I'm going to lay low until they leave. Are you guys going to be okay a bit longer?"

"We'll manage. Call me when they leave." I hung up the phone. "Looks like we're stuck here awhile longer." I sighed. I was eager to breathe in the fresh air above ground, to feel the sunlight on my face, and of course to see Steph. I settled into my place on the stairs and passed the time daydreaming about what my life would be like next fall at Penn State.

Bzzt, bzzt. My phone pulsated on the step. I reached over and snatched it up.

"Hello," I answered. "They're gone? Okay great. Can you get into the building? It is? Lucky for us." I laughed. "You're in the basement. Okay, the next part is going to be tricky. You're going to have to find a hidden panel and spin the dials to get the right combination. Here, it will just be easier if I let Grant explain it." I handed the phone to Grant. "Explain to her how to set the dials."

"What about the hair comb?" He asked as he took the phone from me. He held his palm over the mouthpiece.

"Crap, I forgot about that part." I pulled the comb from my ponytail. I held it up to the edge of the door. "There's no way I'm going to be able to slide it through the crack. The door is sealed tight."

"Are you still there?" Grant held the phone up to his ear. "We're having a bit of a malfunction. Hold on a minute." He dropped the phone to his side. "So, what should I tell her to do?"

Everyone threw out ideas.

"None of those are going to work." Grant shook his head. He lifted the phone to his ear. "I can tell you how to set the dials but it's not going to do any good. We have a piece of the puzzle in here with us and there's no way we can get it to you."

"Maybe there's something in here I can use to Macgyver it with," Steph suggested. Grants eyes lit up. "What does the piece look like?"

Grant explained what the hair comb looked like. "I think that might work," He said after a long pause. He turned to us and explained how she'd crafted a mock hair comb out of some bobby pins she'd found laying around on the make up tables and an old shoe. She'd jammed the bobby pins into the rubber sole making sure they lined up with the correct holes on the dials. "First you have to put in the right symbols," He listed off the symbols to her. "You're going to need two hands for this next part so I'm going to explain it then hang up." He waited for her to agree. "First position the bobby pins over the holes, then press evenly on the shoe with both hands so that all the pins slide in at once. You got it? Okay." he hung up the phone and handed it back to me. "Let's hope that works."

"By the way, how did you know what symbols were the right ones?" I asked, putting my phone in my back pocket.

"The stick figure is the symbol for family, the open shell means treasure, and the triangle means home. Dad is always saying our family is the greatest treasure in our home. After studying the symbols closely, it dawned on me. The saying must have been passed down from generation to generation. Family, treasure, home," he explained.

"Impressive." I patted him on the back. "And how did you know the stick figure symbol meant family?"

"Dad insisted Robert take a semiotics class in college." I stared blankly at him. "The study of signs." My eyes widened with acknowledgment. He continued to explain. "Robert would have me hold up flashcards to help him study. I ended up picking up some of the meanings. No big deal." He nervously picked at his fingernails. It was the first time I'd ever seen him humble. Every once in a while Grant surprised me. There was more to him than the clown he showed to the world. He wasn't just a goofball. He had real knowledge.

I was about to compliment him when the basement wall, somewhere over our heads, vibrated and let out the awful grinding hum. The same hum we'd heard when we first opened the door.

"She got it!" I exclaimed happily. I can always count on Steph to come through when I need her. I stared up at the ceiling in anticipation of it opening.

"Step down a few steps," Kaylin suggested in my ear. "It might get messy." I frowned at him. His comment puzzled me, but I did what he said. As we stepped backwards down the stairs the door began to slide open overhead. A flood of water poured onto the stairs right where Kevin and Grant were standing. The water gushed down over their heads barely missing Kaylin and me. Kaylin let out a quick chuckle.

"How did you know that would happen?" I whispered leaning closer to his ear.

"When we opened it the first time I could hear the water in the wall when I placed my ear against it, then I noticed the top steps were wet when I walked down them. I wasn't sure that's what would happen but I had a good idea it would," he whispered back. "I figured they deserved to get wet, too."

I smiled at him. The other two had been pretty rude earlier in the day and they didn't jump in the well like Kaylin and I had, but they did perform CPR and save his life. Did they really deserve to get water dumped on them? It was nice to know Kaylin could joke about everything that happened. I decided having a little harmless fun wasn't a bad thing. That's what friends did.

"Aurora are you all right?" Steph said, peering down the stairway. She rushed down the steps, throwing her arms around my shoulders, before I could answer. "I missed you so much." She swung me from side to side her arms pinning mine down to my sides.

I wiggled my arms loose and returned her hug. I squeezed her tight. "I missed you, too."

"Can we get out of here?" I asked, pulling away. I grabbed her arm and placed my foot on the next step up. She stayed put, glancing down the tunnel. She bent over and peered towards the town. "Come on." I tugged on her arm. "I don't want to spend another second down here. She turned, and I led her up the stairs.

"I need to tell you something," she said, stopping at the top step. She glanced over at the box with the dials in it. "The shoe worked but it destroyed the box," she confessed.

I hurried over to the box. Two of the dials inside the box were broken into tiny chunks. I reached in and poked the only remaining dial intact. It broke into two pieces and fell from the center rod. "You better come look at this," I called to the boys.

"It's ruined," said Kevin. "We'll never be able to open it again."

"Now what are we going to do?" asked Grant.

"We can't do anything right now," said Kaylin. He shut the lid to the box. "We're gonna have to close the door to the town. Seal up the stairway forever, and get out of here before the cops come back." He walked sadly over to the opening. "Give me a hand pulling this shut." He grabbed ahold of the edge and pulled. It took the three of them several minutes and a lot of grunting to pull the floor back in place.

"I'm a little mad at you, Aurora," Steph said as we waited for them to finish.

"What? Why?" I asked as I turned to go up the stairs and out of the basement. We strolled through the costumes to the stairs. Kevin and Grant rushed past us. I stopped just before the staircase and looked into Steph's eyes. "Why are you mad?"

"I'll wait for you by the Jeep," Kaylin said to me as he forced himself between Steph and me on his way to the stairs.

"We'll be right there, handsome, just a little girl talk," Steph answered him. He glanced at me. I nodded, confirming I'd be all right. He continued up the stairs and disappeared through the door.

"How could you go on this adventure and not tell your best friend?" Steph asked once he was out of earshot, her hands on her hips.

"Oh!" I said dropping my eyes to the floor to keep her from seeing how guilty I felt for keeping it from her. "I had to," I said. "We made a pact, I'm sorry." I placed my hand on her arm. "But I'm glad you're here now." I gave her another big hug and whispered in her ear, double checking to make sure Kaylin was out of earshot before admitting, "The boys are driving me nuts. All they do is argue."

"Speaking of boys, what's going on with you and Mr. Scrumptious?" She asked. "Give me all the dirt, have you guys, you know?" She winked. "Is that why he isn't wearing any pants?"

"No," I thought about Kaylin's lifeless body floating in the water and shivered. I reminded myself that he was all right now and forced a smile. "We haven't had a second alone." "I was hoping this trip would be a little more romantic than it's turned out to be."

"Have you even talked about things? Are you dating? Are you just friends with bennies? Well obviously not that." She corrected herself. She playfully bumped my hip with hers. "Otherwise you'd have more dirt to spill." She laughed as she stepped up onto the first step.

"He suggested we needed more alone time before we left for Roanoke but other than that we haven't spoken about it." I stepped up next to her. "He hasn't even asked me about what happened in English class. I thought for sure he'd bring it up on our first date but he never did."

"Maybe some things shouldn't be talked about." She laughed. Her eyes glistened. "Regardless, it sounds like you guys need some time to talk, or other things," she said, her insinuation obvious, as we continued to make our way up the stairs.

"Did the robbers do this?" I asked, touching the broken latch on the door. I ducked under the police tape as I exited the doorway.

"Looks like they hit it with a crowbar doesn't it?" replied Steph. She picked a chunk of loose wood from the frame. "Did a real number on it." She tossed the chunk on the ground. "Made my job easier though."

I gazed blissfully around at the outside world as Steph and I walked towards the Jeep. The sun was already setting on the horizon, the day coming to an end. I breathed in the salty, fall air. It smelled wonderful, fresh and clean, unlike the stale town air. The hidden town was amazing, but I don't know how my ancestors could have lived down there. We were only down there a day and a half and I'd already missed the feel of the sun on my face. I couldn't imagine being forced to hide like that. Steph continued to ask me questions as we made our way to the Jeep. She wanted to know everything there was to know about the Amerii, the town and my relationship with Kaylin.

Something about her had changed since the last time I saw her. Her dark red hair had grown longer, almost to the middle of her back, but that wasn't it. When I peered into her green eyes, I could see something inside her was different. There was something there I had never noticed before, a sort of insecurity hidden behind her fiery personality, something deep inside her. Had it always been there? Had I just never noticed it before? She was always so sure of herself back in high school. I looked up to her, I strived to be more outgoing like her. Had I changed, too?

"What took you so long?" Grant asked as we approached the Jeep. He sat in the backseat of the Jeep, his legs hanging out of the open door.

"We had some catching up to do. Where's the fire?" Steph replied.

"Everyone this is Steph. Steph this is my cousin Grant," I realized I hadn't introduced them yet.

"Well, hello," Steph said looking him over. "You didn't have to take your shirt off just for me." Her voice dripped with notes of flirtation. Grant's cheeks turned pink. His eyes darted around. I suspect he was desperately trying to think of a clever response to impress her. He had a familiar expression on his face. One I'd seen many times on the faces of the boy's back in high school. Steph had a way of getting all the boy's flustered.

"This is Kevin." I directed Steph's attention away from Grant. Taking the spotlight off of him and giving him a chance to compose himself.

"What happened to you?" She exclaimed noticing the gash under his eye.

"You should see the other guy," he replied, not bothering to look at her. He continued to rummage around in the back of the Jeep in search of something. Steph rolled her eyes. I was impressed. It wasn't often Steph found someone immune to her charms. She was going to have to try harder if she wanted to get Kevin's attention. Kevin pulled a pair of jeans from the back and handed them to Kaylin. Kaylin slid them on.

"Awe," Steph said. Her disappointment was clear.

"And this is Kaylin," I said, saving the best for last. I grinned at him. "I'm so glad the two of you are finally meeting."

"Sounds like you and my girl need to figure some stuff out." Steph gave him her infamous smile, quickly recovering from the damage Kevin had done to her ego.

"We need to get out of here before the guy who locked us in comes back." Kevin said before Kaylin had a chance to respond.

"Or the cops," I said, reminding him. "Where did you park, Steph?" I asked glancing around for her vehicle.

"Just over there." She pointed up the road about half a mile. I could barely see the back of her Explorer peeking out from the branches. She'd done a good job hiding it in the trees, even taking the time to drag a large branch from the woods over the back of it.

"Hop in," Kaylin said "We'll give you a ride up there." He opened the driver's door and slipped inside.

I walked around to the passenger side and hoped in the front seat. Steph situated herself between Kevin and Grant in the backseat.

"You two are with me," she said motioning to Kevin and Grant as we pulled up behind her Explorer. "You two do what you need to do, we'll meet you back at the hotel." She put a hand on Kaylin and my shoulders, turning her head from me to him then back to me. Winking at me the second time she glanced at me before sliding across the seat to the door. I glanced at Kaylin as she exited the door and bounced over to her vehicle. His cheeks were flushed and he kept his gaze forward to avoid looking me in the eyes.

We waited a minute to make sure Kevin and Grant got into her Explorer okay before backing up and heading to the hotel.

"I can't wait to see what new things we discover now that we have the second stone," Kaylin said, trying to break the awkward silence. We'd been sitting there uncomfortably quiet for the first few minutes of the drive.

"Oh! Me too." I wanted to talk about us but I didn't know where to start. After another long moment of silence I blurted out in the most non smooth way possible. "Are we dating?"

"Do you want to be?" He asked, both of his hands gripping tightly to the steering wheel as he stared straight ahead, out the front window.

"Yes. Do you?" I brought my knees closer to the center of the car, turning my body towards him.

"Yes." He relaxed his grip on the steering wheel, but didn't take his eyes off the road.

"So...we're dating then?" I reached in the cup holder and riffled through the pennies in it.

"Yes," he answered again, glancing down to see what I was doing.

Steph had advised me not to talk about what happened last fall but I was curious. I had to ask.

"Did you see my paper the last day in class? Did you know I liked you?" The words spewed out of my mouth before I had a chance to think about what I was saying.

"Yes...." he paused. I was beginning to wonder if that was the only word he had left in his vocabulary. Then he continued. "I searched for you after class, but you were gone."

"You did?" I tossed the penny I'd been fidgeting with back into the cup holder.

"Yes... when I couldn't find you I thought I wasn't going to see you again. I thought I missed my chance..." He spoke softly. "I won't be going back to Cary this fall." He glanced over to see my reaction. "I didn't think I was ever going to see you again." His eyes lit up. "Then you stepped into the coffee shop. I couldn't believe it. I had a second chance. It was like fate or something." He turned back to the road and shrugged. "That probably sounds stupid doesn't it?"

"It doesn't sound stupid," I quickly assured him. Fate. There was that word again. Maybe there was such a thing as fate. "I'm not going back to Cary either," I admitted. My heart fluttered inside my chest. He liked me this whole time. I laid my head against the back of the seat and stared longingly at him.

"Where are you going?" he asked hopefully. He turned the radio down. "Are you staying in Stony Creek?"

"No! I'm going to Penn State, where Steph is at."

"Oh." he said, disappointed. He'd gone back to his one word answers.

"Are you staying in Stony Creek?" I asked, trying to elicit more of a response from him.

"Before we discovered the Amerii, I was thinking about joining the army."

"The army?" I was surprised by his answer. "I never pictured you as the army type." I lifted my head off of the seat.

"That was the plan, but then we found the room and I started thinking I would stay in Stony Creek for a while longer before signing up," he explained. "I think the Amerii is important. I feel like with the Amerii I have a purpose." He fidgeted with the seam of his jeans as he waited for me to respond.

I sat there, letting his words sink in. I stared out the window at the trees passing by, wondering if he was right. Was finding out more about the Amerii important enough for me to delay going to college? We had only just begun to learn about them. We knew very little about our family's part with them and what it could mean for us now. Maybe there was something better in store for me than going to Penn State and becoming an editor at Vogue Magazine. Maybe fate had intervened. Maybe our family's past had led Kaylin and me together. Was our relationship destined to be? I dismissed the idea. There is no way that what our families did over two hundred and fifty years ago could affect whether or not Kaylin and I got together. I must be insane for even thinking that.

"Can I show you something without you freaking out?" he asked.

"Why would I freak out?"

"Just yes or no. Do you promise not to freak out if I show you something."

"Okay, I promise. What is it?"

"Look in the glovebox."

I cautiously opened the glovebox, afraid of what I might find. Afraid of whatever it was he thought I would freak out over. He better not have a gun.

"I don't see anything. What am I supposed to be looking for?" I pushed aside his insurance and registration.

"I found something else in the Amerii room the day we found the Dare Stone," he confessed. "It's right here." He reached over and pulled out an old black and white photograph.

"Why would a photo freak me out?"

"Just look at it."

I studied the photo. "Where did you get a photo of me and you? Who is this man?" I pointed to the man in the picture with us. "I don't remember this photo being taken."

"It's not us."

"What do you mean it's not us?" I frowned. I wasn't blind. I could see it was us.

"Those people in the picture, it's not you and me. You don't remember having the photo taken because you didn't."

"But it looks like me. I have my grandmother's necklace on and everything," I said confused. I was looking right at the picture. I think I would know if it was me. "But how are you wearing the ring? We just found the ring not more than a few hours ago."

"I'm telling you, it's not us. Flip the photo over."

Isabelle Vanagteren, Humphrey Becker, Abraham Lincoln, Together we're strong. 1838

"How is this even possible?" I dropped the photo on my lap. I couldn't look at any longer. The people in the photo looked identical to Kaylin and me.

"They're our great, great, grandparents. I traced our histories back. That was Lincoln as a young man." Kaylin reached over, gently lifting the photo off my lap and returning it to the glovebox. "Are you all right?" he glanced over at me.

"I think so. I just need a minute." I started at the glovebox as if he'd just shut a monster in it. "You've had the photo this whole time?"

"I wasn't sure if I should show you. I was afraid you might freak out." He raised his eyebrows and smiled. "Kinda like you are."

"I'm not freaking out. I'm sitting here calmly."

"You're staring at the glovebox like a snake going to jump out of it and bite you." He chuckled.

"Okay, so I'm freaking out a little, but not that much. I promise."

"You're not going to go mad and cut your hair off then run down the streets naked?" he asked. "I mean, I might be okay with you running around naked, but I draw the line at you cutting your hair off."

I giggled. Kaylin had a way of lightening my mood.

"We're here." He pulled into the hotel parking lot just ahead of Steph. He parked the Jeep. "So you're good?" he asked before he opened his door and got out.

"I'm good." I opened my door and got out. I waited for him to make his way around the jeep before grabbing his hand and heading towards the hotel doors.

"I gave you guys a chance to sneak away," Steph whispered in my ear, joining Kaylin and I as we strolled into the hotel. "The boys and I planned out a whole night without you guys in the car on the way here. You two could have slipped off together."

"We talked. We're dating." I turned and whispered back. Slowing down and allowing our arms to stretch out before Kaylin tugged me along.

"Oh good, at least you did that." She smiled sarcastically then quickened her pace to catch up with Kevin and Grant who were eagerly rushing through the lobby to the elevator. "Change of plans boys. Looks like it's gonna be a pizza and beer kinda party tonight instead." She squeezed between the two of them, putting an arm around each one of their shoulders and waiting for the elevator doors to open up.

"Your friend's kind of wild, isn't she?" Kaylin said to me, letting go of my hand and putting his arm around my shoulder as we took our time catching up to them.

"She can be." I replied, resting my head on his shoulder. "But she's a lot of fun." We stopped in front of the elevators.

I was so happy that I almost didn't notice the man standing near the front desk.

"Kaylin!" I whispered. "Look. I told you I saw the guy from the Fort here." I hid myself behind him.

"It does look like him." The doors of the elevator opened. "Come on." he nudged me forward. "Get in." I rushed into the elevator stepping all the way to the back corner and waited for the doors to shut. I prayed the man wouldn't get in the elevator too.

"That guy is here." Kaylin announced to the rest of the group once the elevator doors shut. "We just saw him in the lobby at the front desk. Aurora was right."

"What guy?" asked Steph taking her arms off of Grant's and Kevin's shoulders and turning to me.

"The one I told you about on the phone," I replied. She stepped closer and took my hand in hers.

Kaylin pushed the floor button and leaned against the wall of the elevator next to me.

Steph held my hand as we rode the elevator up to our floor, quickly exiting, and making our way down the hall to our room.

"I don't think we should stay here tonight." I said once we closed the door to the room. "I think we should go back home."

"We haven't slept in days," Kaylin said. I glanced around the room at everyone. Grant and Kevin were already relaxing on the beds. "The guy is here. No doubt about it. I don't know how he found us, but he did. However, I don't think it's a good idea to drive home tonight with no sleep. There's hundreds of rooms in this hotel. There's no way for him to know which one we're in. First thing tomorrow morning, I promise." He stared at me, his eyes pleading for me to understand. I hadn't noticed until he'd mentioned it just how exhausted I really was. If we drove home now, we took the risk of getting into an accident and getting injured.

"I guess we could use some sleep," I said feeling a bit guilty for suggesting we leave. Besides, there were five of us and only one creepy guy. He wouldn't stand a chance against all of us.

"I'm still ordering some pizza from room service." said Steph. She sat down on the bed beside Grant and Kevin, snatching the room service menu off of the night stand. "You guys have to be starving." Steph was right. My stomach had been complaining for the last few hours. The only thing we'd eaten was popcorn and cotton candy. I shook my head yes. Food and sleep. That's what we all needed.

I kept one eye on the door as we watched a few shows on the T.V. and ate our pizza.

"Steph you can sleep with me in my bed," I offered as I got up to use the bathroom. She yawned and nodded her head sleepily in agreement. The lights were off and everyone was under the covers when I exited the bathroom. Steph had climbed in my bed with her clothes still on, not even bothering to change into her pajamas. She must be exhausted, too.

The last thing I remembered when I woke up the next morning, was laying my head down on the pillow. I'd been so exhausted, not even the creepy man lurking in our hotel could keep me awake. I rolled over to see Steph still sound asleep. It really was nice not to be the only girl anymore. I looked around the room. Kaylin was sitting at the table, drinking coffee. He had both stones next to his coffee cup and a stack of old papers in front of him.

"Good morning," he said softly trying not to wake everyone else up. "Did you sleep okay?"

I lifted the covers off of myself, gently slipping out of the bed and trying to not disturb Steph. I tiptoed over to the counter.

"Yes, I guess I needed it more than I realized." I grabbed a styrofoam cup from the stack by the coffee pot and unwrapped it from its protective plastic bag before filling it to the top with coffee. "What are you working on?" I pointed to the stack of papers as I blew into my cup to cool it off.

"Doing some more translating. I haven't found anything leading to the third stone like I had hoped. Maybe once we get back to Grant's there will be something in the Amerii room that will give me a clue."

"I was thinking we should split up the stones," I suggested hesitantly. I knew he wasn't going to like what I had to say.

"What do you mean?" He furrowed his eyebrows as he placed his hands protectively over the stones.

"We don't know why we're being followed. I think if it was the police they would've arrested us already. They wouldn't be lurking around outside our hotel rooms and locking us in an abandoned underground town. Whoever the guy is, he must be searching for the stones. I mean he did trash our last hotel room. He's obviously searching for something. It has to be the stones. Maybe we shouldn't keep both stones in the same place. Just as a precaution. Then if he does catch us he'll only have one cypher instead of two. We could put one in your Jeep and the other in Steph's Explorer." I took a sip of my coffee. "Ouch." It burnt my tongue. I set the cup on the counter.

"She has a point." Grant grumbled from under his covers.

"Okay, sure." Kaylin shook his head. "We can do that, I guess." he said, reluctant to let one of the stones out of his sight.

"Good," I smiled "Let's get around and head home," I said, eager to get on the road. Everything that had happened over the last few days had left a knot in my stomach. I just wanted to get back to Uncle Rob's house. To someplace safe. "Grant, Kevin you up? Steph time to get up." More grumbling sounds erupted from under the blankets where Grant lay. "Come on guys. Let's go home."

"Is there coffee?" Steph asked as she sat up in bed, wiping the sleep from her eyes. The three of them looked like zombies rising from the grave, but instead of searching for brains to eat, they called out for coffee.

"Yep, so up you go." I motioned for her to continue to get out of bed.

With the aid of multiple pots of coffee, I managed to get everyone up and packing. It was creeping on ten o'clock before we had the cars loaded and departed the hotel parking lot. There was no sign of the man anywhere, which both comforted and worried me. We'd split the stones like we'd agreed, as well as the books we'd brought with us, and the treasures we'd acquired in our searching. In just a few hours we would be driving down the bumpy dirt road leading up to Uncle Rob's house. I couldn't wait.

Kevin and Grant rode in Steph's Explorer ahead of Kaylin and me. I suspected he let them go ahead of us so he could still keep an eye on the other stone. He wasn't as worried about someone taking them like

I was. No, he had become, well for lack of a better word, obsessed with the Amerii. Feeling like it was his duty to protect the stones. I'd even heard him refer to himself as the Stone Keeper.

Sometime around eleven thirty, my phone rang. "Grant says they need to stop for gas," I told Kaylin, pulling the phone away from my ear.

"Tell them okay. We'll stop, too."

I informed him of the plan and hung up. We drove another fifteen miles before we saw a sign for a gas station.

"Next exit there's a gas station. I bet they're going to get off there." I pointed out the sign to Kaylin. "You might want to get back into the right lane," I warned as he passed a large line of cars trying to keep up with Steph's lead foot.

"Okay." He glanced over his shoulder at the cars in the other lane. "I'll try to sneak in between them." He turned his blinker on and started to pull into the right lane. The car behind us honked. He jerked back into the left lane.

Steph sped up and pulled over in front of the line of cars.

"They're turning off," I warned watching Steph turn.

"I'm trying, no one will let me in," he said frantically. He kept searching for an opening between cars.

"You're missing it." I watched the exit pass us by along with our chance to follow them.

"Thanks, Captain Obvious. Call them and tell them to stay there. We will take the next exit and meet back up with them."

They agreed to wait for us at the gas station. We took the next exit a few miles up the road.

"There should be a side road around here that will take us back south," Kaylin leaned forward scanning up the road for a street sign. "Pull up Google maps and see what you can find."

"I found one. We need to turn right on Webster in a quarter mile. That should take us back."

"Should or will?"

"It will." I rolled down my window. "Take a right at that road." I put my arm out the window and pointed. Kaylin took the right. I rolled my window back up.

"What do you think the odds are someone else missed their exit?" Kaylin adjusted the rearview mirror.

"Probably slim. Why?"

"The guy behind us was also behind us on the expressway. He got off when we did. Now he's turned onto Webster just like us."

"Could be a coincidence." I glanced behind us. "Maybe he lives down this way." I adjusted the head rest. "He does seem really close."

"He's been right on my tail since we got off." Kaylin checked his mirror again. "Should we pull over and let him go around?"

"I'm not sure if that's such a great idea." I turned to Kaylin. "What if he stops when we do and gets out of his car." I reached into the backseat and shoved the bag with the Dare Stone in it under the seat. "Hey, I think he's getting closer." The gap between his car and ours quickly grew smaller. "Something is wrong." I knew it in my gut. "He's not slowing down!" I dug my fingernails into the seat cushion. "He's going to hit us." I barely got the words out of my mouth before the car rammed into the rear end of the Jeep. Kaylin grabbed on tightly to the steering wheel. The loud screeching sound of metal rubbing together pierced my ears. Kaylin managed to get the Jeep under control, narrowly missing an oncoming truck. The car behind us slammed into the bumper again. This time with more force, launching our bodies forward. My right shoulder smashed into the glove box, causing me to lose my grip on the seat cushion. I found the seat again and dug my nails in deeper.

"What's going on?" Kaylin screamed in fear. "Why does he keep hitting us?"

"He's coming at us again!" I warned trying to brace myself for the third impact. The car behind us roared as the driver stepped on the gas. The car sped up. The driver was determined to push us off the road. I glanced helplessly over at Kaylin as he desperately tried to keep the Jeep on the road. Everything was happening so fast. The world outside the Jeep blurred as the third hit sent us spinning out of control. My arms flailed around in search of something stronger than the seat cushion to hold onto. I clung tightly to the first thing I touched. Kaylin was no longer in control of the Jeep. The Jeep's tires veered off the edge of the road. Gravel flung up, pelting the windows. Each stone left tiny chips in the glass. The soft sand along the edge of the road sucked us in, flipping the Jeep over, tossing me helplessly around the inside of the cabin like a leaf blowing in the wind. My head slammed hard against the side window. The glass exploded. Shards flew everywhere. Something warm ran down my cheek. Then nothing.

Chapter 9

Where Are They?

"Did you try calling them?" Steph looked across the Explorer hood at Grant. "It's been over an hour. How long are we supposed to wait?"

"I've tried both of their phones. Neither Kaylin or Aurora are answering," he replied resting his arms on the hood.

"Did Aurora say what way they were coming? Do you think we should go search for them?"

"She just said they would take the next exit and come meet us," Grant explained stepping around the front of the Explorer.

"I think we should wait. Maybe Kaylin got them lost," offered Kevin from the concrete curb behind Steph.

"But why aren't they answering their phones?" Steph pointed out turning to face him. "It's not like Aurora to ignore her phone. The last time she didn't answer it was because you guys were locked in an underground town."

"Maybe they're getting it on in the bushes somewhere," Kevin suggested jokingly as he chewed on a weed stem. "I know he wants to. He couldn't stop talking about her when she first got to town. I mean you should have heard him going on and on about her, it was kinda pathetic, if you ask me."

"Or, they don't have a signal." Grant opened the driver's door and reached across the seat for his phone. "We are in the middle of no-where." Grant checked his phone. "No calls."

"Let's give them a half an hour. If they're not back by then, we'll go search for them," Kevin stood up, throwing the chewed up stem on the pavement. He rubbed Steph's shoulders. "You'll see. They'll pull up any minute," he said and patted her back.

"Okay," she said, reluctantly agreeing. "Maybe you're right. Maybe Aurora finally took my advice and the feeling in my stomach is just hunger." She rubbed her belly.

"There's a diner across the street." Kevin pointed. "We can go get a sandwich or something. We'll be able to see the gas station from the window. If they show up we'll know." He opened the back door and got in.

"I'm famished," Grant said, walking back over to the passenger side and getting in. "I'm sure they're fine, Steph. Stop worrying."

"Fine! But if they show up you're both putting your sandwiches down and running back over here." She got in the driver's seat and started the engine.

They headed across the street to the diner.

Steph's phone buzzed as they entered the diner. She picked it up expecting to see a text from Aurora. She sighed. It wasn't from her, it was Peter, again.

"Was that Aurora and Kaylin?" Grant asked as they followed the waitress to their seat.

"No it was Peter."

"Who's Peter?" Kevin asked as he sat down and picked up a menu. "I'll have a cup of coffee," he said to the waitress.

"Nobody you need to worry about." Steph turned to the waitress. "I'll have a soda please."

"I'll take a soda as well," said Grant.

The waitress left to get their drinks.

"Is he your boyfriend?" Grant pressed for more information.

"Yes, if you must know," she said, while Grant's face grew long. "But not for long if he can't figure out how to take care of things on his own." Steph rambled on as she opened the menu and scanned over the items. She was completely unaware of the emotional rollercoaster Grant was riding as she spoke. "I gave him one task to do." She shook her head. "He's worthless."

"So there's a chance you might break up?" asked Grant hopefully.

"Maybe."

He grinned at her reply.

The waitress returned with their drinks. "Are you ready to order?" she asked.

They ordered their food, then chatted nonchalantly as they waited for the waitress to return with it. Their conversation continued after the waitress brought their food.

"Time's up boys." Steph said placing the crust of her sandwich on her plate. "It's been a half an hour and they're not here yet. Take your last bite and let's go." She wiped the corners of her mouth.

"I think we should get back on the highway then take the next exit and follow the way they would have come back to us," Grant suggested as he laid two twenty dollar bills on the table.

"Sounds good to me," Steph replied. A bell chimed as they exited the diner. "Grant you're up front with me. I need a navigator of your caliber," She playfully teased.

He climbed into the passenger seat. His blond hair had become scruffy, dislodged from its normally well groomed placement. The soft autumn breeze sent it fluttering about. Steph reached over and jostled it back into place.

"There," she said and put the Explorer in reverse. She sped onto the highway and followed it to the next exit then got off like they'd discussed.

"Okay up ahead there should be a road to your right," instructed Grant. "It's the only one for miles that leads back to where we were at, so it has to be the one they took."

"Webster? Is this it?" Steph asked. She slowed down to read the street sign.

"Ah...." He picked his phone up from his lap and turned the screen on. "Yep. Webster." He put his phone back in his pocket. "It goes straight back down to where the gas station is."

They'd only been driving a few minutes when Steph spotted the tire marks on the road.

"Holy crap," said Grant spotting them too. "Someone was driving like a maniac."

"There's glass too." She pointed out the front window.

"Stop!" Kevin's voice boomed from the back seat. "Look over there, off to the side of the road. There's a car smashed into the trees." His words were heavy with concern. "It looks like Kaylin's Jeep."

Steph strained to make out the vehicle from the pile of twisted metal against the tree. "It is the same color as Kaylin's Jeep." She quickly pulled off the shoulder of the road.

Kevin had his seat belt off and the door opened before she had the Explorer fully in park. He ran over to the wreckage, darting from one side to the other. He peered into the wreckage anywhere there was an opening.

"It's his Jeep!" he exclaimed in horror.

"Are you sure?" Steph asked. The pile of metal didn't resemble a vehicle anymore. "How do you know it's Kaylin's?" The front end had been nearly split in two by the enormous oak tree. The sides were folded downward accordion style. It looked like it had rolled over several times before coming to rest on the tree. Most of the back end was missing and there were glass and metal pieces littered along the roadside for nearly a half a mile back.

"I'm positive." He could hardly get the words out as he frantically searched for his brother. "I don't see them. I can't find them. There's blood all over the ground but I don't know where it's coming from."

Grant ran to the wreck, leaving Steph standing on the shoulder of the road. He made his way down the small embankment to the edge of the tree line. The sight was horrific.

"They're not here," yelled Grant from the opposite side of the twisted pile of metal. "Kevin, they got out. They must still be alive. Kevin!"

Kevin clawed at the side of the Jeep trying to find a way into the car. Grant ran over to him and jerked him away. "Kevin look at me. They got out. They got out."

Kevin resisted Grant, continuing his fruitless efforts to get into the Jeep. "Kevin!" he yelled again putting his hands on Kevins shoulders. "They're not in there!"

Hearing Grant's words, Steph fell to her knees right there on the gravel edged roadside. Tears formed in her eyes.

Kevin stepped back. "We have to find them. They could be bleeding out somewhere." He started searching around in the trees.

"Maybe they're at the hospital?" Steph said hopefully.

"I don't think so," Grant replied bending down and picking up a blood soaked leaf. "If the cops had been here they would have towed the vehicle away."

"Maybe a passer-by picked them up and took them to the hospital." She insisted, holding on to the hope that they were somewhere getting the help they need.

"But didn't call the cops? Highly unlikely," he replied standing up and walking over to a tree.

"Where's Kevin?" Steph said. Kevin wasn't anywhere around the crash.

"Oh crap, he must have taken off into the woods to look for them." Grant said scanning the trees. "Kevin," he yelled. "Where are you?"

"I'm right here." Kevin yelled back.

"Where?" Grant yelled stepping closer to where Kevin's voice was coming from.

"Here." Kevin stepped out from behind a tree, revealing his location. "I think I found a trail."

Steph got up off her knees. The small pieces of jagged gravel that had mashed themselves into her knees left tiny dents as they fell off. She brushed at the few pieces that refused to fall off on their own. She hurried down the embankment, meeting Grant next to Kevin.

"Look there's blood on this tree." Kevin pointed at a large smear of blood, about shoulder height, on the tree trunk.

They inspected the smear, their eyes followed the trail of dark red blood down the trunk to the puddle on the ground. "That's a lot of blood, more blood than I've ever seen before," said Steph. She grabbed ahold of Grant's shoulder to steady herself. "I think I'm going to be sick." She covered her mouth with her hands and bolted behind a tree.

"We need to spread out and search for more blood," Kevin said. "Hurry!"

"Are you okay?" Grant checked on Steph before beginning his search.

"I'm fine." She stepped out from behind the tree. "I felt sick looking at all that blood but once I got away I was fine."

They spread out and frantically inspected the trees and plants for signs of more blood. Hoping they would find Kaylin and Aurora in time, that it wasn't already too late.

"I found more over here," hollered Grant a few feet from the tree. "There's a few drops over here."

They continued combing the area. Each drop of blood they found led them deeper into the woods and one step closer to finding their friends.

"There's a cabin up ahead." Kevin pointed through the trees at the back of a small cabin. "Maybe they're in there."

Steph and Grant peered through the branches. The cabin was well hidden amongst the trees, almost impossible to see if you weren't looking for it.

"Let's check it out," Grant said, running off through the trees towards the cabin. He carelessly mowed through the saplings with no disregard for who was behind him. The branches snapped back into place, whipping Steph as she followed.

"Slow down," she cried, holding her hands out in front of her to catch the tiny branches before they swung towards her face. "We don't know if someone is living there."

"You're right," replied Kevin, blazing his own trail through the trees a few feet to their right. "Grant, you and Steph circle around that way to the left. I will go to the right. Don't get too close." He slowed his pace, proceeding around the right side of the cabin with caution.

Grant stopped running and crouched down, concealing himself behind a bush. Steph carefully inched her way around the cabin, peeking out from behind each tree, before darting to the next one and then the next. Grant crawled along the ground in the underbrush.

"I don't see anyone," She told Grant once they'd made it to the front of the cabin.

"Shhhh!" he replied holding his finger to his lips. He stood up and pressed his back against a tree trunk. "I hear something."

The door to the cabin opened up and a man stepped out. The man was too far away to clearly see his face but the knife in his left hand glistened in the sunlight clearly visible.

"I have them," he told the other person. They'd been so focused on the knife they hadn't noticed the phone he held to his ear. "Yes, it's all taken care of. There won't be any way of tracing it back to us."

"What does that mean?" Steph whispered to Grant leaning out from behind the tree.

"Shhhhh!" Grant stayed hidden. "He's going to hear you." He brought his shoulders together and his arms closer to his sides.

Steph leaned back against the tree waiting for the man to finish his conversation and go back in the cabin. His shoes clacked up the wooden steps before the screen door slammed shut. She peeked out from behind the tree. The man was nowhere in sight. Grant stepped out from behind the tree and nodded for her to follow him over to the tree Kevin was hiding behind.

"Did you hear what he said?" Steph asked Kevin once they'd met up with him. "He has them. What do we do?"

"I'm going to try to get closer," Kevin said leaving the safety of his hiding spot. "See if there's others in there with him."

"Be careful," Steph whispered crouching down in a small depression next to Grant.

Kevin slowly approached the cabin. He stepped out into a clearing, no longer able to hide himself behind the trees, while Steph and Grant kept a lookout for the man. Kevin was completely exposed as he made his way up to the cabin's small window.

"He made it," Grant whispered.

Kevin sat with his back against the side of the cabin just under the window.

"Why is he just sitting there?" She asked Grant. "What's he waiting for?"

"Steph!" Grant said loudly. His voice filled with panic.

Steph quickly spun around and faced Grant. The man was standing behind him, his knife tip against Grant's shoulder blade.

"Who are you?" the man demanded, grabbing Grant's arm and pulling him to his feet. "Don't try anything or I will gut your friend," the man said. He glared at Steph. She peeked in Kevin's direction without turning her head. Kevin was already climbing the front steps, his hand reaching out to open the screen door. "Tell your friend to stop." The man dug the tip of his knife into Grant's back. Grant grimaced, letting out a cry.

"Kevin," Steph screamed and waved her arms high into the air as she tried hysterically to get his attention. "He has Grant."

Kevin froze in place, his arm still stretched out reaching for the door handle.

Chapter 10

Who's There?

My head throbbed. An intense piercing pain radiated from my temple, down my neck and throughout my entire body. I reached for my head. "Aaah," I moaned. The slightest movement of my arm intensified the pain. What happened?

I scoured my memories for an answer. I remembered we'd missed our exit and had turned off on the next one. We'd found a road to take us back to Steph and the boys when, a car, there was a car! Someone rammed into the back of us. I'd hit my head on the window. Instinctively I reached up to touch the side of my head. "Aaah."

"She's waking up," a man said. I didn't recognize his voice. I opened my eyes. The soft light in the room stung them. I blinked. I couldn't make out where I was. Everything I saw was blurry and out of focus. Was I still in the Jeep? Where was Kaylin? I stared at an object close to me. What was it? I focused on the shape of the object, using all of my mental energy to figure out what I was seeing. Slowly, my eyes began to adjust and the object came into focus. It looked like teeth—large teeth and brown fur. An animal? Yes, an animal. A bear!

Oh my God, a bear's after me, I screamed, but nothing came out of my mouth.

I kicked my legs. Nothing happened. Why wasn't my body working? Why couldn't I run away?

"Don't try to move," the man said again.

Didn't he see the bear?

"Kaylin!" I screamed out his name, finally able to form the words with my mouth.

"I'm here, Rory. It's all right." He touched my left shoulder. His touch, although gentle, sent a shocking pain throughout my body. I grimaced.

"Sorry." He quickly withdrew his hand.

As I glanced around, the soft edges of the objects began to sharpen. I was in some sort of cabin, maybe a hunting lodge. I glanced back in the direction of the bear. It was just a stuffed bear mounted on a platform in the corner of the room. I exhaled. The cabin was filled with taxidermied animals—a deer head mounted on the wall next to the bear and a rabbit posed on a table next to an old couch. My gaze came to rest when I found the door. My way out. I turned to see Kaylin seated next to me. His face was peppered with tiny cuts. There was a large patch of flakey dried blood crusted across his forehead, extending from his right eyebrow up into his hairline. His top lip was twisted and swollen. He smiled. His eyes flickered from the pain it caused.

"You had us worried," he said softly. His words slightly malformed. I didn't get the feeling he was scared. Were we safe?

"She should be fine with some rest and a little bit of time," the unfamiliar voice said. I peeked over Kaylin's right shoulder to see who the voice belonged to.

It wa the man, the man from the lobby, the one who had run into me at the Fort. It was him. Panic took over my body. He had us. We were his prisoner. Did he get the stones? In my head I was shouting, but all that came out was, "It's him!" My voice, raspy and dry.

"I'll get her some water," he said and left Kaylin's side.

"It's okay, Rory." Kaylin leaned closer. "He saved us." His eyes were gentle and comforting. "I will explain everything to you, but right now you need some rest." He studied my face. He reached up and softly brushed the hair out of my face. "You got pretty banged up in the accident."

The man returned with a glass of water. He gently lifted my head and held the glass to my lips. I resisted.

"You need fluids." The man tilted the glass. The cool water touched my lips.

"It's okay, Rory," Kaylin said.

I parted my lips and let the water slide down. I didn't trust the man, but the coolness of the water soothed my sore throat. Once I was finished, the man gently laid my head on the pillow then set the glass on the table nearby. I closed my eyes unable to keep them open any longer and drifted off to sleep. I journeyed on the edge of deep sleep and full lucidity for quite some time. During one of the times I was awake, I heard Kaylin and the stranger discussing the Amerii. Kaylin was explaining to the man what we had found. The man understood the things Kaylin was telling him and reciprocated with knowledge of his own. He knew things about the Amerii that we didn't. Was he an Amerii? I drifted off to sleep again.

"How ya doin, Cuz?" Grant said cheerfully, sitting next to me when I opened my eyes the next time.

"What are—" My throat was still dry. I motioned for the glass of water next to the bed. My pain had lessened. Moving my arm was bearable now, creating only a small twinge of pain. I realized the pounding in my head had also stopped. How long had I been out? Grant held the glass up, placing his hand on the back of my head and helping me take a sip. "What are you doing here?" I managed to ask between gulps.

"We're just hanging out, having a party," he said sarcastically. His wisecrack comforted me. "We're here to find you." His face became serious. "You guys had us really worried. It was lucky dad had Mr. Truedell follow us."

"Uncle Rob had us followed?"

"Yep, you were right the whole time, Cuz, we were being followed. Even from the very beginning. You can say I told you so if you want. I deserve it. I should have believed you when you said you saw someone outside the window." He closed his eyes and waited for the I told you so.

"No," I wanted to say, I told you so. He deserved to hear it but knowing he was sorry was enough for me. "Why did he have us followed?" I asked instead.

"Oh, that! I forgot you don't know what's going on. So, dad had us followed by Mr. Truedell." he nodded towards my left, at a small kitchen area. The man, presumably Mr. Truedell, sat at the kitchen table between Kaylin and Kevin. I scanned the lodge for Steph and found her sitting on the old couch near the foot of my bed, intently staring at me.

"Hi!" she said, putting the magazine in her hand down on the coffee table in front of the couch. "I thought I lost you." Her eyes started to fill with tears. She stood up and stepped over to the side of the bed. "I want to hug you but I don't want to hurt you." She held her arms out. Her eyes glassy.

"It's okay." I lifted my arms. Something tugged at the back of my neck. I looked down at the sling over my right arm. "When did this get here?" I questioned. Everything felt surreal.

"Mr. Truedell did it while you were out," Grant said. "Like I was saying, you've missed a lot. Dad suspected we were up to something so he asked Mr. Truedell to keep an eye on us, and it's a good thing he did." He pointed to an IV in my arm. I hadn't even noticed it was there. "Otherwise you might not have been so lucky. You lost a lot of blood. Mr. Truedell found you after the accident and saved your life."

"Where's the guy that hit us? Did he get the Stones?"

"Mr. Truedell took care of him." Grant had a funny expression on his face when he answered.

I wondered what he meant. Did he kill him? Was that what Grant was saying? How long had I been unconscious?

"What day is it?" I asked looking from Grant to Steph for answers.

"Tuesday," replied Steph. "You've been asleep for two days."

"I've been out for two days!" No wonder everything felt surreal. I was missing two days.

"Yep, now can I finish?" asked Grant, getting agitated about being interrupted. "So dad had us followed. Mr. Truedell's family were once Amerii, just like ours." He leaned in closer. "They're real," he whispered excitedly.

Of course they're real. What did he think we'd been doing the last month, playing a game of clue?

"Are the Amerii still around?" I asked excitedly. I pictured walking into a large room, men and women seated around an enormous round table, discussing their plans. Maybe we could even become part of them.

"Well kinda, but not really," answered Grant. My heart sank. Go figure there were no more Amerii around.

"The stones were hidden to protect the Amerii secrets, right? But it also led to their destruction in a way. Because they no longer had a way of communicating in secret, their plans were intercepted, leading to the assassination of the head of Amerii. Mr. Truedell and Kaylin have been discussing all this stuff." Grant scooched forward, sitting on the edge of his seat. "Oh! Guess what, America is named after the Amerii. Plus the original U.S. flag Betsy Ross claimed she made, it didn't represent the thirteen colonies, it represented the original thirteen men and thirteen women that founded the Amerii. One star for the men and one stripe for the women. There's actually a lot of meaning behind the number thirteen throughout the Amerii history." He leaned even closer. "The flag was actually sewn by Anna VanAgteren, Eleanor Hunt's daughter in 1658. Over a hundred years earlier as a tribute to the Amerii founders. George Washington grew up in an Amerii home and thought the flag would be better used to unite the country, so Betsy Ross was paid to make a replica of it and claim she was the creator of it. It was all a big cover up to keep the Amerii a secret." Grant did a mic drop motion with his hand.

"Get back to the destruction of the Amerii," I said. "While the flag is fascinating I'm more interested in hearing why the Amerii isn't around anymore."

"Right. There's the Amerii massacre in 1692 in Salem. It was the first attempt by the George Party to dissolve the Amerii."

"I thought that was the Salam witch trials and what? George party? Who is the George Party?"

"Lovers of King George. Mortal enemies of the Amerii, you know, good and evil, that sort of thing. They used witches as a cover up but that's not what ended the Amerii though. It only diminished their numbers. The end eventually came when they succeeded in the assassination of President Lincoln."

"Lincoln was the head of the Amerii?" My eyes widened.

"From 1855 until his death he was."

"Why didn't someone take over after him?" I questioned. How could an organization as large and as powerful as the Amerii just cease to exist?

"You have to be a descendent of the original thirteen men or women to be an Amerii Leader or prove yourself an exceptional leader through great acts of heroism like Lincoln did. Not just anyone can lead the—"

"Not in front of the Ameriilite." Mr. Truedell said stepping up to the bedside. He began fiddling with the IV bag.

"What's an Ameriilite?" So many things about the Amerii were still a mystery to me. I felt like the kid in class the teacher calls on when she catches him sleeping at his desk. Everyone around me knew what was going on. Everyone, except me.

"Me," Steph answered with disgust. "They make me wear headphones when they're discussing the Amerii." She tugged a pair of earbuds out of her pocket and held them up for me to see.

"An Ameriilite is someone who knows about the Amerii but has not been properly inducted. There must be a ceremony held. If Stephanie is chosen to become part of the Amerii and participates in the ceremony then she can be privy to our discussions but not until then," replied Mr. Truedell placing two fingers on my neck and watching the clock.

"I'll fill you in when you're feeling better." Grant winked at me then meandered over to the kitchen table and sat down next to Kevin.

"You had quite the concussion." Mr. Truedell lifted a pen out of his chest pocket. He clicked the end. It was a flashlight. He shone the light into my eyes. "Looks like you're doing better. Your pulse is back to normal. You've got a sprained shoulder muscle and plenty of bumps and bruises, but you're going to be okay." He inspected the wound on my temple. Satisfied I would be making a full recovery, he shuffled back into the kitchen.

Who was this guy? I wondered. Was he a hit man, a doctor, or a spy? He told the others Uncle Rob sent him but was it the truth. Maybe he lied and he's really part of the George Party.

I glared at Mr. Truedell's back as he walked up next to Kaylin. Kaylin glanced in my direction. He rose from his seat, keeping his eyes locked with mine as he strolled over to my bedside and sat down in the chair. He gently slipped his hand under mine, intertwining our fingers. Lightly stroking my arm with his other hand. I took a deep relaxing breath. His touch put me at ease.

"How are you feeling? Do you need anything?" His eyes showed his concern.

"I think I'm a little hungry," I answered. "My tummy hurts." I lifted my right arm to touch my stomach. The sling tore at the back of my neck. A sharp pain shot across my shoulder. "I guess I'm going to have to get used to this thing." I slipped my good hand from Kaylin's to rub my shoulder.

"What would you like to eat?" Kaylin stood up to head to the kitchen. "There's not much in the cupboards but I can rustle something up, I'm sure."

It was at that moment I realized I wasn't wearing my clothing any longer. Someone changed what I was wearing. Was it Mr. Truedell? Did he see me naked? Or worse, was it Kaylin?

"Whose clothes are these? Why am I wearing them? Who changed me?" I glanced from Kaylin to Steph, demanding to know the answer. Steph hadn't left my side since I'd woken up.

"They're mine," she said. "I changed you. You were covered in blood."

"Oh!"

"Don't worry, I made everyone leave when I did it." She smiled, twisting a lock of her hair in her fingers. "Nobody saw anything."

"Steph's been tending to you, making sure you were comfortable and had everything you needed. We pretty much had to fight her to even get near you," Kaylin explained. He glared at Steph.

Steph ignored his glare. "Only the best for my bestie," she leaned in closer to me when she said it.

"Now how about some soup? Something easy for your tummy to digest," Kaylin said.

"That sounds great," I replied.

Kaylin wandered into the kitchen and started rummaging through the cabinets.

Steph propped me up into a sitting position to eat, doing her best to fill me in on what happened during my missing two days. They wouldn't let her be a part of the conversations and it bothered her a great deal. She told me about the bits and pieces she'd heard over her headphones or when they didn't think she was around.

She leaned in close to me and said, "I don't like Mr. Truedell. I mean I'm thankful he saved your life but something about him gives me the creeps."

I agreed. His story about Uncle Rob was too convenient. Plus some of his stories didn't add up. Like if he was there to help us then why didn't he save us when we were locked in the Amerii town?

"Do you know where we are?" I quietly asked her before she sat back down.

"It's some old hunting cabin. I guess there's still people out there who support the Amerii. People who are trying to find a new leader. He said he called out a distress call to the Amerii supporters and one of them happened to have a cousin who owned a cabin near by where you crashed. He says they told him he could use it to lay low." She shrugged her shoulders then glanced into the kitchen to see if anyone was paying attention to us before whispering. "Seems awful convenient, don't you think? What are the chances there would be a cabin of an Amerii supporter a few miles from where you were run off the road? Like I said, I don't trust him." She sat back down glancing over her shoulder into the kitchen again. I spotted Grant smiling at Steph before she turned her attention around to me. "I think he's the one that ran you two off the road. Then he loaded you into his truck while you were unconscious, drove into the woods, found a cabin then murdered the owner. When Kevin and Grant and I first found the cabin we overheard him talking on the phone to someone. He said he had you two and that he'd taken care of it. That there was no way it could be traced back to him." She leaned back and folded her arms in front of her. "I don't trust him at all."

Was Steph right?

Kaylin returned with a bowl of chicken broth. "It's not much, but it should help." He held out the bowl for me. The spoon spun around in the bowl. Steph quickly snatched it from his hands.

"How's she supposed to hold this with a sprained shoulder? Give it to me and I'll feed her."

"See what I mean." Kaylin shot an angry glare in Steph's direction. He returned to his post at the kitchen table, peering over every once in awhile.

"I've been keeping an eye on Mr. Truedell while you were out. He didn't get near you without me saying so." She scooped a spoonful of broth out of the bowl and blew on it before holding it to my lips. "Just be careful around him," she warned then didn't say another word about it.

I finished my soup. The warm broth in my belly had me feeling pretty good. Well enough in fact to try and get up.

"Can you take this stuff off me?" I hollered at Mr. Truedell. "I'd like to get up."

He walked over and tugged at the tape holding the tubing in my arm.

"Take it slow at first. Your muscles are going to be a bit weak," he said.

I swung my legs over the side of the bed. They'd become stiff from lying in bed for the last two days and ached now with the movement. I slid my rear closer to the edge of the bed, slowly putting pressure on my feet. I'm not sure why, but I became very nervous. Maybe it was because everyone stopped what they were doing when they saw me moving and were now intently watching to see what I would do. Even Kevin, who hadn't said one word to me since I had woken up, was staring at me to see if I could stand.

"Could someone give me a hand?" All three of the boys stood up. Steph stared at them. Grant and Kevin sat back down. Kaylin continued to stand there, helpless. I noticed a glimmer of sadness in his eyes. Steph hooked her arm around me and gently raised me to my feet. "I think I'm good now, thank you." She reluctantly loosened her arm and I took a step. My legs wobbled under me like jello, but I was determined to walk without help. I cautiously made my way from the bed to the table, stopping to take a rest as I passed the couch. Steph took each step with me, the whole time her arms ready to catch me if I fell.

"Would you mind if Kaylin and I stepped outside?" I asked Steph finally reaching the table in the kitchen. I asked her more as a courtesy to her for helping then as an actual question I needed answered. The last time Kaylin and I were alone together, I was peering over at him and the Jeep was spinning in circles then everything went black. I didn't even know if he was all right. I could see a few cuts on his face but honestly the gash on Kevin's face from when we were in the Amerii town appeared worse.

"You better not let anything happen to her," Steph warned Kaylin before agreeing to my request.

Kaylin took my arm and led me to the door. I desperately wanted to get away from all of the prying eyes and eavesdropping ears. The cabin was so small that even the most discreet conversation could be overheard. I stepped out of the cabin and took a deep breath. The musty smell of decaying leaves mixed with the sweetness of pine sap greeted me, giving me the extra boost I needed to make it off the landing and down the three steps to the ground.

"Are you okay?" I asked Kaylin as soon as my feet touched the hard packed dirt. The yard around the cabin was comprised of packed red clay, speckled with tufts of grass and weeds.

"For the most part," he replied. He lifted his shirt to expose an enormous bruise in the shape of a seatbelt strap across his chest.

"Oh my god!" I touched his chest.

"It's fine, nothing's broken. Just a few bruised ribs, that's all."

"Are you sure? It seems bad." I gently traced the edge of the bruise with my finger.

"I'll be fine, I promise." He lowered his shirt. Pushing my hand away. "How are you?"

"Other than this stupid thing on my arm, I feel okay," I lied. I couldn't let him know that walking around on my stiff leg muscles was causing me a great deal of pain. "I'm ready for our next adventure...

Where is our next adventure?" I bit my lip to keep from wincing.

"Maine," he said with a silly grin on his face. "I love lobster." He rubbed his belly.

"Maine? That's not at all where I thought you'd say. I figured it would be DC or somewhere, I don't know, more political."

"We could go to London, if you'd prefer. The Houses of Parliament are there," he replied kicking a small branch out of my path as we strolled around to the side of the cabin.

"London sounds better than Maine, let's go there ...Wait: London? How did we go from Maine to London? What do the two have in common?" I asked, confused.

"That's where the map is."

"A map of what?"

"Maine," he said laughing.

"So, I'm guessing we're not really going to London," London sounded way more fun than Maine. If I ate seafood, Maine might be fun, but I don't. I hated the stuff. The smell, the feel, everything about it. Maine didn't tantalize me.

"We don't really need to because we have something better than the map in London. We have John Hunt's personal journal, thanks to Mr. Truedell. Mr. Truedell has been an enormous help. He's filled us in on so much of the missing information. Like, we now know how John Hunt fits into the Amerii, besides his marriage to Eleanor, I mean. In John's journal are detailed descriptions of Fort St. George." He paused. "The Fort's in Maine."

"Gotcha, Maine."

The descriptions include the underground tunnel system that was built by the Amerii." His eyes lit up. "The tunnels connect one building to the other. They were kept a secret to even the colonists who lived there. Only a select few knew of their existence or how to access them. John Hunt was an Amerii member."

"Okay, so Maine it is then. Do you know what led the Amerii to go to Maine?"

He ignored my question and continued to explain how John Hurt became part of the Amerii, "In 1607, Sir Walter Raleigh funded another expedition to the New World. This time to Popham, Maine, which is now Phippsburg, Maine. Among the colonists was John Hunt." He explained how John Hunt ended up in Popham. Then went on to connect the dots between John and Mr. Huerta. "In Hunt's journal, he refers to a Mr. Huerta as a true friend of the Amerii. Mr. Huerta is Eric Dupont's grandfather. Anna asked for Mr. Dupont's help in the letter that led us to Roanoke. Remember?"

"Right, of course I remember. The bump on my head didn't give me amnesia. The letter said there was a trader and she told Mr. Dupont she was taking the stone to her great-grandmother's home."

"Yes, sorry." His cheeks were pink. "I didn't mean to imply there was something wrong with your head."

"I know." I touched his arm. "I was just giving you a hard time." I giggled. He smiled and the pink faded from his cheeks. "But why did they go to Maine, of all places?" I asked again.

"Oh! I'm not sure." He laughed. "They don't give an exact reason. My guess. They didn't feel like living in a cave anymore. I think nineteen years in a cave would drive just about anyone batty." He chuckled at his own joke.

"That joke was almost on Grant's level," I said, teasing him. I hid my smile as I bent over and picked a pinecone up off the ground. "So you think Eric followed Anna's example and took a stone to his grandparents' home?" I peeled several pieces of the pinecone off and tossed them to the ground, like you would with flower petals. Only I wasn't trying to figure out if he loved me or not. I just liked the crunching sound the pinecone made.

"Seems like a logical thing for him to do, right?" Kaylin stared at the pinecone pieces as they fell to the ground.

"Sure, I guess. Plus, a tunnel system would be a great place to hide a stone. Now that we know where to search, finding the third stone should be a piece of cake."

"Don't jinx us, geesh," said Kaylin. I should've figured him the superstitious type. After all, he did believe in fate.

We walked a complete circle around the cabin while we'd been talking and were standing in front of the door again.

"When are we leaving for Maine?"

"As soon as you feel well enough to go." Kaylin kissed my cheek before climbing up to the landing and opening the door.

"I think I'm ready." I tossed what was left of the pine cone into the trees and climbed the stairs.

"Good." He held the door open for me. "We can pack up and get going," He said, pleased to be able to search for the last stone.

I stepped back into the tiny cabin, Kaylin followed closely behind me.

"Get your stuff together." Kaylin informed everyone of our plans to leave right away. Steph protested, arguing that I was in no shape to go anywhere. I assured her I was fine. She hesitantly gathered her stuff and loaded it into her Explorer.

"We aren't all going to fit in Steph's Explorer," I said.

"You and I will go in Mr. Truedell's truck," Kaylin replied.

"Are you sure that's a good idea?" I asked. I didn't like the idea of being stuck in a truck for the next thirteen hours with a man I wasn't sure I trusted.

"Why wouldn't it be?" asked Kaylin. He tossed his backpack into the cab of the truck.

"Do you think we could swing by my house?" I followed him as he moved from door to door on the truck, situating the bags. "You guys didn't grab any of my stuff from the Jeep."

"It's not like Mr.Truedell had a lot of time Aurora," Kaylin defended him. "He was trying to stop the guy who ran us off the road from getting the stone. And save your life. We're lucky we got what we did."

"I'm just saying, we're only about an hour from Cary. It would be nice to have some of my own clothes to wear." I tugged the hem of my shirt down, trying to cover some of my midsection.

"Sure," Kaylin said over his shoulder. "We can get you something to wear. I guess it's not that far out of the way."

"Good." I smiled. I'd gotten what I'd wanted. "I feel really uncomfortable in Steph's stuff," I whispered. I didn't want to hurt Steph's feelings. Her style was a bit too revealing for my taste. I didn't dress like a nun or anything, but I liked my clothing to fit properly, not so tight. Steph looks great in it. She has the figure for it, but it makes me feel too exposed.

"It's sexy," he said playfully. The irritation in his voice was gone. He kissed my bare shoulder before leaving me at the driver's door and walking over to the passenger side. He leaned across the front seat. "But you're right, it's not you. I like you better as you. You don't need to dress up like she does to be sexy. You're sexy no matter what you wear." He winked at me then hopped into the front seat. I pushed the driver's seat forward and climbed into the rear of the cab.

I smiled as I watched the cabin, out the back window, disappear from view. Mr. Truedell turned the truck down a winding dirt trail that led us back onto a paved road. My smile faded when I realized we were on Webster Road.

In order to get onto the highway heading north, we had to pass by the scene of the accident. Luckily for me, someone had removed the Jeep already. I didn't think I could handle seeing it all twisted and mashed up against a tree. Steph had told me of her frantic search for Kaylin and me and what a horrific experience it was for her to pull up to the site of the accident. With the Jeep gone, the only indication of an accident left was some overturned dirt down the embankment towards a scraped up tree trunk and the wavy black tire marks down the road. Even those had begun to fade, almost like it never happened. Had the cops cleaned up the mess?

"Aren't the cops going to be searching for Kaylin?" I asked, slouching down in the back seat.

"The Amerii has a few friends on the force," replied Mr. Truedell. "The accident report has already been lost."

"How did you know where we were?" I asked Mr. Truedell.

"I slipped a micro tracker into your phone's headphone jack when I bumped into you that day at the fort," he replied. "I needed a way to know what you were doing." He grabbed a bottle of water from the center console and took a sip. "You guys moved around so sporadically I was having a hard time keeping up."

I reached for my back pocket. "Where's my phone?" I asked, realizing I hadn't seen it since the accident.

"It got destroyed in the crash." Kaylin turned back towards me and reached for my hand. "We can get you a burner phone when we stop at a gas station and you can use that for now until we get back to Stony Creek and can buy you a real one." I nodded. He let go of my hand. "Can you reach that bag for me?" He pointed to his backpack on the seat next to me. "I want to do some research on our drive." I handed him the bag.

"Where you placing a bug or something when you trashed our hotel room?" I continued my line of questioning. It irritated me that he'd invaded my privacy.

"That wasn't me," he denied my accusation. "Why would I trash your room? If I wanted to plant a bug in your room I would be secretive about it. You wouldn't have even known I was there." He gripped the steering wheel tighter. His knuckles turned white. My questions were getting to him.

"Was it you outside the window the first night?"

"Yes." He grunted. "You saw that? I didn't think anyone was awake. Guess my skill set isn't what it used to be." He shook his head in disgust. "That was my first attempt at sneaking a tracker into your stuff," he admitted. He loosened his grip on the wheel. "But I couldn't get the window open. It was painted shut. I'm sorry if I scared you." He adjusted the rear view mirror so that it reflected my face.

"You didn't," I lied. Kaylin glanced over his shoulder. I leaned closer to the door, avoiding Mr. Truedell's eyes in the mirror and held my finger up to my mouth. "And it was you watching me in the hot tub."

"Yes. You guys had switched hotels on me. I was waiting for you to go back to your room so I could follow." He scratched his head. "I really am out of practice. First thing I'm going to do after we find the third stone is begin training."

He had a logical explanation for every one of my questions. I increased the difficulty in my line of questioning.

"Why did you steal the corpse?"

"What corpse?" He became agitated again. He stared straight ahead, out the window and twisted his hands around the wheel.

"The mummified corpse in the cavern. The one in the Amerii town."

"There was a body down there?"

"Yes!" I said. As if he didn't already know that.

"What possible use would I have for a body?" he asked.

That was the million dollar question. None of us had any idea why someone would steal an old mummified corpse from a secret underground town. It just didn't make sense. If they were after the ring why didn't they just take it off the corpse like Kaylin had. Why steal the whole body? I needed him to have the answer.

"Cavern, huh? Is that where you were? Were you there overnight?"

"Yes," I replied, becoming irate. I wasn't getting the answers I'd hoped for from him. Instead he kept turning the conversation around and asking me the questions.

"That explains why I lost you!" he shifted his position in the seat and relaxed. "I thought the tracker in your phone wasn't working."

"Let me see if I've got this straight. You're claiming it wasn't you who trashed our hotel room, and that you didn't steal the body or beat up Kevin when he caught you, and then locked us in the cavern..." I paused giving him one last chance to confess.

"No," he repeated himself. "I mean yes." He looked confused. "I mean no. Look, I told you I didn't do that stuff. Phrase it however you want but my answer is still the same. It wasn't me."

I was quiet for a moment. Then asked, "Was it the guy who ran us off the road?"

"It's hard to say for sure, but I doubt it."

"What makes you think that?" asked Kaylin. He had been sitting silently during my questioning.

"He was a young guy, around your age. He didn't seem to have a clue what he was doing or even what he was searching for. As soon as I confronted him, he started rambling on about how this isn't worth it and how he'd just killed someone. He was hysterical. If it were him, he's not alone. He definitely isn't the one calling the shots. Doesn't have the brains for something like that."

"Did you kill him?" I asked point blank.

"Kill the guy who ran you off the road? No. I chased after him. Made sure he wasn't going to come back but then I turned around to help save you." He glanced back up in the rearview mirror. Our eyes met. I was grateful for his help. "I wasn't able to catch him. Whoever's after the stones. They're still out there, Aurora. We are all still in danger." His words frightened me. "Don't worry," he assured me in a softer, more sincere tone. "I won't let anything happen to you." He adjusted the mirror back to its intended position.

"One more question," I said. I took a breath and spit it out. "Did you kill the owner of the cabin or is it really the cabin of an Amerii supporter? Because it seems highly unlikely that there would be a cabin right where we needed one. It seems more likely that you killed the guy."

"What on earth are you talking about?" Kaylin spun around in his seat. "Where are you getting this stuff from?"

"Steph said, the cabin belonged to a cousin of an Amerii supporter or something like that."

"We don't know who owned the cabin. Steph knows that." Kaylin shook his head in disgust. "After the crash I blacked out for a few minutes. When I woke up the guy that ran us off the road was trying to climb in the window and take the stones. Mr.Truedell showed up at that time and yanked the guy from the window and tossed him on the ground. The guy ran back in his car and sped off. Mr. Truedell tore after him in his truck. I managed to get myself out. I don't know how I did it but I managed to pull you from the wreckage and carry you into the woods."

"When I returned to the accident You and Kaylin had disappeared," Mr. Truedell cut in. "I followed Kaylins trail into the woods. When I found you, you were in rough shape. There wasn't enough time to carry you back to my truck and drive you to the hospital."

"That's when I saw the cabin," continued Kaylin. "Mr.Trudell helped me carry you the rest of the way to the cabin." Kaylin and Mr.Truedell glanced at each other. "I broke the lock on the door." He turned to me. "We were prepared to offer the owner money to fix the door and pay for our stay but they never showed up."

"I left a note on the kitchen table with some cash before we left," said Mr. Trudell.

"Oh," I said ashamed. Steph lied to me? Why hadn't she just told me the truth?

I slipped a road map out of the cubby beside me pretended to study the route. I was too embarrassed to ask anymore questions. An awkward tension grew between us as we rode the rest of the way to Cary in silence.

"Take a left up here. My house is the gray one about halfway down the block." My words cut through the heaviness in the air surrounding us. Mr. Truedell did as I instructed. The sight of my house lifted my spirits. Everything about the house seemed the same as the day I'd left it. Mom's tacky lawn ornaments were thoughtfully placed throughout the front yard just like they always were. I'd normally cringe at the sight of them, but today they comforted me. I'm home. It had been nearly nine months since I'd been here. It was Christmas in fact. I'd headed straight to Uncle Rob's from college not bothering to stop off at home first. Now, I wish I had. I could use one of my mom's overbearing hugs right about now. Even my dad's relentless hounding about how I need to do this or I shouldn't do that, would be welcomed right now. I missed them terribly.

"It doesn't look like anyone's here," Kaylin said. "Are there normally cars in the driveway?"

I leaned forward. I grabbed the back of Kaylin's seat and stretched my neck to get a better view of the driveway. He was right. The driveway was empty. On the bright side, it meant I would be able to run in and grab the stuff I needed without interruption or questioning, but on the dark side, I wouldn't get the hug I so desperately desired. Mr. Truedell pulled into the driveway and parked the truck. He opened the door and stepped out. He stretched his arms then pulled his seat forward to let me out. I stepped out onto the familiar ground. The pebbles made a comforting crunching sound under my feet. A sound I was very accustomed to.

Steph pulled up at the end of the driveway, with the passenger window rolled down. She hollered out across Grant, "I'm going to swing by my place. Be back in a second." Then she sped away. I was glad she hadn't wanted to come in the house with me. I wasn't ready to confront her yet.

I entered the house and made my way from the kitchen down the hall of our average sized ranch home to my bedroom. My bedroom was the second door on the right, just beyond my mom's craft room. I found an old backpack, from high school, in the bottom of my closet and stuffed it with as much of my clothing as I could fit. I pulled off Steph's flashy red tank top and replaced it with something of my own. I shimmied out of the tight fitting shorts, tossed them on my bed, and searched through my drawers for my favorite jean shorts, forgetting that I had taken them with me to Roanoke and that I was wearing them the day of the accident. My necklace. My grandmother's necklace was in the pocket of my shorts. I ran over to my bed and checked the pockets of Steph's shorts. I prayed she'd put the necklace back in my pocket when she'd changed me, nothing. Kaylin said the guy who ran us off the road hadn't taken anything, but where was it then. I didn't recall seeing it with anyone's stuff back at the cabin. Had it fallen out of my pocket as Kaylin and Mr. Truedell carried me to safety or did the guy in fact steal it? My heart sank in my chest. It wasn't just a key to unlocking the Amerii's secrets. It was something my granny had given me. It was special to me. Maybe Kaylin had it and just forgot to tell me. I told myself. Trying not to panic, I quickly threw on the first pair of shorts I grabbed out of my drawer, finished packing, and ran out to the truck.

"Do you know where my necklace is?" I asked Kaylin as I threw my bag across the back seat of Mr.Trudell's extended cab and slid in behind it.

"No, I haven't seen it," he replied. "I have the hair comb. I found that but I never saw your necklace."

"My necklace is lost." The tears formed in my eyes. I couldn't hold them back.

"Don't cry," he said reaching into the back to comfort me. "Maybe Steph found it when she changed your clothes."

I jumped out of the truck, hoping he was right. I rushed back to where Steph had parked on the side of the road.

"Was there a necklace in my pocket when you changed my clothes?" I asked, desperately wanting her answer to be yes.

"I didn't see one," she replied. "I still have your clothes though." She pointed to the back of the Explorer. "Maybe it's still there." She popped the latch before exiting the driver's seat and heading to the rear of the vehicle. She rummaged through her bags searching for my clothing. She located a plastic grocery bag tied off at the top. "Here you go." She handed it to me. Dried blood flaked off of the plastic as I untied the knot. I dumped my clothing out on the grass and knelt down beside them. They were saturated with blood. So much so that I could no longer make out the graphic design on the front of my t-shirt. The blood had completely distorted the image. My shorts weren't any different. I shoved my hand hopefully into the pockets but each time came out empty handed. I returned my clothes to the bag, tied the bag back into a knot, then stood up and tossed it all into the garbage tote on the curb.

"Did either of you see my necklace back at the cabin?" I asked Grant and Kevin.

"Not me," replied Kevin, leaning over the backseat.

"Me either," answered Grant from the passenger seat.

"Sorry, Aurora." Steph offered her sympathy. She shut the hatch.

"It's okay," I said softly. But it wasn't okay.

My head hung low as I made my way back to Mr. Truedell's truck. My heart, heavy with sadness. I'd lost something very dear to me. I climbed into the back seat of the truck and shut the door. Kaylin watched me as I buckled my seatbelt. Mr. Trudell put the truck in reverse and began to back up.

"Stop," Kaylin unbuckled his seatbelt. Mr. Trudell stopped the truck. Kaylin opened his door, slid out then turned, pulled his seat forward and climbed into the backseat. He pushed my bag onto the floor and pulled me as close to him as my seatbelt would allow. I laid my head on his shoulder, we had a long drive ahead of us, one I wasn't looking forward to at all.

So far, Grant was the only one of us that hadn't been injured. This was not how I'd imagined our trip would go. I thought back to the day we'd left Stony Creek. How happy we'd been and how excited we were for the adventure.

Chapter 11

Popham

We drove through the night and into the next day, each of us taking a turn behind the wheel to let the others rest. Kaylin was driving when we arrived in Brunswick, Maine late Wednesday afternoon. We were about twenty minutes away from Phippsburg, previously Popham. I was in the passenger seat and Mr. Truedell was resting in the back.

It was nearing the end of August. The summer was quickly coming to a close. Popham would be all we had time for before I had to leave for Penn State. If we didn't find the stone here we'd have to wait until next year to look again.

Kaylin picked a hotel and while he was waiting for a car to pass by before pulling into the parking lot, he caught me rubbing my shoulder. "Is it feeling any better?"

"It's fine." I adjusted the brace. "I'll be back to myself in no time."

Kaylin shifted the truck into park. "I'm glad to hear that," He said softly. He leaned over and kissed me.

"Get a room," said Mr.Truedell. I turned around and glared at him. His face wore a big grin. His teeth, perfectly straight and very white, peeked out from between his thin lips. It was the first time I'd seen him smile. As quickly as the smile appeared, it disappeared. His face returned to its normal unfriendly glare.

Steph parked a few spots down from us. She and the boys were already unloading their bags when Kaylin and I opened the truck doors to get out.

"We should see if there's anything fun to do in this town," Steph hollered over the tops of the cars. "The boys and I were talking on the way up here. We think we deserve to have some fun, maybe eat some lobster," she suggested.

What was with everybody and lobster?

"This is fun," Kaylin answered from the back of the truck as he rummaged around under the tonneau cover.

"Maybe for you, little bro, but the rest of us need a little more spice," replied Kevin. "We've been going at this for days. It wouldn't kill you to have fun for one night. Oh, by the way, we saw Illinois, Indiana, and Iowa on the way here," he added. I had to give it to them, they were certainly dedicated to playing the game.

"We want to go to a bar or a club. We also saw Kansas," Grant said, reminding Kevin.

"See, the boys want to have some fun," said Steph with a smug I told you so look on her face.

"Bet she's always up for fun," Kaylin scoffed. I nudged him.

"She's my best friend," I reminded him.

"Sorry." He shivered then tilted his head from side to side, cracking his neck. "She just gets under my skin."

"You kids may go have your fun. I'll stay here and guard the things," Mr. Truedell said as if he was giving us permission to go. He waved us on. I rolled my eyes. What we did had nothing to do with him.

"Thanks, dad," Steph said sarcastically as she passed by us with just her purse on her shoulder.

"Where's your stuff?" I asked, observing her lack of bags. Kaylin shook his head disapprovingly.

"The boys are getting it for me." She continued on her way to the front doors of the hotel.

"She thinks she's some kind of goddess, doesn't she?" Kaylin said loudly so that everyone could hear.

I pointed to Kevin and Grant. "Is she wrong? If boys did every-thing I told them to do, I might start thinking I was a goddess, too."

"Well I'm glad you're not like that. I don't really see why you two are friends." He forcefully pushed the bags around in the bed of the truck. "She's such a lying bitch," he said, not holding back his hatred for her.

"She's there when I need her," I said, defending her. I couldn't be-lieve he called her a bitch. "She got us out of the Amerii town didn't she?" I reminded him. "She has good qualities too."

"Yes, then she complained about it the entire time you were un-conscious."

"What are you talking about?" I asked. I didn't believe him. Steph wouldn't complain about saving me.

"Let's just say she's not the person you made her out to be." Kaylin grabbed the last bag from the back and slammed the tailgate shut. "She acts totally different when you're around than she does when you're not round."

His comment enraged me. Who did he think he was, talking about Steph like that? I tore my bag from his hand and hurried to catch up with her.

I couldn't even look at him while we waited at the hotel desk for our room keys. I made sure we got two rooms this time. One for Steph and me and one for the guys. I didn't cool off until Kaylin and I parted ways after getting off the elevator.

"Aren't you going to unpack?" I asked, noticing Steph just sitting on the bed staring at her phone. The boys had thrown her bags on the floor by the door then headed off to their room to settle in.

"I don't figure we will be here much more than a day. Why bother."

"We don't always find what we're searching for that quickly." I pulled my toiletries out of my backpack and carried them into the bathroom.

"Let's talk. It's been so long since we've had girl time." When I re-turned, she gestured for me to sit on the other bed. "Remember when we used to have sleepovers and stay up all night talking about boys?"

"I remember." I remembered Steph going on and on about the new boy she liked. Her newest crush. They changed every week.

"What was that one guys name? The one you had a crush on. Was it John or something?"

"You mean Jeff?"

"Yes, Jeff, that's what it was."

"The one you stole from me?" I said. She's a bitch. Kaylin's words repeated in my head. My anger returned.

"I didn't steal him from you. You know that. You were never going to ask him out. Besides, it's a good thing you didn't date him. He was a loser, with a capital L, and still is." She picked up her phone. "Here look." She rotated her phone to show me his profile picture. "Still a loser." I took her phone in my hand and scrolled through his profile.

"He's studying to be a Veterinarian. What's wrong with that?"

"Did you see his girlfriend? A real dog. Maybe that's why he wants to be a Vet." She started laughing. I tossed her phone on the bed next to her. "Lighten up Aurora, it was a joke."

"I'm going to finish unpacking."

"Fine, you unpack. I'm going downstairs to take a peek in the gift shop." She grabbed the door card from the night stand between the beds and headed out the door. It was the first time I'd been alone in what felt like ages. It seemed strange not having one of the boys around. I finished unpacking then sat on the end of the bed and enjoyed the silence. It wasn't long before there was a knock on the door. I opened the door expecting to see Kaylin there with an apology. Instead Steph burst through the door.

"I found a bar in the hotel lobby. I've already told the boys. They're going to meet us down there. Do you still have your fake ID from back in high school?"

"No," I replied. "I threw that away. I never use it anymore, besides I will be twenty-one next spring. Why didn't you use the door card?" I asked her annoyed.

"What? Oh! I don't know." She yanked the card out of her back pocket. "I guess I didn't think about it."

"What if I was in the bathroom or something?"

"Then I would have used the key. What is this the Spanish Inquisition? Is it really that big a deal? God Aurora, I forgot. Is that okay?"

I didn't feel like arguing. I'd done enough arguing for one day. I grabbed my wallet and headed out the door with no idea of where I was heading to. I paused at the guy's door. I thought about seeing if Kaylin was in there then changed my mind before knocking. I didn't want to end up arguing with him again, so I walked to the stairway at the end of the hall. I strolled down the three flights of stairs to the lobby and out the front doors. I continued past the cars in the parking lot, past the restaurant next door, then a shopping center, and another one after that. I kept walking. I walked for hours up and down the streets of Brunswick. Fathers were grilling in their backyards, their children playing games, and the wives chatted with each other at the edges of their properties. Every single family blissfully unaware of what was going on in the world around them. I doubted any of them bothered to stop and think about the town they lived in or how it came to be. They were most likely unaware of the sacrifices that were made, the lives that were lost, the secrets that were told to form this nation. Hell, most of them probably hadn't even heard of Roanoke, let alone knew who the Amerii were. They believed what their history teachers taught them to be true. Eating up the stories that had been fed to them by the spoonful. They didn't bother to question any of it. What would America be like if there had been no Amerii? Would it be worse, would it be better? I asked myself as I walked on. What about other countries? Do similar organizations exist in other countries? How deep does the rabbit hole go?

"There you are." I glanced up to see Mr. Truedell standing in front of me. His stern expression reminded me of all the arguing from earlier. Where was I? I glanced around, recognizing the doors to the hotel. "Everyone's out searching for you."

"I'm sorry," I said as I stepped past him into the lobby. I still needed to be alone.

"Wait a minute. Your friends have been worried sick about you." He said following me through the doors. He grabbed my arm.

"Thanks for letting me know," I said, trying to jerk my arm away.

"Don't thank me, what's wrong with you?" Don't you care that your friends are out searching for you?" He shook my arm.

"Does it really matter? Nothing any of us do really matters does it? It's all been predetermined by the Amerii?" I struggled to get away from him.

"That's what this is? You think the Amerii has decided your life for you. You've only just begun to understand who the Amerii are and what they actually did for you." He forced me to a corner of the room, far away from the other hotel guests who were lounging about in the lobby. "The Amerii is not the enemy. They haven't chosen your life for you. Just the opposite. They've given you your freedom, your ability to make your own choices. You're not controlled. You're not told where you will work, how much you will be paid, whom to love, or how many children you can have. You've been given the right to voice your opinions, without fear. These are just a few of the gifts your ancestors gave to you." He let go of my arm. "Now call your friends. Tell them you're okay." He handed me his phone. I did as he instructed. He was right. I owed it to my friends to let them know I was all right.

"Thank you," I said, hanging up the phone and meaning it this time. "Thank you for helping me see the truth." I wrapped my arms around him. I needed a father figure to remind me what was important.

"You're welcome." He smoothed out his shirt. "We will have a meeting to discuss tomorrow's events in our room when everyone returns. You will let the others know." He pivoted and calmly strolled to the elevator. I found an empty, black leather couch in the lobby and strolled over to take a seat while I waited. The leather released a farting noise as I sat down. I nervously glanced around to see if anyone else heard it. Sweet. No one had heard the awful rumble.

Grant and Steph were the first ones to return to the hotel. I watched them pull into the parking lot through the enormous glass windows on the front of the hotel. That's how Mr. Truedell had known I'd returned. I kept my gaze glued to them as they strolled through the parking lot to the lobby. Steph had herself draped all over Grant, running her fingers through his hair, and shamelessly flirting with him. She was making a spectacle of herself in front of everyone in the lobby. I'd sat back and blindly watched as she'd perfected her technique throughout high school but now she was using her skills on my cousin. Could I continue to sit back and let her? Grant was enchanted by her, completely under her spell. How could I tell him she'd blow through his life, leaving him heartbroken before he even knew what hit him. Watching them made me realize It wasn't Steph that had changed over the last year, it was me. I had changed during our time apart. I wasn't oblivious to her manipulation of the opposite sex, anymore. I shook my head in disgust as she and Grant made their way into the lobby. Grant quickly separated from her the second he noticed me on the couch. He stepped away from her, slipping out from under her arm and straightened his hair. She stared blankly at him. He nodded in my direction. Steph followed his gaze. Her expression changed the moment she realized I was watching them. She immediately forgot about Grant, plastering a concerned smile on her face and hurried over to me. Grant nonchalantly strolled up behind her. We all pretended I hadn't seen their raunchy public display of affection.

"You had us worried, Cuz." He sat down and put his arm around my shoulder. "Kaylin went off the deep end. You should have seen him." He gave my shoulder a quick squeeze before letting arm fall from around me.

"He did?"

"Yep, he thinks he made you leave," Steph said. She stood near the end of the couch, a shameless grin on her face.

"Did you tell him it wasn't him?" I glared accusingly at her. She pretended to be shocked by my accusation. I knew her better than that. She couldn't fool me. She knew it was our argument that had sent me over the edge not the one with Kaylin.

Kaylin burst through the lobby doors. He stood at the entrance and frantically scanned the lobby before she had a chance to answer. His interruption pleased her. She grinned and waved him over. He ran across the lobby to me as soon as he spotted her arm in the air. Kevin calmly strolled into the lobby a few seconds behind him. He didn't appear to share Kaylins eagerness to see me. Grant made room for Kaylin as he approached. There was an expression on Kaylin's face that I had never seen before. Was he angry? Worried? Both? I couldn't tell.

"Don't do that again," he said. It sounded like anger, but the way he knelt down in front of me and placed his hands on my knees felt more like worry. "Not when there could be people out there wanting to harm us." His voice now reflected the worry I felt in his hands.

"I'm sorry." I met his gaze with mine. Our eyes locked. I placed my hands on his.

"Ouch." I said recoiling back, ruining our special moment. Stupid shoulder. How long was this going to be sore? I tried to reconnect with him, to gaze back into his eyes.

He slid his hands from my knees up the outside of my thighs to my back. Then in one quick movement he slid me forward to the edge of the couch, bringing my body against his. The couch let out the obnoxious noise again.

"God, Aurora, did you have to?" Grant laughed, lightening the mood.

"Way to go, Aurora," Steph chimed in. She relaxed onto the arm of the couch, crossing her legs so that no one could see up her short skirt.

"Good one," Kevin said. All three of them chuckled at the noise.

"Guess that wasn't as romantic as I had hoped it would be," said Kaylin trying not to laugh with the others.

"It was the stupid couch," I said, defending myself. "You all know that right?" I couldn't help but giggle a little myself. That was enough to get Kaylin laughing. He shoved me back on the couch, making the noise again. Everyone exploded. No one could keep their laughter from bubbling out. Grant slid himself along the couch, letting out another enormous rumble.

"Mine's better," he sputtered out between fits of laughter.

"Is everything okay over here?" The man behind the check in desk approached us. "What is all the commotion?" He clasped his hands in front of himself and waited for an answer.

"Sorry, yes, we're fine." I managed to compose myself just long enough to answer.

"You might want to think about getting some different furniture for the lobby," Kevin suggested. He pressed his lips tightly together. "Bah ha ha." The laughter rolled out of him.

"I think we should go up to our rooms," Kaylin said. He changed the expression on his face to that of a serious one. A few chuckles still slipped out but he did his best to be in control. "Uhm," he cleared the laughter from his throat.

"Oh, that reminds me, we're supposed to meet Mr. Truedell in your room for a meeting. I was supposed to tell you guys. When you got here."

"We'd better go then," said Kevin loudly. His face was bright red and blotchy.

The rest of us corralled our laughter and adopted Kaylin's serious expression. Grant and I stood up from the couch at the same time, letting out the loudest rumble yet. The rumble sent everyone back into an uncontrollable fit of laughter. Even the desk clerk laughed this time.

"Oh my god, I'm dying," roared Steph. "We have to get away from this couch. I can't breathe."

Our laughter and energy was contagious. The groups of people we passed on our way to the elevators smiled and giggled as we strolled by. The mood of the whole lobby lifted.

"I can't tell you the last time I laughed so hard," Grant said, wiping the tears away from his eyes as the elevator doors shut behind us. He pushed our floor button, then cleared his throat.

"That was fun," said Steph. She stood confidently between Kevin and Grant. They each reached out to put a hand around her waist. Their hands touched and they both flinched. Kevin dropped his hand to his side. Grant glared at him. Steph beamed. She had them right where she wanted them.

"I don't think the front desk clerk was all too happy with us." Kaylin positioned himself behind me. He wrapped his arms around me and held me while we rode up to our floor. The whole time whispering playfully into my ear. Once the elevator doors opened, he released his arms from around me and took my hand in his. We exited the elevator and strolled, hand in hand, to the boys' room.

"Open the door, dude," Kevin said impatiently to Grant. The five of us were clumped together outside the door, eager to get in.

"I must have left my key card in the room," he replied, patting his back pockets. "I could have sworn I had it right here." He checked his front pockets.

"Step back, I've got it," said Kevin. He pushed Grant to the side. Grant folded his arms in front of him. Kevin slid a key card from his back pocket and swiped it along the door. The light on the door flashed green. Kevin pushed down on the handle and swung the door open. "Ladies first," he teased Grant.

"I ain't too proud." Grant strutted into the room.

We entered the room behind him to find Mr. Truedell sitting at the small table in the corner.

"What's wrong with you? Is someone hurt?" He asked us, pushing his chair back to stand up. We glanced at each other. Our faces were red and puffy from laughing so hard. The trail of a tear here or there on a few of our faces.

"No, no one's hurt," replied Kaylin. He smiled and squeezed my hand.

"It's a long story," I added, holding in a stray giggle.

"Okay, as long as everyone's fine. He scooched his chair in and picked up his pen. "Can we get to work then?" He put the pen to the paper and stared at us.

We each found a seat on one of the pieces of furniture somewhere in the room. Kaylin and I sat at the table with Mr. Truedell, Steph and Grant sat together on one of the double beds while Kevin sprawled out on the other. Kaylin and Mr. Truedell had hashed out a plan of action days earlier, in the cabin, while I was unconscious. This meeting was more or less to inform the rest of us of the plan and to make sure they hadn't missed any minor details in their original formulation of it.

"Most of the hard work has been done for us," Kaylin started off. He flipped opened John Hunts journal to an earmarked page then set it face up on the table. "In 1997, Jeffrey Brian excavated three of the eighteen buildings that formed the fort. The liquor storage building, the storehouse, and the Admiral's house. The rest of the remaining buildings are still buried. Some of the buildings are on private land and some of them have been paved over, under a public road. But

that's fine. We can enter into the tunnel system from one of the excavated buildings and as long as the tunnels are still in decent enough
shape for us to climb through them, we should have no problems
finding the buildings that haven't been excavated yet. Does everyone
understand?"

"Yep. We go to the dig site, find an entrance to a tunnel, search the
tunnels. Piece of cake," replied Grant.

"There should be an entrance here." Mr. Truedell pointed to a spot
in the liquor storage building and one here in the Admiral's house,
as well as one here in the storehouse. We have three possible entry
points."

"Because we can't be certain what shape the tunnels will be in.
We've decided it would be best to split up into groups, each group
taking an entrance. The entombed buildings themselves may be in-
accessible. Possibly caved in with dirt and rocks. So be careful when
you're down there. We think the Dare Stone should be somewhere
around here." Kaylin took the map from Mr. Truedell, pointing to one
of the larger buildings on it. "This building was the town's chapel. Mr.
Dupont's father was the town's clergyman. It stands to reason that
the stone should be somewhere in there." He laid the map down on
the table and coaxed his hair back behind his ear.

"I think it's time for everyone to get some rest," Mr. Truedell said,
gathering the papers on the table into a neat pile.

"Meeting adjourned," Grant said jokingly. He flirtatiously banged
his fist down on Steph's thigh.

I slowly rose to my feet, stretching as I did. Between the long car
ride north and my impromptu soul searching walk around the town
this evening, my body was screaming for a nice, comfy bed.

"Can I talk to you in the hall?" Kaylin asked, walking me to the
door. "Alone?" He glanced over at Steph.

"Sure," I replied. I turned to Steph. "I'll meet you back in the
room." Steph wandered away down the hallway to our room. She
glanced back at us before opening the door and stepping inside.

Kaylin waited for the door to close behind her before shoving me
up against the wall. He silently stood inches from me, staring lustful-

ly into my eyes. I could feel his breath on my cheek. His hands forced my shoulders firmly against the wall. I wasn't sure if he wanted to hit me or kiss me. My pulse quickened. He slid his right hand down to my breast, gently running his thumb over my nipple before continuing down to my hip. He followed the curve of my body around my side, across my back and down to my rear. His left hand still firmly on my left shoulder. He pulled my waist against his. I could feel his excitement, growing hard, against my pelvis. He clenched the back of my thigh tightly as he encouraged my leg up around him. He began grinding his hardness against my body. I let out a soft moan. He placed his left hand gently on my chin, lifting it slightly. I trembled. I held my breath. He traced my bottom lip with his thumb before leaning in and kissing me. He began thrusting his hips upwards. His body repeatedly pressed harder against mine each time. He lifted me slightly off the floor. I tightened my leg around his waist as I rocked him inward over and over. His breathing grew heavier, he let out a moan.

"I'm sorry." He released his lips from mine long enough to say the words.

"No! Don't stop!" I grabbed the back of his head encouraging him to kiss me again.

"I was so scared something happened to you earlier." He resisted my kiss, his eyes shifted down at our tangled bodies. He placed his forehead against mine. "You feel so good." He continued to rock his pelvis into me. I needed to taste his sweet kisses again.

"Kaylin."

"We have to stop or I'm going to rip your clothes off and take you right here," he whispered back. He slowly released his grip on my thigh, letting my leg return to the floor.

"I don't care if someone sees," I protested. I wanted him.

"I do."

I tipped my head back and stared at the ceiling. How could he just stop like that? My body ached with desire. I wanted to feel him inside me. The elevator dinged announcing someone getting off on our floor. Kaylin inspected himself, quickly adjusting his pants to hide the enormous bulge before the couple exited the elevator. We didn't say a word as they passed us on the way to their room.

"I want you with me, when we break off into groups tomorrow," Kaylin said once the couple was in their room. He took my hand and led me to my room. I followed reluctantly. "That wasn't fair of me back there. I'm sorry." He grinned sheepishly.

I sighed, then pulled my wallet from my pocket and rummaged around in search of the key card.

"Hmmm, I've lost my card as well," I said confused. I pulled out a stack of random business cards I'd collected over the years and fanned them out. "I know without a doubt I had it in my wallet.

"Are you sure you're not just trying to get me to stay in the hall with you longer?" Kaylin said, teasingly. He knocked on the door then gave me a quick kiss and stepped away before I could persuade him to come in. I shoved the cards back in my wallet.

"No, I really lost it." I insisted. "It wasn't a ploy. I promise." He turned and jogged down the hall to his door.

"I will see you tomorrow," he called to me, before entering his room.

Steph opened the door just as Kaylin closed his. I leaned against the door jam, slightly out of breath.

"That must have been some talk," She said, her eyes inspecting me from top to bottom.

"It was." I shoved my way past her into the room. She closed the door behind me before following me to the bed. She sat down on the bed next to the bag I was searching through to find my pajamas.

"I would just like to point out that you didn't use your room key either." She had a smug smile on her face.

"I lost it." I stared into my bag randomly grabbing articles of clothing. I was searching for my pajamas but couldn't keep my focus long enough to remember what they looked like.

"Wanna talk about it?"

"Losing the room key?" I asked puzzled. Still staring blankly into the bag. Why would I want to talk about that? I frowned.

"No. Your little talk in the hall with Kaylin. What do I care if you lost the room key?" She chewed on her cuticle. "I only pointed it out because you made such a big deal earlier about me knocking." She held out her hand and inspected her well-manicured nails.

I thought about her question for a minute then blurted out. "I think I'm in love with him." The spontaneous confession momentarily cleared the haze from my mind and I found my pajamas. I scurried into the bathroom to get ready for bed. The words sounded strange to my ears, as if someone else had said them, but it felt good to finally say them.

"You can't just drop a bombshell like that then walk away," she said through the door. I opened the door just enough to poke my head out. "I love Kaylin." I said the three little words. I'd never said those words to anyone. I had a few boyfriends in high school, but none of them made me feel the way Kaylin did. "That's it. I love Kaylin." I said, confirming out loud what I was feeling inside, more for my benefit than for hers. I shut the bathroom door again.

Steph was already under the covers by the time I exited the bathroom.

"Good night," she said as I slipped into my bed.

"Night," I mindlessly replied. My head was swimming. I'm in love with the boy of my dreams.

Chapter 12

The Traitor

The early morning sunlight had just started to come in through the window when the alarm sounded. I rolled over in bed, my eyes still closed and clumsily felt around on the table for my phone. It couldn't be morning already. I was having the most wonderful dream. It was springtime. I was walking down a path of rose petals through the field of daisies and black-eyed susans at my uncle's place. My friends and family were seated in rows of white folding chairs. Large Roman pillars spaced evenly apart formed a barrier around the rows of chairs. Flower garlands draped from one pillar to the next. I was standing at the end of the aisle, searching for Kaylin in the crowd, but he wasn't seated with everyone else. I looked to the other end of the aisle. He was standing there holding his hand out for me to join him. I started running towards him but my clothing weighed heavy on my body, making it difficult. The heels of my shoes sank deep into the earth with each step I took. I glanced down. I was wearing the most beautiful white gown I had ever seen. Piles of smooth, white satin rippled down an enormous train out behind me. I lifted the skirt revealing a pair of white, heeled sandals. It took me a minute to realize what was happening. I was getting married. I was about to marry Kaylin.

I tightened my eyes, squeezing out the light that tried to force me out of my dream world. Just a few more minutes and I would have made it down the aisle to Kaylin.

"Aurora, the boys will be here in a minute. You better get up and get ready." Steph's voice interrupted my fantasy. I felt for the covers to drag them up over my head.

"I don't want to."

"Okay, but don't you want to at least brush your teeth before Kaylin gets here? I love you won't have quite the same effect on him if your breathing morning breath into his face."

"You can't tell him! I'm not ready yet." I sat straight up. Steph was standing next to the bed, brushing her hair.

"I'm not going to tell him, you are." She slid the brush from root to tip.

"Nope. Not going to do it. Nope not telling him."

"Why not?"

"I'm not ready yet."

"What do you have to be ready for?"

"I don't know. I want it to be perfect when I say it."

Steph laughed. "If you're waiting for perfection, you're going to be waiting forever. There's no such thing, Aurora." She tossed the brush onto the table.

"Hey that's my brush." I snatched it off the table and held it up in the air. "Put it back where you found it." She took the brush from my hand and strolled onto the bathroom with it. "I disagree. I know the right time to tell him I love him will present itself, and when it does, I'll be ready." I flopped backward and lifted the covers up over my head.

Steph returned from the bathroom. "Regardless of whether or not you're going to tell him today, you still need to get up." She yanked the covers completely off the bed into a big pile on the floor.

"Fine, I'm up." I slid one leg off the side of the bed. "See, I'm up."

I reluctantly got out of bed and made my way to the bathroom. Maybe a shower would bring my mind back into focus. I slipped off my pajamas then stepped under the warm water. I'd barely shut the curtain when the bathroom door opened.

"Geesh Steph can I have a minute?"

"It's me."

Kaylin, in the bathroom with me, and I was naked.

"Steph said you had something important to tell me and it couldn't wait."

Now was my chance. Should I fling open the curtain? Pull him in the shower with me and confess my love for him? I couldn't do that. What would he think of me?

"She's just trying to set us up," I replied. "She thinks she's clever." I grabbed the edge of the curtain.

"Oh, sorry! I should have figured that out. I'll be outside." Kaylin exited the bathroom.

Damn her. I was going to kill her for this. I let go of the curtain. It wasn't the right time. I heard him say something to Steph, but I couldn't make out what it was through the door. I lingered in the shower longer than I needed to. Standing under the water, letting it run down my face, helped me think clearly.

"Hurry up," Steph yelled through the door. "Everyone's ready to go."

"Fine," I yelled back. I shut the shower off and stepped out.

It didn't take me long to finish getting ready. I wore very little makeup—mascara and a little lip gloss was my everyday routine. My go to outfit was a pair of jean shorts and whatever cute tee I found in my bag that day. Most of the time I didn't even wear socks, just an old pair of converse that I refused to get rid of even though the tread was completely gone.

"Okay, let's go," I said, exiting the bathroom. Everyone was standing around the room, their backpacks packed and slung over their shoulders.

"About time, Cuz," Grant said, making his way to the door.

"I saved you a bagel and an apple juice." Kaylin held out my backpack. "I put them in your pack."

"Thank you." I finished putting the ponytail holder in my hair then grabbed the bag from him. We made our way through the hotel to the parking lot.

"I gave you the perfect moment," Steph whispered in my ear before she headed off to her vehicle.

"Yes, perfect," I replied sarcastically. "Remind me to return the favor someday."

"Can't say I didn't try," she hollered back, over her shoulder.

It took us twenty minutes to reach the Popham dig site. I stood at the edge of the embankment, taking in the vastness of the site. A large section of the earth at least a half a mile wide and approximately six feet deep, had been removed, revealing three partially intact buildings. The building farthest to the right had three of the outer walls remaining, as well as stone remnants of where the interior walls would have been. That must be the Admiral's house. The second building, almost directly across the dig site from where I stood, didn't have much more than a stone foundation left, and the third building farthest to the left had one partial wall, along with something that resembled the hearth to a fireplace protruding up from the ground. According to the map the second building would be the liquor storage, making the third the storehouse. The archaeologists had crafted a wood-planked stairway that led down the side of the steep hill to the bottom. We cautiously made our way down the stairs. Square plots of land dotted the floor of the dig site. They ranged in size from one foot by one foot to as large as ten feet by ten feet. Each plot marked in the corners with wooden stakes hammered into the ground. Every square carefully dug into the ground by an archeologist in search of artifacts. While I found it fascinating, our main focus was on the unearthed buildings, not the centuries old artifacts. The six of us fanned out over the site, peering momentarily into the missing plots of land as we made our way to the buildings.

"Split up into teams of two," Mr. Truedell said. "Each team focused on the areas of the buildings we showed you last night."

Kaylin made his way over beside me. Steph veered in Grant's direction. Kevin glanced around at the couples pairing up then reluctantly headed in Mr. Truedell's direction.

"Kevin and I will take the Admiral's house. Kaylin and Aurora you go to the storehouse. Steph and Grant you take the liquor storage.

Once you've located the tunnel entrances let everyone else know before heading in."

We did as he directed.

Grant and Steph were the first ones to find an entrance.

"We've found one," Grant announced. "We're going in."

"The tunnels connect. Once we've all made it inside, we should be able to meet up. Keep an eye out for the stone until then." Mr. Truedell informed everyone.

Kevin and Mr. Truedell were the next ones to find an entrance. "We're going in," they hollered.

"Okay, we suck," I said to Kaylin.

"We don't suck," he replied. "I wanted to have a few minutes alone with you so I haven't been looking that hard." He smiled at me as he strolled up beside me. "I'll look. After I do this!" He put his arms around my waist, manipulating my body closer to his and kissed me passionately. "I couldn't stop thinking about you last night," he said. "I almost returned to your room for more."

"I couldn't stop thinking about you, either," I said breathlessly. I kissed him again. "I wish you'd come back."

"Let's find this entrance so we can get the stone and go back to the hotel."

"While you were stalling I was actually searching but I haven't found anything."

"On the map the trap door in the floor was located somewhere to the right of the fireplace." Kaylin stepped over to the remnants of the stone hearth. He began stomping on the ground as he walked in tiny arcs, each one further away from the hearth than the first. "I think the ground sounds different here." He stomped harder where he stood. He dashed over to the corner of a plot and yanked out the wooden stake, then hurried back to the spot and, using a rock, began hammering the stake into the ground. The stake abruptly stopped about an inch and a half into the ground.

"Do you think you hit a rock?" I asked. I hovered over him.

"I don't think so." He tapped the stake with the rock. " Hear that?"

"I do. It sounds like it's echoing."

Kaylin pulled the stake up and used it to dig. I rushed over and grabbed another stake then knelt down beside him and scraped at the dirt.

"There's some wooden planks here," Kaylin said excitedly. He brushed the loose dirt away with his hand. "Continue to scrape this way along the board." He kicked a line on the ground. I dug at the earth while he pulled the loosened dirt away from the board. Then we did the same with the board next to it. In no time, we'd uncovered both boards. "That should be wide enough for us to fit through." He jammed his stake between two of the boards and began to pry the board up. The board creaked as the old, rusty nails loosened at the ends of the boards. "I've got it," Kaylin grunted.

Snap! The board sprang up. Kaylin fell backwards onto the ground. He dusted himself off and peered into the hole.

"We found the tunnel," he announced proudly. He clasped his fingers around the edge of the next board and pulled upward.

I slid in closer to him and grabbed the board. I pulled with all my strength. The second board cracked in half. Kaylin stood up and stomped down on the broken board sending the pieces down into the tunnel.

"Do you want to go first?" he asked, taking a headlamp out of his pack, and slipping it onto his head. He centered the light then flipped it on.

"Got anymore of those?"

"I thought you might like one." He fished a second one out of his pack. "Pretty cool, huh?"

"I don't need to go first. You can go." I said, pulling the light over my head.

"Okay." He sat at the edge of the hole, his feet dangling into the darkness.

"Shine your lamp in there for me would you?"

I stood across the hole from him and peeked in. The light from my headlamp illuminated his legs.

"A little more in the hole than on me please."

"Is that better?"

"Perfect." He slid himself into the hole, disappearing beneath the ground.

"Are you okay?" I hollered into the hole.

"Come down." His voice echoed out of the hole. I sat at the edge of the hole and dangled my feet in just as Kaylin had done.

I wished I were as brave as he was. Why did everything with the Amerii have to be underground? That's where the spiders and snakes lived. Something touched my legs, and I quickly jerked them out of the hole.

"It's just me," Kaylin said and laughed. "Who did you think it was?" I peered down into the hole to see Kaylin standing under me. "I'll catch you." He held his arms up.

I put my legs back in the hole and slid in. Kaylin's hands grabbed my waist as I dropped into the tunnel.

"Check it out," he said glancing around. His headlamp revealed bits of the tunnel as he spun his head.

We'd entered into a long section of the tunnel. It stretched farther than our headlamps were able to shine in each direction. I inspected the walls of the tunnel. It was in better condition than I'd expected. The walls and ceilings were constructed of stone reinforced by large wooden beams spaced out every six feet down the tunnel. There were a few spots here and there where a stone had come loose and fallen to the gravel floor, bringing a pile of dirt down with it, but over all the tunnel was still in good condition.

"Let's see if we can find the others." Kaylin said, retrieving the map that Mr. Truedell had sketched out for everyone.

"That way should lead to the Chapel." He stared down the tunnel behind me. "Ready?"

"As ready as I'll ever be," I replied. We headed off down the tunnel, the darkness always just ahead of us. We stopped at a cross section of the tunnel to examine the map.

"We keep going straight," Kaylin said.

"Wait! I hear something."

"I hear it, too. Kacaw," he called down the tunnel to our right.

"Kacaw," someone called back.

"It's Kevin and Mr. Truedell,"

"Kacaw? What's kacaw?" I asked. "I've heard of marco, polo, but never kacaw."

"It's how our mother would round us up when we were little," Kaylin explained. "When we were at the store and she couldn't find us she'd holler out kacaw."

"She did that in public?"

"Little Bro?" Kevin shouted out. He sounded unusually chipper. A beam of light bounced along the stone walls towards us. "There you guys are," Kevin said as he and Mr. Truedell approached us.

"Have you guys seen Steph and Grant?" I asked, stepping out of Kevin's blinding light. "I have a feeling that the two of them are fooling around somewhere and not searching for the chapel."

"We have not," replied Mr. Truedell in his usual respectable manner. "We best keep going." He said stepping down the tunnel to our left.

"We need to go this way." Kaylin gestured down straight ahead of us. Mr. Truedell stopped. Kaylin stepped over to him and showed him where we were on the map.

"I believe you're right," said Mr. Truedell. He adjusted his pack and led the way down the other tunnel.

"It looks like there's something blocking the tunnel up ahead," Kaylin said, a short way down the tunnel.

I peered around Kevin. The narrow tunnel was barely wide enough for two people to walk side by side. Kaylin and Kevin were shoulder to shoulder behind Mr. Truedell leaving me to bring up the rear.

"It's collapsed." Kaylin's head lamp shone from top to bottom, then bottom to top as he scanned the rubble.

"We can dig our way through it." Kevin climbed onto the pile.

"Get down from there," shouted Mr. Truedell. He stepped closer to Kevin and swatted at his pant leg. "You could cause the whole tunnel to collapse."

Kevin tugged on the debris, ignoring Mr. Truedell's warning. "It's fine." He reamed on a piece of broken beam. "You guy's worry for nothing." A trickle of sand poured from between two stones in the ceiling like an hourglass that had just been flipped over.

"You must stop," Mr. Truedell yelled. The trickle grew into a steady stream. "Stop now." A boulder the size of a watermelon fell from the ceiling where the stream of sand was pouring out and crashed to the ground. A cloud of dust bloomed into the air. Kevin fell backwards onto the pile of rubble. A second, slightly smaller bolder fell onto the pile next to Kevin. The dirt and stone slid out from under him.

"Kevin!" Kaylin shouted in fear. "Get out of there." He lurched forward to save his brother. Mr. Truedell caught Kaylin by the shoulder and dragged him backwards away from the collapsing section of tunnel.

I spun around and sprinted down the tunnel as fast as I could. The sound of splintering boards and crashing rocks chased me as I ran. A thick cloud of dust rushed ahead of me, filling the tunnel and making it impossible to see. I ran into something, someone, and they let out a painful scream. Steph! I reached out for her as our bodies collided, wrapping my arms around her and bringing her tumbling to the ground with me.

"The tunnels coming down," I shrieked. My mouth filled with the taste of dust. We scrambled to the closest wall.

Kaylin shouted Kevin's name from somewhere down the tunnel. Grant found Steph and me huddled together.

"What happened? Are you hurt? Where is everyone?" Grant rapidly fired off his questions. He cleared the dust from the air with his arms. "You guys okay?" He crouched down in front of us and placed one hand on my shoulder and one hand on Steph's.

"It's Kevin!" I coughed. "We're okay."

He glanced towards the cave in. He patted our shoulders then hurried down the tunnel towards Kaylin.

Steph and I separated. She found her flashlight that had been flung out of her hands when I ran into her and shone it down the tunnel. I sprung to my feet and went to find Kaylin. The tunnel was littered with debris. I carefully climbed over the fallen pieces of stone and wood as I made my way to where Grant, Kaylin, and Mr. Truedell were. The three huddled around Kevin.

"Is he okay?" asked Steph, coming up behind me.

I'd been too afraid to ask. I wasn't sure I wanted to know the answer. Grant gazed up at us.

"I'm fine," Kevin said from the center of the circle.

Oh thank goodness. I buckled over, placing my hands on my knees and let out a sigh of relief.

"He's lucky," Mr. Truedell said. He stood up from the huddle and stepped away.

I knelt down beside Kevin, in Mr. Truedell's place. Kevin's body was caked from head to toe with a thick layer of dust. The dust fluffed off of him, poofing into the air every time he moved. I inspected him thoroughly with my eyes. The small cuts on his arms didn't concern me but the blood on his chest inside one of the tears on his shirt did. I lifted his shirt.

"Does that hurt?" I pressed on his chest next to the cut. He winced in pain and pulled his shirt down.

"I'm going to take him up top," Grant said, helping Kevin to his feet. "You guys keep searching for the chapel."

"Thanks, man." Kevin leaned on Grant for support as he stepped over a fallen rock. He turned and glanced over his shoulder at me. Our eyes met. I'm okay, he mouthed to me.

I watched them navigate around the debris until they disappeared into the darkness of the tunnels then turned to the group and asked, "How are we supposed to find the chapel now? The tunnel's caved in."

"Lucky for us, there are multiple routes to and from each building." Mr. Truedell slid the map out of his pocket. "We'll have to take the long way around."

Kaylin and Mr. Truedell guided us through the maze of tunnels to the chapel entrance without any more complications.

"The chapel should be just on the other side of this door," declared Mr. Truedell coming to a stop.

"A door! How convenient." Steph flipped her hair over her shoulder. "How come we didn't have a tunnel door in our building?" she complained, bringing her hands to her hips.

"Aurora and I had to dig up a trap door in the floor and then drop into the tunnel through a narrow opening." Kaylin took off his pack and set it on the ground next to the door. "I don't know what you're complaining about."

"Your building didn't have a basement," replied Mr. Truedell. He joined Kaylin at the door. The two of them inspected the wall around the door for signs of structural integrity.

"Right, no basement," she responded to Mr. Truedell as she glared at Kaylin. "I guess that makes sense." Kaylin returned her glare with a smug grin. Steph turned to me. "I can't wait to get in there and find the Stone. Today is going to change our lives forever." She sounded relieved, as if she'd been waiting for this day to come.

"You're awfully excited about the stone," I said. If her interest in the stones was genuine, perhaps it would give her and Kaylin something to bond over.

"More than you know." She smiled and sauntered over to the door. "Shall we open it?" She tugged on the door handle.

"Wait," shouted Kaylin and Mr. Truedell. They put their hands up to stop her but it was too late. She'd already twisted the knob and pulled on the door.

I cringed, expecting the walls of the tunnel to come crashing down around us, but the door swung open easily. She turned and smiled then shrugged her shoulders and stepped inside. Kaylin shone his light into the damp room. I hurried over to the door and peered in. The room had been pristinely preserved, untouched all those many years by the elements. Not a speck of dust anywhere. We stepped through the door into the seventeenth century. Four large, gold crosses draped in sheer linens rested against the wall to our left. An assortment of chalices and other utensils used during services were neatly divided and placed on two tables opposite the door. An old, leather-bound bible, prominently displayed on an easel between the two tables, had been left open to Matthew 6:21. I strolled across the room to the bible. "For where your treasure is, there will your heart be also." I read the verse to myself.

"This is out of this world!" Steph said. She ran her fingers along one of the linens on the crosses before wandering over to a table and picking up an incense burner.

"More like out of this century," Kaylin corrected her.

"Are we in the chapel?" She leaned over and asked me.

"No," replied Kaylin as he passed by us, making a circle around the room. "We're under the church, in a cellar or a basement."

"What are we searching for?" Mr. Truedell asked. He'd made a beeline to the farthest right corner where a stack of books were piled on a shelf. He thumbed through the pages of the top book.

"We found the first stone in a locked chest, the second was hidden in a sculpture of a chalice, but both of those were hidden by Anna... Try to get in the head of Mr. Dupont," Kaylin said. He leaned over Mr. Trudell's shoulder and glanced at the page then continued on.

"I think this might be a clue," I said reading the bible verse to the others. It reminded me of the riddles Uncle Rob used to make for me and Grant to solve.

"If I were Mr. Dupont, where would my heart be?" asked Steph. She set down the incense burner and picked up a new object. "Who did he love?" She carelessly dropped the object back on the table and turned to me. I frowned and warned her to be more careful.

"He loved his parents," Kaylin answered for me. "That's why he hid it here." He scurried up behind Steph and picked up the object she'd dropped. She shot him a devious smile then sauntered over to the other table. He inspected the object then carefully put it back in its place on the table.

"I think it's more than that," I said, watching the two of them wage their silent war. "It's obvious he loved his parents. I think it's a deeper love."

Steph sighed. "Okay, was he married?" She rearranged the chalices on the table, then strolled over to the book shelf and watched with amusement as Kaylin hurried to put things back into place.

"I don't remember reading anything about a wife," Mr. Truedell said oblivious to their squabble.

I glared at Steph. "Stop it."

She laughed and shrugged her shoulders. "Maybe he loved Anne. Maybe he had a thing for her." She leaned against the wall. "He did hide the stone for her."

I turned back to the bible and read the passage aloud again. "For where your treasure is, there will your heart be also." I tapped my finger on the page as I thought. "He loved his country!" I blurted out. "Anna trusted him enough to hide the Dare Stone and John Hunt says he was a trusted friend to the Amerii in his journal. He must have been very loyal to his country. To be that loyal to something you have to love it. Even treasure it."

"He didn't love his country, he loved the Amerii," Steph said angrily. She pushed herself away from the wall. Her anger seemed sudden and out of place. "You're confusing the Amerii and America. It really gets me the way you guys go on and on about the Amerii."

"What's wrong with loving the Amerii?" I asked, turning in her direction. The light from my headlamp shone right into her eyes. Not everyone in this country was part of the Amerii. I would bet some people were even against the Amerii."

"Nothing if you're into brainwashing." Her tone grew more fierce. She held a hand up to shield her eyes from my light. Where was this sudden hatred towards the Amerii coming from?"Not everyone in this country was part of the Amerii. I would bet some people were even against the Amerii." She stepped out of my light.

"This isn't the time for arguing," Mr. Truedell said. He'd moved away from the books and was intently inspecting the objects on the table to my left. "Right now we need to find the stone. If you are not here to support the Amerii then leave. No one is stopping you."

"Believe me as soon as we find the stone I'm out of here." A spark flickered in her eyes before she turned away. What was she up to?

Kaylin had been considerably quiet for the last few minutes. I glanced around to see where he'd gotten off to. I found him crouched down in a corner sifting through a pile of old robes. I joined him.

"Did you find something?"

He shook his head no and tossed the robes back into a pile and asked, "What in this room represents country or the Amerii? It all looks like religious stuff to me."

"We have to remember this was before the Declaration of Independence was written, while the colonies were still under Great Britain's rule. Part of what the colonists were fighting for was the freedom of religion. The right to choose which religion they believed in or if they even believed at all. Freedom wasn't just about governing themselves, voting, taxation, property ownership, it was also about being able to decide for yourself what your beliefs were in all aspects of your life," said Mr.Truedell. He pointed around the room. "Look at this stuff. While this does appear to be a Catholic church, I'm sure what Mr. Dupont loved about his country, about the Amerii was that they gave him the right to choose his religion without persecution."

"I know where it is! It's in the Bible!" I ran over to the Bible. I carefully flipped through the pages. "Look!" I pointed to a section of the Bible that had been removed. Everyone stopped what they were doing and joined me. The stone lay inside the section.

"How did you know it was in the Bible?" asked Kaylin.

"Religion was where his heart was. What represents religion better than a Bible?"

Steph forcefully grabbed the stone out of the bible, not bothering to care if she destroyed the pages.

"Let me see that." Kaylin tried to snatch the stone out of her hands.

"I'm looking at it right now." Steph spun her body, making the stone impossible for Kaylin to grab out of her hands. She started heading back to the tunnel.

Kaylin chased after her pleading for her to give him the stone.

"You don't even know how to read the stone," he argued as he hurried out of the room. "I'm not one of your boy toys that will do anything you say, Steph. Now give me the stone."

Kaylin's backpack, with the other stones in it, caught my eye as Mr. Truedell and I exited the room. I couldn't believe he'd left it there. I grabbed it by the strap and hurried down the tunnel after them.

"I know more about the stone than you do," she hollered. "You don't even realize what you've done, do you?" She picked up her pace.

"What do you mean? What I've done!" Kaylin asked. Her statement stopped him dead in his tracks.

Steph took the opportunity to place the stone in her pack, then climbed out of the tunnel. Kaylin caught his breath. "Stop right now and give me the stone," he said. He lunged through the opening of the tunnel. His outstretched arm grazed her pant leg.

"You're not in charge anymore." Her words were cold. She kicked dirt at him as he pulled himself the rest of the way out of the tunnel. " I have the stones. I'm in charge now."

"You have one of the stones."

"Better check again."

I saw Kaylin reach for his backpack, forgetting he didn't have it on him from inside the tunnel. He looked back at the tunnel opening. "I will use force if I have to," he warned.

Steph laughed. "You and what army?" She turned and confidently walked off.

I squeezed through the opening of the tunnel just in time to see Kaylin spring forward. He grabbed ahold of her pack and yanked her backwards. She spun around, fist clenched and punched him hard in the jaw. He stumbled backwards dragging her along with him. The zipper on her pack split open. The stone, along with her belongings, spilled out onto the ground.

"What the hell, Steph," I shouted. Running to Kaylin's side.

She quickly grabbed the stone, leaving her pack and the rest of her things on the ground then ran towards the steps on the embankment. I glanced down at her stuff. A gold chain caught my eye. I bent over and slid it out from under her clothing. My necklace.

"You said you didn't know where this was," I shouted after her, holding the necklace up in the air.

She stopped running and spun around. She slowly walked back toward me, stopping a few feet from me.

"Why did you steal my necklace? My grandmother gave this to me." She knew what it meant to me.

"Do you have any idea how hard I've been working to stop all this from happening. To save you from making a huge mistake? I hoped it wouldn't come to this."

"Save me from what mistake?" I asked confused.

"The Amerii.... You guys came out here in search of these stones but do you have any idea what you're doing?" She shook her head. "I hoped you'd give up, That it wouldn't come to this, but you just kept going. Even after Peter ran you off the road. I mean take a hint." She stepped closer. "Your life was in danger Aurora." She paused and stared compassionately into my eyes. Her tone softened. "Most people would stop doing what they were doing once the security of their life was put in danger." She sighed. "But not you. Oh no, you just kept searching for your precious stones." She shook her head in disbelief. "It's really not that hard to figure out." Her face twisted into a smirk. I didn't recognize the face of my best friend anymore. Where had she gone?

"You know who ran us off the road?" I asked, closing the gap between us.

"Know him? Yes, I know him. Hell, I'm the one who told him to do it," she said with no remorse.

"You told someone to try to kill me?" I felt the rage boil over inside of me. Who was this person standing in front of me? The Steph I knew wouldn't send someone to kill me. Had she lost her mind?

"Peter, come on out," Steph shouted over her left shoulder. "You think your man is hot? Wait until you see mine," she bragged.

That confirmed it, she had lost her mind. I scanned the dig site. It dawned on me that Kevin and Grant should be nearby. Where were they? "I don't care about what the guy looks like." I told her. "Why would you brag about him right now?"

"You can't always have the best of everything, Aurora," she said, then spewed a line of hurtful insults at me. "Get out here, Peter," she yelled impatiently once she'd finished belittling me.

"Keep moving," a man growled. I turned to see who it was. Kevin and Grant stepped out from behind the wall of the Admiral's house, their hands bound together behind their backs. A man, not much older than me, rounded the corner behind them, holding a gun against the back of Grant's head.

"Run, Aurora," Grant's voice trembled.

The man shoved him forward with the barrel of his gun. "Don't think about it." he warned.

"Grant!" I shouted and took three steps in his direction.

"I'm okay," he said. His words didn't offer me any reassurance. The man maneuvered Grant and Kevin forward with the threat of his gun until they were standing next to Steph.

Kaylin, who'd been at my side the whole time I'd been arguing with Steph, stepped out in front of me. He clenched and unclenched his fists in preparation for the fight of his life.

"Hey, babe," said the man. He leaned over and kissed her cheek. His gun pulled slightly away from Grant's head. Grant twisted but the man caught him before he could escape.

"Pay attention, Peter." Steph rolled her eyes. "Did you have any problems getting their stuff from the hotel?"

"Nope the key cards worked just like you said they would. I loaded everything into the back of your Explorer."

"You took my key card. I didn't lose it." I began to put the puzzle pieces together in my head. "I can't believe I never saw you for who you are." I stepped out from behind Kaylin. The anger inside me had built up to the point that I could no longer contain it. "Why are you doing this to me?" I lurched forward after Steph. Kaylin caught me by the arm and held me back. I wanted to make her hurt. To feel the pain I felt.

"You still don't get it." She shook her head. "I will use small words so you can understand. The Amerii stole my family's rights. Took everything from us. We were forced to live like dogs." She grabbed the gun out of Peter's hand and pointed the barrel at me. I stepped back. Kaylin grabbed my hand. He motioned to Kevin and Grant to hold their places. Steph was unstable. There was no telling what she'd do. "What do you think happened to those families loyal to the crown? Huh? We were royalty before we came to the New World. Had money, power, prestige, and the Amerii took that all away. Equal rights for everyone, they said." She laughed. "My family worked hard to get where they were and now...we're nothing. We're the same as everyone else." She waved the gun around. "We stopped the Amerii once. I'm not about to let them rise again." She stood perfectly still, both arms stretched out in front of her. Her hands firm around the grip of the gun. "Bang." She pretended to pull the trigger. I stood strong without flinching. She stared into my eyes. "I wouldn't waste a bullet on an Amerii scum like you." She handed the gun back to Peter.

Kaylin squeezed my hand "Keep her talking, we have a plan," he whispered in my ear. His facial expressions communicating nonverbally with Kevin.

"How could you give up our friendship just like that?" I asked her. Not just to keep her busy but because I really did want to know the answer. From the corner of my eye, I saw Mr. Truedell sneak up behind Peter.

"We were never friends."

Never friends? What about all those hours we spent chatting on the phone? All the sleep overs? All the laughs?

"My family has been watching the Amerii for centuries. I was sent to watch you," she said with no remorse, no sadness, no feeling whatsoever. I kept my focus on her so as not to betray Mr. Truedell's whereabouts. He was seconds away from grabbing the gun.

"It was all a lie?" I hunched over and glanced down at the ground. "The last three years have been a total lie." I muttered to myself. I straightened my back and took a single step toward her. "What kind of person could pretend to be someone's friend for three years?" How could I have been so ignorant? My stomach churned. I swallowed hard in order to keep from vomiting.

"Now!" shouted Kaylin. He lunged forward, knocking Steph to the ground. She fought him off of her, scrambling to her feet. Kaylin swung his leg around, tripping her and sending her flailing forward helplessly. Her body smashed into the hard dirt. She rolled onto her side in an attempt to escape. Kaylin leapt forward, coming down on her body with all of his weight. She let out an agonizing scream. At the same time Mr. Truedell wrestled the gun out of Peter's hand. Peter spun around, fist clenched and swung at Mr. Truedell. He missed. Mr. Truedell's didn't miss. His fist connected with Peter's gut. Peter grabbed his stomach and stumbled backwards. He quickly recovered, resuming his stance and charged at Mr. Truedell. A shot rang out. Who was hit? Grant and Kevin dropped to the ground on their knees. Both of them fell forward, their hands still bound behind their backs as they landed face first in the dirt. I spun around. Was anyone hurt? Mr. Truedell and I were the only ones standing. It all happened so fast. I ran over to Grant. Grant rolled onto his side. He's all right. I turned to Kevin. He was trying to push himself up onto his knees. They are both all right. I looked to Mr. Truedell for answers. Peter lay, crumpled over, on the ground at his feet. A small pool of blood formed around him.

"Did you?" I asked horrified.

"Yes." Mr. Truedell stepped away from Peter's body. He helped Grant and Kevin get to their feet. He then took out a knife and cut their bonds. Kaylin had Stephanie pinned to the ground, face down in the dirt, his knee placed firmly between her shoulder blades.

"She's a bitch, Rory! Just like I said." Kaylin stared at me. "What do we do with her?" he asked Mr. Truedell. She squirmed angrily under his leg.

"Hang her," Grant said with no affection towards her. He kicked dirt in her face. She spit at his shoes.

"We can't kill her—" I yelled. She may very well be a sociopath but I couldn't just forget the last few years like that. It had been real to me.

"I know you think she was your friend, Rory, but we have to do something with her. She did try to kill us," Kaylin said.

"Twice," Kevin said. "Well, three times if you count locking us in the Amerii town.... But she did also rescue us, so." He shrugged his shoulders. "That one might even out."

"Only because she needed us to finish finding the stones," Grant said, not taking his eyes off of her. He spit back at her.

"We'll take her back with us to your father's house." Truedell circled around Grant and knelt down beside Stephanie. "You will hold a trial and sentence her according to Amerii law." Truedell bound Stephanie's hands behind her back.

"I'll hold a trial?" Kaylin said, moving his knee off her back.

"You all will," Truedell replied. "You are the new leaders of the Amerii." He lifted Stephanie to her feet and struggled with her as he led her towards the stairs out of the dig site. The four of us stared at each other with a puzzled expression. Leaders of the Ammerri? What is he talking about? How are we the new leaders of the Amerii?

"Hold up!" Kaylin jogged off to catch up with Truedell. He grabbed Truedell's shoulder to stop him from walking any further. "What do you mean we're the leaders?"

Truedell paused for a moment. "Everything will be explained when we get back to Stony Creek." Stephanie fought him. He pushed her to the ground. "Gather up all of your stuff. Don't leave any trace we've been here." She tried to crawl away. He pushed her again, toying with her like a cat plays with the mouse just before it eats it.

"What about the body?" Kaylin asked, stepping after them.

"His name is Peter," Stephanie said.

Truedell lifted her off the ground, shook her and said in a deep voice, "You don't have a voice anymore."

"What should we do with him?" Kaylin asked again standing between Truedell and the stairs. He purposely didn't use Peters name to further anger Stephanie.

"Check his pockets. Make sure he doesn't have anything of the Amerii's, then dump him in the tunnel." He shoved Stephanie around Kaylin and led her up the stairs to the vehicles.

I packed Stephanie's clothes back in her pack, while Kevin and Grant dragged Peter over to one of the tunnel entrances. Kevin knelt down and shoved his hands into Peter's pockets then stood and with his foot pushed him in. They filled the hole in with dirt while Kaylin and I searched the dig site for anything we may have left behind.

"I don't like this," I said to Kaylin as the four of us met up. "We killed that guy."

"Me either." His face was somber as we climbed the stairs.

"Did you find a set of keys?" asked Truedell when we joined him. He held Stephane between his body and his truck. "We need to get rid of this guy's car."

"Yes." Grant guided a keychain out of his pocket. He held the keys in the air.

"We'll drive the car back to Stony Creek and find someone to dispose of it there. Grant, you drive the car, Kaylin, you and Aurora take the Explorer. Kevin, I'd like your help in transporting the prisoner back in my truck."

Chapter 13

Homecoming

"Looks like we don't need to go back to the hotel," Kaylin said lifting the back hatch of the Explorer. "He really did load everything into the back here." He opened his bag and rummaged through his belongings to see if anything was missing. "Even the little hotel shampoo bottles and bars of soap are in there." He zipped his bag and tossed towards the back of the seat.

"What were you guys planning to do once you got the stones?" Grant got in Stephanie's face. "Kill all of us?" he yelled. Hatred flickered in his eyes. Truedell pulled her away from the side of the truck. He opened the door. Kevin tilted the seat forward for him. He shoved her forcefully into the backseat. "Grab the rope from the bed of the truck," he told Kevin. Then bound her feet with it when Kevin returned.

"I'd like to see you try and run now," Grant said, spit flying from his lips.

Kevin shoved the seat back into place and hopped in.

"Get in the car, Grant. We will interrogate her back at your house," said Truedell. Grant stepped aside to allow him by. Kevin yanked the door shut. "Now," Truedell insisted as he walked around the truck to the drivers side. Grant glared in the window at Stephanie. Stephanie turned her face from him. Kevin nodded towards Peter's car. Grant gave in and stomped angrily to the car. He flopped into the driver's seat, closed the door behind him and stared out the windshield to avoid making eye contact with the rest of us. Kaylin closed the hatch to the Explorer, then hurried up into the driver's seat. I watched in disbelief as Truedell closed his door and started the engine. How had we gotten here?

"Rory, get in the car." Kaylin leaned over into the passenger seat trying to get my attention. He knocked on the inside of the window. "Come on." He patted the seat. I opened the passenger side door. "I know it probably doesn't seem like it now, but you're better off without her," he said as I sat down. I glanced over at her one last time, then buckled my seatbelt and closed the door.

"What am I going to do now?" I asked him. The reality of my uncertain future setting in. "We had plans together."

"College?" He asked as he fiddled with Stephanie's cluttered keychain. He found the engine key and placed it in the ignition.

"And other things. She was going to design clothing and I was going to write about her styles at Vogue." I tried to keep the tears from rolling down my cheeks. I cleared the lump in my throat. "Now what am I going to do?"

"You can still write for Vogue." He wiped my cheek with the back of his hand. "You don't need her." He gazed softly into my eyes. "I don't like to see you so sad."

"You'd better go." I pointed to Truedells truck as it pulled out of sight.

"I know where they're going." He placed his hand on my thigh. "I don't need to follow. Right now, I'm worried about you."

"I will be fine," I lied. I pushed his hand away and I stared out the window. "There goes Grant." Kaylin stared at me. His eyes filled with concern as he turned the key in the ignition. I did my best to ignore him. He placed the Explorer in drive and rolled away from the dig site.

"Who's going to be there for me when I do something stupid?" I sobbed. We hadn't even driven a quarter mile down the road.

"Rory, you don't do stupid things." He pressed on the brake and veered to the side of the road. " I knew you weren't all right."

"No keep going."

He jerked the Explorer back on the road. The person in the car behind us honked his horn. Kaylin checked the rearview mirror as he tried to console me.

"Look at all the stuff you've done this summer." He patted my arm. "You didn't need her for any of it."

"Really?" I said sarcastically. I touched my arm where he'd patted it. "I seem to remember having to call her after I saw Truedell spying on me in the hot tub and I needed someone to talk to."

"You have me to call now." I glanced up at him through my tears. He smiled. "I'm here for you, Rory. I always will be." His offer was caring and sincere.

"I know you are." I found a kleenex in the glovebox and dabbed the end of my nose. "Can we talk about this later?" I crumpled the tissue up and held it in the palm of my hand. "I'd like to just listen to the radio for a while." I laid my head back on the seat. My eyes were puffy and sore from crying.

"Sure." He touched my leg before turning the music up. I let the songs wash over me. I hoped they would erase the last twenty-four hours from my mind. That their rhythms would pound away at the sadness inside me and leave me numb.

The sun had faded behind the mountains several hours before, taking with it today's horrific events and we were approaching DC when Kaylin finally spoke again.

"Are you feeling any better?" he asked, turning the music down.

"Better," I replied.

"Only a few more hours to go. Then we will be back in Stony Creek." He said excitedly. "Ah! Kentucky!" He pointed to the illuminated license plate on the car in front of us. His excitement faded when I didn't respond. "Sorry, I was just trying to lighten the mood."

I closed my eyes. I didn't want to think about Stony Creek. Being back there meant the summer was ending.

"Rory, you better take a peek at this." I opened my eyes. The morning sun streaming in the windows stung my eyes. How long had I been asleep? I felt a string of drool dripping from my chin. "Uh," I muttered in disgust. I searched my seat for the tissue I'd held in my hand earlier.

"Look at what?" I wiped my chin then tucked the tissue into a cup holder.

"Look!" He pointed out the passenger window, his arm bobbed in front of me as we bumped along on the familiar dirt road. I turned my attention in the direction he pointed, gazing out over the field. There were no more daisies or black-eyed susans left. Not even the empty green stems from summer were visible anymore. The field was alive with color but not from the flowers like it should've been. I blinked, making sure the rainbow of campers and tents scattered about were real and not a hallucination. I gazed out my window in bewilderment at all the people. They stood around their campfires, cooking breakfast as the children climbed in the trees and played games with each other. I rolled my window down and stuck my head out of the car. I still couldn't believe what I was seeing.

"They're back!" one man exclaimed. He dropped the carton of milk in his hands onto the ground.

The woman sitting next to him in a lawn chair, with a baby on her lap, turned to see what he was talking about. She quickly stood up, holding the baby close to her chest, while she ran to the nearest camper and began pounding on the door. A man burst out of the camper, followed by a teenage boy, both of them ran to the nearest tent or camper, spreading the news to everyone they passed on the way. Each time sending the person receiving the news running off in a different direction. A roar of voices burst out over the field. I quickly shut my window and slid down in my seat.

I turned to Kaylin. "What's going on?" I asked him. "Why are all these people here?"

"I have no idea." Kaylin slumped down behind the steering wheel.

The people began to line up along the edges of the drive. Kaylin slowed down to avoid hitting anyone. A few of the men were down on one knee with their heads bowed. The women curtsied and waved as we drove by and the children bounced around pointing at the vehicle. Clumps of people sprouted up like crabgrass, eager to take over the driveway in front of the house. I glanced up to the front porch. Mom!

"My mom and dad are here!"

They stood beside my aunt and uncle on the porch. Grant's brothers, Danny, Robert and Christopher were also there as well as some other people I didn't recognize.

"So are mine," Kaylin said. "Up there, on the porch." He pointed.

"That's your mom and dad up there?"

"Yep."

Our families started to make their way down the steps. They greeted the smaller clumps of people with hand shakes and waved to the larger crowd continuing to spread across the field towards the house. Kaylin pulled up behind Truedell and shut off the engine.

"Should we get out?" Kaylin asked as I placed my hand on the door handle. I let go of the handle and shrugged.

Truedell wrestled with Stephanie, trying to get her to come willingly out of the backseat of his truck. Kevin made his way to the Explorer. He knocked on Kaylin's window.

"What's going on?" Kaylin asked, rolling down the window. Kevin leaned forward and stuck his head in.

"They're here for us," he said. "I guess we're some sort of big deal." He turned to the crowd and threw up his arms. The people burst into cheers. "See," he said, turning back to face us.

Grant pulled up behind us and hesitantly got out of the car. I opened my door. My mom and dad pushed their way through the crowd, greeting me with open arms once they'd gotten to me.

"We're so proud of you, honey," my mom said. She squeezed her arms tight around me.

"You did good, kid." My dad rubbed my head.

"What's going on?" I asked, turning out of the hug to see the crowd but keeping one arm wrapped around my mother's waist.

"We'll explain inside," Dad said. He put his arm around me and him and my mom led me through the crowd. People reached their hands out to touch me as I walked past them.

At the top of the stairs, I turned to see if Kaylin was behind us. My eyes fluttered from face to face seeking his, but I couldn't find him anywhere.

"Wait, Kaylin!" I shouted over the noise of the crowd.

"He'll be okay," said my mother, tightening her arm around me. "We need to get you inside."

Without warning, the crowds rejoicing cheers turned to hateful threats.

"Kill her," a man shouted.

"Traitor," yelled another.

I quickly located Truedell. The crowd had shifted their focus from me, solely on him and the prisoner he was escorting. They moved together as one big unit, as if a strong wind had uprooted all of them and blown them towards Truedell. He stood in the center of them, holding Stephanie tightly with one arm, while trying to control the pressing crowd with the other. My father forced me through the front door into the house. I rushed to the window.

"They're going to kill her!" I said, terrified that they actually might.

Uncle Rob and Aunt Theresa burst through the door with Grant between them. His older brothers close behind them.

I ran to Grant. "Where's Kaylin?"

"He and Kevin are trying to help Truedell."

I ran back to the window to see the three of them trying desperately to hold back the mob of angry people.

"Someone's got to do something. They need our help." I stared at Grant, my eyes pleaded for him help.

"What can we do?" he asked. "There's hundreds of them."

"I have an idea. Follow me." I ran to the front door. The front porch was empty. No one there to try and shake my hand or touch me as I passed by. Their hatred for Stephanie had made them forget about Grant and me. I ran to the neatly wound up garden hose at the edge of the porch and took it in my hands. "Turn the water on," I told Grant. I waited for the water to build up pressure in the hose before twisting the nozzle attached to the end and aiming the steam of water into the crowd. The cold water got their attention. They spun around to see where it was coming from. Some of them retreated but others held their ground. "Grant, it's not working," I hollered over my shoulder.

Grant ran into the house then returned a moment later with a shotgun. He fired into the air. People gasped. "Come on," I shouted, still spraying anyone who got near me with cold water as I slowly backed through the crowd. Stephanie, aware of the danger she was in, gave no resistance and allowed Truedell to quickly lead her through the crowd with Kevin and Kaylin on their heels.

"I can't believe it worked," said Grant. He slammed the door closed behind us. "That things so old I didn't think it would fire." He hung the civil war-era shotgun back in its display on the wall.

"Where would you like me to put her?" Truedell asked Uncle Rob. He swung Stephanie around in front of him.

"Follow me," he replied. Uncle Rob and Truedell guided Stephanie out across the room.

Safe inside the house, behind locked doors, away from the threat of the crowd, Stephanie's desire to escape had returned. She twisted her body, kicking Uncle Rob in the shin. Truedell threw her against the wall, his forearm pressed firmly across her chest. Stephanie smiled a devilish smile at me, ignoring what was happening to her, her eyes penetrating me. I got the feeling she wanted me to watch them hurting her. That she somehow liked it. Uncle Rob pulled Truedell off of Stephanie and the two of them hauled her out of the room. I continued staring blankly down the hallway, long after they disappeared out of view.

"Let me get you boys a towel," Aunt Theresa said. She sauntered away, impeding my view of the empty hallway and bringing me back to reality.

I turned around. In my attempt to free them from the crowds grasp I had accidentally soaked them. "Sorry about that." I apologized. They shrugged and tried to convince me it was nothing.

"Here you boys go." Aunt Theresa returned with the towels.

"Where did all these people come from?" Kaylin asked. He patted his face with the towel.

"All over the country. They wanted to see if the rumors were true," Dad said. Kaylin dried his hands off then extended one to my dad. "It's nice to meet you, Mr. VanAgteren. I'm Kaylin."

My dad accepted Kaylin's hand. "Nice to meet you too, Kaylin. You can call me Bill. This is my wife Alice." My mom stepped away from the window and joined my dad.

"Thank you for keeping my daughter safe," she said, touching his arm. Kaylin nodded.

"Aurora." Kaylin turned to me. "I would like you to meet my mom and dad." I was terrible with introductions. They made me feel incredibly uncomfortable. "Aurora this is my mom Cindy and my step dad Jack." I shook both of their hands. "And this is my dad Travis." Before I could I could extend my hand out Travis wrapped his arms around me embracing me in a big hug. "Dad!" Kaylin said, blushing a little. "My dad's a hugger." He glared at his dad. "Okay now that the introductions are out of the way, you were saying something about rumors, Mr.—um, Bill?" Kaylin focused his attention back on my dad. "What rumors?"

Before my dad had a chance to answer there was a knock on the door. Aunt Theresa peered out the window. "Oh, It's just Mr. Witherson." She wandered over to the door and unlocked it. Mr. Witherson hobbled through the front door.

"I knew it!" he exclaimed, making a beeline straight to me. "I knew the day you stopped and asked me for directions. Your aunt and uncle didn't believe me but I knew you were the one." He put his hands on my face and gently kissing my forehead, then got down on one shaking knee in front of me.

"What's he talking about?" I scanned the room for answers.

"The rising of the Amerii, child," Mr. Witherson said, trying to get back up. Kaylin offered him a hand. "I knew you would be the one." He said, steadying himself.

"You silly old fool! You didn't know anything," said Aunt Theresa. She took his arm and led him to a chair. The very same one I'd sat on waiting for Kaylin to take me on our first date. So much had happened since then.

"I did so," he argued. "My pansies told me so. They started growing the day I met you, Aurora, and haven't stopped since." He patted the arm of the chair with his fist. "They're the most beautiful pansies

I've ever grown." He leaned forward and held up a bony finger. "It's a sign."

"Could someone please explain to me what's going on around here?" I asked again. Mr. Witherson's crazy explanation only confused me more.

"Why don't you have a seat, Aurora?" Uncle Rob said, coming back into the room.

"Where's Truedell?" I asked. I'd expected to see Truedell return with him.

"He's guarding the prisoner," Rob said, his eyes full of sympathy. "I don't think we're going to be able to convince your friend the Amerii weren't the bad guys. Her parents have her brainwashed." He shook his head in disbelief then glanced at me. "I'm sorry." Then he turned to the boys and said, "All of you should have a seat." The four of us did as he requested. Grant, Kaylin, and I settled down on the couch, while Kevin nestled into a chair to our left. The rest of our families situated themselves around the room. Everyone stared at Uncle Rob, eagerly awaiting an explanation.

"I'm going to tell you a story, when I finish I will answer any questions you have," he said. "Before this country became the United States of America, before the Constitution was signed, before we declared our independence from Britain, your ancestors founded a secret society called the Amerii—"

"We know about the Amerii," Grant said impatiently. "We want to know what happens now."

"Please just let me tell the story, Grant," Uncle Rob continued. "The Amerii were made up of thirteen men and thirteen women from all over the globe. Most of the members came here to the New World to escape the hardship and oppression in their countries. They were in search of a place where all men were created equal, not just the wealthy or the over privileged. Only to find the conditions here to be worse than where they had fled from. Hundreds of miles across the ocean, Queen Elizabeth had made promises to the settlers of the New World. She encouraged them to come, spinning wild tales of opportunity and freedom. But she was unable to keep those promises forever and after her death in 1603 her successors forgot about the Queen's promises to her people. By the time the Mayflower set sail in 1620 under the rule of King James the first, the New World was looked at only as a way for Great Britain to expand its territory. The settlers were just pawns in King James's plans.

The Amerii had grown stronger by this time. The members reached into the upper hundreds. They carefully set a plan into motion. A plan that would enable them to take back the rights they'd been promised. They spread out, implanting themselves amongst the settlers of the newly forming colonies along the coastline and began to recruit new members. They took on positions of power, becoming leaders or men of importance in each of the settlements. They taught their children the ways of the Amerii to ensure that the Amerii legacy would continue on long after they'd passed away. By 1690, the Amerii had been instrumental in shaping the New World. Of course as with any organization there's always going to be those that oppose. Those who were still loyal to the British crown plotted to eliminate the Amerii, coming up with ridiculous accusations of witchcraft. Scaring the people of the colonies into believing there were supernatural forces at work. The loyalist to the crown frightened the settlers so far past the point of logic that when mass executions were suggested it seemed to the settlers that it was the only way they could be safe. They agreed. The witches must burn. Thus creating an opportunity for those loyal to the crown a way to destroy the Amerii in full view of the colonists under false pretense. While their attempts were unsuccessful in completely eliminating the Amerii, their attacks did weaken the Amerii's numbers. These British loyalists became known as the George Party.

The Amerii rebuilt their numbers and eventually succeeded. America became an independent nation and in 1776 they wrote the Declaration of Independence. The George Party didn't relent, even though the Amerii had accomplished what it set out to do. They continued their efforts to destroy the Amerii, eventually succeeding when Booth, a loyalist to the George Party, assassinated Abraham Lincoln in 1865. With no one left willing to lead the Amerii, the secret society eventually dissolved and the remaining Amerii members wandered aimlessly through time, hoping they would be alive to see the next Amerii leaders be revealed. It's been prophesied that the sons and daughters of the original Amerii founders would rise again. When the country needed them the most, They would reveal themselves and take their rightful place as Amerii leaders. They would restore uphold the Amerii beliefs and make America the nation it once was." He paused and peered over to the window then back to us. "The people out there in the yard. They believe you're their new leaders." He exchanged glances with my dad then nodded at Travis, Kaylin's dad.

"How did they know what we were doing?" I asked.

"News this fantastic travels fast," Mr. Witherson said.

"Especially when there's gossip in town," Uncle Rob said, looking at us, but his comment was meant for Mr. Witherson. "You guys weren't as sneaky as you thought you were. Your aunt and I had a feeling you were up to something. At first we thought you guys were sneaking off to smoke a joint or whatever it is you kids do these days. Vaping? Is that what you call it?" He waited for one of us to respond. We stared at each other.

"Yes, that's what it's called," I finally answered. "But none of us do that."

"Right. Anyway, when I caught you acting strange in the hallway that day, Aurora, I realized it was something more, so I started following you." He grinned from ear to ear. "I couldn't believe my eyes when I saw you open the hidden door. Your grandma always said our ancestors had hidden Amerii secrets in this house." He let out an envious laugh. "She said if I was worthy of leading the Amerii I'd find them." He glanced down at the floor. "I searched this place from top to bottom with no luck. Of course I was looking for something smaller. Like a hidden meaning in one of the paintings or an inscription on a plaque. " He shrugged and glanced back at us. "I never dreamed it would be an entire room of secrets." He slapped his knee. "How on earth did you guys find it so easily?"

"It wasn't easy," said Grant.

"The roof," I said. "I noticed something about the towers didn't add up. So one night we went looking. We couldn't figure out how to get into the second tower from the inside of the house so we climbed the roof and got in from the outside."

"Genius!" he shook his head in disbelief. "All this time I should've been thinking bigger?" he said.

"Do you think grandma knew of the Amerii room?" asked Grant's brother Robert.

"You know, I think she did." Uncle Rob turned to Robert. "I remember hearing the strangest noises coming from inside the walls at night."

"So you caught us. Then what?" asked Kaylin, bringing the conversation back to us.

"Oh! Okay, after I saw where you guys were sneaking off to, I called your father." He motioned to me. "We knew we wouldn't be able to talk you out of going on your little adventure, but we wanted to make sure nothing bad would happen to you, so we called Mr. Truedell to keep an eye on you. It's a good thing we did, too. You all look like you've been through a tornado."

I peered over at boys. He was right, the boys were a mess, the last two weeks had been like going through a tornado. I could only imagine what I must look like.

"Mr. Truedell kept us updated on your progress. He let us know when you found the stones as well as if you were eating and sleeping, that sort of thing." Uncle Rob added. "Your mom was in a panic when we heard about the accident." He smiled at Aunt Theresa. I glanced over at my mom. She smiled, causing me to wiggle in my seat. I could tell she wanted to wrap me in her arms.

"When did all these people start showing up though?" asked Kevin.

"The day after you guys left," Aunt Theresa said. "The first camper arrived around noon. It's been a steady stream after that. More and more people just started arriving each day. They pitched their tents wherever, building campfires in my daisy field. Each day I would get up and gaze out the window to find the crowd had grown. On the third day, I called your parents, Kevin...and I called your brothers home, Grant. Bill and Alice were already on their way here, but that wasn't going to be enough. I needed more help with all these people."

"They stopped living their lives just to see us return?" I asked.

"Yes," she replied. She raised her eyebrows and took a deep breath. "They've also been bringing gifts for you."

"What kind of gifts?" asked Grant.

"Money, mostly. Some of them have also expressed their interest in becoming part of the council." She wandered over to the end table and pulled a notepad out of the drawer and handed it to me. "I have been compiling a list of names for you to go over if you accept the position." She directed her attention to Kaylin and me. "You and Kaylin will be the new leaders of the Amerii," she announced.

"Hey, what about us?" asked Grant. He stood up and looked over at Kevin. "We helped, too."

"It will be Aurora and Kaylin's decision to place you in the council position they feel is right for you." Aunt Theresa's answer didn't make Grant very happy. He stared blankly into her eyes. "There will be a ceremony held tonight to inaugurate our new leaders," she said then did the strangest thing. She bowed. It made me feel awkward. I scanned the room for some sort of normalcy but everyone was bowing, even my parents. In a few short weeks, I had gone from plain old Aurora to the leader of the Amerii. Kaylin stood up. He turned and offered me his hand. I took it and pulled myself up into a stand next to him.

"We need to talk about this," he said to everyone. "Please excuse us." He led me upstairs. I peered over my shoulder as we left the room. They were all still bowing.

Chapter 14

Leaders
of the
Amerii

"This is crazy! Did you see everyone bowing to us down there?" I asked, pushing the wall closed behind me.

"I think we should do it," Kaylin said with a serious expression on his face.

"You want to be the leader of the Amerii?" I aimlessly wandered around the room, imagining what my life might look like if I accepted the position.

"Why not? I'd already planned to take a year and learn more about the Amerii. What better way than as their leader?" he said, crossing his arms and sitting down on the edge of the table.

"What about Penn State?" I stopped walking and pivoted on my heels. "Should I just give up on being an editor?" I waited for an answer.

"No. Never give up on your dreams." He frowned and shook his head. "I would never ask you to do that." He stepped beside me and took my hands into his. "But do you really want to go to Penn State after what happened with Steph?"

I had asked myself that very question multiple times on our ride home.

"No, not really. It was our dream to go together. Or well, it was my dream. She may have been pretending the whole time. I don't know.

Maybe she doesn't even like fashion. Maybe everything she said was a lie." I cut myself off. The anger threatened to bubble up inside me again. I had a decision to make and getting worked up over Stephanie wasn't going to help me make it.

"Okay so why not be the leader?" He raised his eyebrows and grinned. His eyes sparkled.

I slipped my hands from his and stepped away. "What about us? What if it changes us, our relationship?"

"What about us?" He returned to the table and pretended to flip through a book. "Is there some rule that the leaders can't date?"

"How would I know? You're the Amerii expert. Is there?" I nervously laughed.

"No...in fact most of the former Amerii leaders were married to each other." Kaylin shut the book and stared at me. The expression on his face reminded me of the day he'd asked me to the picnic in the park celebration.

"Married!" My eyes bugged out of my head. I recalled the dream I'd had after our rendezvous in the hotel hallway. My cheeks felt hot. I still hadn't told him I loved him.

"I'm not suggesting we get married," Kaylin quickly said, noticing my embarrassment.

"No!" I held up my hand. "I don't want to marry you," I said quickly, not wanting him to misinterpret my expression. I got the feeling he thought I wanted to marry him. At least I didn't think I wanted to marry him.

"Okay, a little harsh don't you think." Kaylin hid his disappointment of my blunt reaction.

"No, that's not what I meant either." I stepped towards him.

"So you do want to marry me?"

"Maybe, someday." I turned my attention away from him. "This is getting all messed up," I explained. I rested my hands on my hips. "I didn't mean to hurt your feelings." I looked at him squarely.

"Let's forget I mentioned it," he said, waving his hand in the air.

"I'm sorry." I tilted my head to the side and lifted my shoulder. "I think we should take things one step at a time." I kicked the dust on the floor. "First, we need to figure out if we're going to accept the positions as leaders then let's start with a second date."

"I'm going to accept." He crossed his arms and stared at me. "I don't need to think about it. It feels right to me." He waited for my reply.

"Well I'm not like you. I need some time to think about it." I opened the door and stepped out into the hallway. "I can't just make a decision that fast." I left him standing in the room.

How could anyone make a life changing decision that fast? I slipped into my room, closing the door tightly behind me, and sat down on my bed to mull it over. That's when I saw the picture of Stephanie and me on the bedside table. I grabbed the picture and threw it as hard as I could across the room. The picture hit the wall with a loud thud. Shards of glass flung in all directions. I buried my face in my pillow and sobbed. How could she have lied to me for all those years? A lump grew in my throat. I tried swallowing, but I couldn't. The tears poured from my eyes, soaking the pillowcase. I could hold back the pain any longer. I gripped my pillow tightly in my fists and allowed the sadness to pour out.

"Honey, can I come in?" My mom poked her head in the door. "Are you all right, honey?" She sat down next to me on the bed and gently stroked my back like she had when I was a little girl. "I know this is a lot to take in," she said, comforting me.

I lifted my head from the pillow, wiped the tears from my eyes, and cleared my throat but kept my gaze distant. "Why didn't you and Dad tell me about the Amerii?" I asked, not ready to face her.

"We didn't want you to get caught up in it." She sighed. "Your Uncle Rob has spent his whole life doing what he thinks the Amerii would want him to do." She pulled me into her arms and stroked my hair. "He even tried training you and his boys to be ready if the Amerii should ever call on you." She stopped stroking my hair and lifted my head. Do you remember all those riddles he used to make you solve as a child?" I nodded. "They were to prepare you for the day the Amerii would rise again." She laid my head back on her chest.

I knew it, he had been training me.

"I never imagined it would be you that would make that happen," she admitted. "I don't think your Uncle Rob even thought it would be you kids to reunite the Amerii. I believed your Uncle Rob was foolish for still following the old Amerii ways." I pulled away from her, sitting up straight on the bed next to her. She looked me in the eye and said, "I was wrong Aurora. I should have had faith."

"Is that why you got so mad when he gave me those riddles the solve?" I sniffed. Because you lost faith in the Amerii?"

"Yes, and why we stopped coming to visit." She glanced up at the ceiling. " I convinced your dad you would be better off not knowing about the Amerii." Her words were soft and hard to hear. "I didn't want you to waste your life chasing a dream that wouldn't come true." She stood up and bowed. "But you have to believe me. I know how wrong I was. Please forgive me."

"It's okay, Mom." I touched her shoulder. She raised her head. Her eyes were filling up with tears. If she started to cry, I was going to cry again. "Mom." I pushed her shoulders up. "I'm okay, Mom. A little beat up," I laughed at my state. "but I'm okay. I forgive you, I promise."

She relaxed. "I was afraid you'd hold it against me. I didn't want the wrath of the Amerii coming down on me and your father for not upholding the beliefs." She smiled and opened her arms. "I was so worried about you." I stood up and hugged her. She swayed me side to side as she tightened her grip around me. "Everything's going to be all right." She loosened her arms and pulled away. She touched the side of my face. "You're here and you're okay." She composed herself. "Do you know what you're going to do?" She asked.

"I'm going to accept," I said, sure in my decision.

"Are you sure?"

"Yes." Becoming the next leader of the Amerii was my family's legacy. "It's in my blood," I said proudly.

"Then we better get you ready." She strolled over to the door. "Theresa, you better get in here!" she hollered down the hall to where my Aunt had been waiting.

Aunt Theresa rushed into the room. "Is she going to do it?" she asked excitedly.

My mother looked at me before confirming. I nodded yes. "She's doing it," my mother answered, her voice jubilant.

"Oh! I'm so happy you decided to do it, dear. I've been waiting for this moment for so long." Aunt Theresa's excitement was contagious. It filled the whole room with an electric buzz. I smiled. My family loved and cared for me. No matter what the future held, everything was going to be all right. My decision to become the leader of the Amerii was going to change my life forever. I feared it might be for the worse.

"First thing we need to do is get you cleaned up," Aunt Theresa said, pulling my towel off the hook on the back of the door. "Your mom and I will get everything around while you shower," she reassured me, thrusting the towel into my arms. "Off you go!" She shooed me out the door.

They began planning what to do with my hair and which outfit I was going to wear as I left the room and headed down the hall into the bathroom. Being back here, surrounded by the familiar voices of my family, comforted me.

I slipped out of my clothing and into the shower. I let the warm water run over my body, washing the painful memories of Stephanie's betrayal down the drain along side the filth from the tunnels. The water not only cleaned my body, but also my mind and soul. I started to see things clearer. My future was going in a new direction, with hundreds of possibilities laid out in front of me, just waiting for me to grab hold of them. So what if I wouldn't be going to Penn State anymore? I had something far more important to do. I had the chance to make the lives of millions of Americans better. I jumped out of the shower with a new sense of purpose, wrapped my towel around me, and waltzed back to the bedroom with my head held high.

"Amazing what a shower can do, isn't it?" my mom said when I entered the room, my newfound confidence evident to her.

"We picked out a dress for you." Aunt Theresa held up a gown. It was gorgeous, the most beautiful shade of royal blue I had ever seen. Not even the tropical waters of the Caribbean, with their vast array of blues, could compare to this single shade. The gown's lace bodice was delicately embroidered with small flowers and crystal beads that shimmered when the light reflected off them. A layer of chiffon, split up the center of the skirt, revealed the continuing lace pattern from the bodice all the way down to the floor. The gown fluttered in the air, like drooping rose petals fluttering to the ground, with even the slightest of movements from Aunt Theresa. "It was your Grandmother's," she said extending her arms out for me to take the gown. "Do you like it?"

"I love it!" I exclaimed. I was speechless. I'd never worn anything that beautiful in my life.

"Go try it on," my mother said. She clasped her hands together and brought them to her mouth. "I can't wait to see how beautiful you look in it." She bit her knuckle.

I carefully took the gown from Aunt Theresa and ran back down the hallway to the bathroom. I couldn't wait to put it on. I dropped my towel and slipped the gown over my head. It's silk lining, so soft and smooth, slide effortlessly down my body.

"You look beautiful," said Kaylin. His voice startled me. I peered into the mirror to see Kaylin leaning against the doorframe behind me. I had been in such a hurry to try on the dress that I had forgotten to close the door behind me. I quickly made sure none of my naughty bits were exposed then spun around to face him. "I didn't see anything, I promise." His cheeks took on a rosy color. "I was just coming by to see if the shower was available and there you were." He held his arms out, motioning to the gown. He took in a deep breath and shook his head in disbelief. "It's amazing." He ogled the dress. "You look stunning."

"Thank you!" I replied softly. I felt amazing in it.

He took a step towards me. "I'm glad you decided to do it with me," he said. My mind drifting to dirty thoughts. "To become the leader of the Amerii," he added, realizing what he'd said.

"Oh! Right, right." I grinned. " I decided it was the right thing to do," I replied, glad I hadn't said something seductive before he'd finished. "Could you help me zip up my dress?" I turned my back to him.

"Sure." His hands nervously grasped the zipper and gently pulled it upwards. "There how's that?" I melted as his hands came to rest on my hips.

I cleared my throat. "It's perfect." I admired myself in the mirror. The gown fit flawlessly, accentuating all the right parts of my body. The sweetheart neckline and cap sleeves showed off my figure without making me feel uncomfortable and the waistline flared perfectly at my hips. I felt like a princess.

Kaylin kissed my bare shoulder. "You're the most beautiful woman I've ever had the pleasure of kissing."

"You are certainly radiant ," my mom said from somewhere behind us.

Kaylin let go of me and I turned to see my mom standing in the hall. "The dress is perfect for you Aurora. Your grandma would be so proud of you." She pushed past Kaylin and stepped into the bathroom. He stepped back and winked at me. "Now we just need to do something with your hair. I think we should put it up like this." She gently gathered my hair in her hands, twisting it atop my head. "Let's let Kaylin use the bathroom," she suggested. "We can finish your hair in the bedroom." She let my hair fall down around my shoulders and stepped back into the hallway. I followed her out, smiling at Kaylin as I passed him. He gently brushed his hand across mine. Our pinkies twisted around each other for a split second then we let go and continued on our way.

"I can't wait to see you tonight," Kaylin called after me before closing the door.

After several minutes of manipulating my hair into the perfect bun, Aunt Thresa said, "There, I've created a masterpiece!" Then handed me a mirror. "What do you think? Do you love it as much as I do?"

I gazed in the mirror, turning my head from side to side to see every angle. "It is perfect." I gave her an approving smile and patted my hair just above my ear.

"Oh, I'm so glad you like it, honey!" My mom's voice cracked. Her eyes glistened as she leaned down to hug me. "My baby is the leader of the Amerii. I never could have dreamed this would ever happen," she said and wiped the corner of her eye. "Not in a million years. I'm so proud."

"We have more work to do downstairs, Alice." Aunt Theresa took the mirror from me and set it on the bedside table then touched my mom's shoulder. "We'd better get to it. It's getting dark outside already." She nodded towards the window.

"It's almost time. I can't believe it. Where has the day gone?" my mom said as she took me in one last time. "Take a minute for yourself. We'll see you downstairs when you're ready." She kissed my forehead before following Aunt Theresa out of the room.

Where had the day gone? I stepped over to the window and peered through it. The sun was setting off in the distance, and darkness had swept across the field. Hundreds of campfires illuminated the field, sputtering tiny sparks into the air above the tents and campers, like someone had set a million tiny Chinese lanterns loose into the air. It was magical. It had been easy to forget the hundreds, maybe even thousands, of people spread out across the field when I was safely tucked away inside the house, but peering out over the field, I could no longer ignore them. Panic tore through my body, shredding my confidence. What had I agreed to?

"Breathtaking," said Kevin. I turned my attention away from the window. Kevin leaned against the door frame.

"Yes it is," I replied and glanced back out the window for a moment, temporarily mesmerized by the flickering lights.

"I meant you." He stepped through the doorway. "Kaylin's a very lucky man." His voice was low and full of hidden meaning.

I noticed the drink in his hand. "Are you drunk?" I asked. His behavior was making me extremely uncomfortable.

"What, this?" He held the glass up, continuing to step closer to me. "Just a drink to calm my nerves before the big event tonight. Do you want some?" He offered me the glass. My nerves were on high alert, a drink sure would be nice. I took the glass from Kevin and gulped the rest of it down.

"Thank you," I said, handing the glass back to him and wiping the corner of my mouth. His fingers lingered on mine as our hands met. I couldn't tell if he had done it on purpose or not.

"We better get downstairs. They're waiting for us." Kevin said, gently touching my arm.

I nearly jumped back. That was definitely on purpose.

"Yes, we better get downstairs," I agreed, slyly navigating around him and quickly leaving the room. I glanced over my shoulder to see Kevin confidently strolling behind me down the hall. Our strange encounter had left me feeling nervous. I hurried down the stairs to find Kaylin.

Kaylin's eyes lit up as soon as he noticed me on the stairs. He stopped his conversation with Grant and met me at the bottom step. "You look so beautiful," he said, luring me closer and kissing me.

I glanced around to see if anyone noticed the kiss. Everyone but Kevin, who was intently staring at us from the top of the stairs, had been too involved in their conversations to notice.

"There's my little Amerii Queen," said my father, holding his arms open for a hug. I ran into his embrace. Kevin strolled to the bottom of the stairs and playfully punched Kaylin on the shoulder as he passed.

"Not queen, the Amerii aren't ruled by a king and queen, Bill," Uncle Rob corrected him.

"What are they then?" my father asked.

"They will be addressed as Dynast Aurora and Dynast Kaylin once the ceremony is over and they have accepted their positions."

"You're still my little Amerii Queen," Dad whispered in my ear.

"Speaking of ceremonies, we best get a wiggle on. Your acolytes are waiting," Aunt Theresa said. "Here are your robes." She handed a white robe to Kaylin and me. The robe reminded me of the painting I had seen in the Amerii room. She made her way to Grant and Kevin, handing them their robes as well.

"How come their robes are white?" asked Grant, commenting on the difference before even taking it out of his mother's hand.

"The Dynast wear white, the council men wear red and the council women wear blue," Aunt Theresa said. "Depending on what position you're appointed to will depend on the sashes you will receive." Grant let out a grunt in protest, but took the robe from her anyway.

"I'm not sure what you have to complain about," said Danny, Grant's oldest brother. He was standing at the kitchen table beside his wife. "You should be proud to be on the council."

"You will all have an opportunity to submit your requests to join the council," said Uncle Rob, addressing Grant's other two brothers who were in the room as well. "Tonight is about honoring these four for their courageous acts and appointing Kaylin and Aurora leaders of the Amerii. I will be presiding over the ceremony for tonight only because a master of ceremonies has not been appointed yet. Give us a few minutes to get into position then the four of you put your hoods up and follow the aisle to the altar. Everyone else, please join the other acolytes in the tent."

Mom kissed my forehead as she passed by on her way out the door.

Tent, Altar, Acolytes, Dynast, Council, the words swam around in my head at a dizzying speed.

"I'm not sure I can do this!" I said, my heart pounded forcefully in my chest and my body began to overheat.

Kaylin took my hand in his and whispered, "I will be by your side the whole time." His words comforted me.

"If you're not up to it, I'll take your place," Grant said. I ignored his jealousy.

"How about another drink," suggested Kevin. Kaylin glanced at me puzzled then glared at him.

"You can do this, Rory, I know you can." Kaylin focused his attention back on me. "Let's talk about something else, try to keep your mind off what's about to happen. Hey, I found out why Kevin and I didn't know about the Amerii."

"Me too," Grant said. "My parents didn't think I was ready for the responsibility. They were waiting for me to prove myself worthy or some shit like that. My brothers have known about the Amerii for years."

"Our parents got divorced because of it," Kaylin said, ignoring Grant's pity fest.

"What?" asked Kevin.

"Yeah, Mom and Dad couldn't agree if they should tell us or not. I guess they fought over it so much they decided to get a divorce."

"I'm sorry," I said.

"It's okay. If they hadn't gotten divorced, I wouldn't have gone to college in Cary and we would have never met."

"I guess that's a good way to look at it," I said. Again I wondered if fate had a hand in Kaylin and me getting together.

They're ready for you guys," Danny said, poking his head in the room.

"It's showtime," said Kevin. "Should we do a huddle or something before we go, like in football?"

"Why not?" replied Kaylin. We gathered in a circle with our arms around each other's shoulders.

"Go team!" shouted Kevin. We repeated after. Go team.

My heart was still pounding in my chest but I focused on putting one foot in front of the other and walked to the door. Danny held it open for us to pass through. I stepped out onto the front porch. A pathway lit with torches guided us from the porch to an enormous white tent out in the yard. Most of the people were already inside. The few stragglers left were rushing to get inside before we made our entrance. I paused at the entrance to the tent to take a breath.

"You can do this!" Kevin said again.

I repeated his words in my head. I can do this.

"Are you guys ready?" Danny asked. I turned to get a glimpse of the others for moral support. I could see Kaylin smiling at me from under his hood.

"Who's missing?" I asked, peering back and only seeing one of them. Kevin lowered his hood.

"Not me," he said. "I'm not missing."

"Where did Grant go?" Kaylin asked, lowering his hood, too.

"I don't know. He was right here a second ago," Kevin said. "Grant," he shouted out into the darkness. Grant stepped out from the shadows, back onto the lighted pathway. "Quit fooling around dude."

"Put your hoods back up," I said, reminding Kaylin and Kevin. "Okay, we're ready." I said. I can do this.

Danny drew the tent flap back, a gush of warm air blew onto my face. The pathway that led us here from the porch continued on into the tent. A hush fell over the crowd as they eagerly awaited our entrance. I turned my head from side to side, but the large hood of the robe didn't turn with me, blocking most of my view of the crowd. The path led us up to a raised platform on the far side of the tent. It was the only thing I could make out clearly. I reached for Kaylin's hand as we made our way into the tent, but it wasn't there. He was too far away and had no idea I was trying to comfort myself. One of the two behind us, noticed me reach out, they gently patted me on the shoulder. I can do this!

We climbed the steps to the platform. Uncle Rob stood in front of an altar, motioning for us to spread out in front of him. Kaylin and I stood dead center, I locked my gaze with Uncle Rob's to keep from passing out. Kevin stood to the left of Kaylin and Grant to my right, or at least I think that's how we were standing. It was so hard to see under the hoods.

"We are here today to honor these four for their brave acts of heroism and to appoint them the new leaders of the Amerii." Uncle Rob's voice boomed out over the silent crowd. "They showed no fear when faced with the difficult task of locating the Dare Stones. Overcoming countless obstacles on their journey and capturing a member of the George Party." The crowd burst into cheers behind us. Uncle Rob patiently waited for them to subside before continuing. "Kaylin and Aurora, do you pledge your loyalty to the Amerii and its people above all else, including the lives of your family as well as your own?"

"We pledge our loyalty to the Amerii," Kaylin and I answered.

"Do you promise to uphold the Amerii laws set by your ancestors before you?"

"We pledge our loyalty to the Amerii," we repeated.

"To continue the Amerii traditions and adopt their way of life as your own?"

"We pledge our loyalty to the Amerii."

"Kaylin, please kneel before me so I may bestow the Amerii blessing on you." Uncle Rob stepped in front of him. Kaylin got down on one knee. "Kaylin Samuel Becker, son of Cindy and Travis Becker, descendant of Thomas Becker, you have accepted the Amerii and they have proclaimed you as their leader." Uncle Rob placed a gold cord around Kaylin's neck. "Stand and be known from this day on as Dynast Kaylin." Kaylin stood up. Uncle Rob walked over and stood in front of me. "Aurora Alice VanAgteren, daughter of Alice and Bill VanAgteren, descendant of Virginia Dare, you have accepted the Amerii and they have proclaimed you as their leader." Uncle Rob placed a gold cord around my neck. "Stand and be known from this day on as Dynast Aurora." Uncle Rob stepped back and addressed the crowd. "I present to you Dynast Kaylin and Dynast Aurora along with the newest members of the acolyte council, Councilman Kevin and Councilman Grant." He raised his hands up. The crowd clapped. Uncle Rob gazed upon the four of us lovingly. "Please lower your hoods and turn to face your acolytes as the leaders of the Amerii," he said.

I slowly lowered my hood and twirled around to face everyone as a new person. I was filled with pride. I was Dynast Aurora, leader of the Amerii. My heart was no longer pounding in my chest. I wasn't nervous or scared. I wasn't the awkward girl I used to be. I had confidence in myself and it was because of the Amerii.

"Please lower your hood and turn around," Uncle Rob repeated louder. I scanned from side to side. Everyone but Grant had followed his instructions.

"Grant! Turn around!" I encouraged him. "I know you're unhappy about not being the leader, but this is not the time to protest."

Grant stood there for a few more seconds then he hesitantly lowered his hood. Everyone gasped, including Uncle Rob. It wasn't Grant. Instead the lowered hood revealed a young woman.

I ran over to the young women. "Who are you? Where is Grant?" I asked, insisting she answer me.

"He told me he would be right back," she answered backing away from me.

"Who told you that? Was it Grant?" I pressed her for more information.

"Yes. I was on my way into the tent when he stopped me. He told me to wear this robe and follow you," she said. I could see the fear in her eyes. "He said he would be back before the ceremony started." She repeated the sentence over and over, each time changing her focus from me to Kaylin then to Kevin and Uncle Rob, desperately trying to get one of us to believe her.

"What's your name?" Uncle Rob asked trying to calm her down.

"Lydia. My parents are over there." She pointed to the couple trying to get our attention at the edge of the stage.

I gazed beyond the couple at the edge of the stage out into the crowd. I could see the worried expressions on the peoples faces. Accusing words passing from lips to ears on heated breath, spreading through the crowd like a wildfire raging out of control. I could feel the crowd's burning anger licking at my cheeks as strongly as if I were standing in front of a furnace.

"What did you do with Grant?" I asked her in a panic. It wouldn't be long before the crowd turned violent.

"Dynast Kaylin! Dynast Aurora!" called a familiar voice from the crowd. I glanced down to see Mr. Truedell. What is he doing here? He was supposed to be guarding Stephanie. Mr. Truedell dashed up the steps to the stage.

He leaned close, his face full of anguish, and whispered into my ear, "I'm sorry, Dynast, but Stephanie has escaped!"

J. W. Christie

After a short stint as a destination blogger, **J.W. Christie** took her writing to the next level. Christie completed her first novel in her hometown, Traverse City, Michigan. She fell in love with writing during her high school years but began a career in the baking industry instead and settled down to start a family. After raising her children, she finally decided it was time to rekindle the old writing flame and sat down to write *The Amerii, Second Rising* (Prospective Press, 2022) and Around The Table (The Ankh Quarterly, 2020). Christie is currently working on her second novel, *Re-Creation* as well as *Hindsight* and *The Amerii, Risen*, the sequel to *The Amerii, Second Rising*. Constantly creating, whether it be in the kitchen or on the page, and a passion for fantasy is what drives her to give to you, what she likes to call fantastic realism—something that's beyond belief yet completely within your grasp.